The
PRESENCE

A Collection of Haunted Stories and Folklore

KINSMAN AVENUE PUBLISHING, INC.
www.kinsmanquarterly.org

Registered with the U.S. Library of Congress

Library of Congress Control Number: 2025900978

Printed in the United States of America

The Presence: A Collection of Haunted Stories and Folklore

Cover Design by Summer Greigh
Interior Book Design by Monique Franz

Senior Editor: Monique Franz
Co-Editors: Sandhya Barlaas, Radiyah Nouman, Sophia Obianamma Ofuokwu, and Dawn Leas

Contributing authors in alphabetical order:
Alishia Dauterive, Anthony Martinez, Arvee Fantilagan, Franka Zeph, Ihsan Sim, Jeff Thompson, John Sieber, Jonathan Brònico, Justin Alcala, Mei Davis, Mir Aziz, and V.M. Sawh

The

PRESENCE

A Collection of Haunted Stories and Folklore

Edited by Monique Franz
Kinsman Avenue Publishing, Inc.
New York

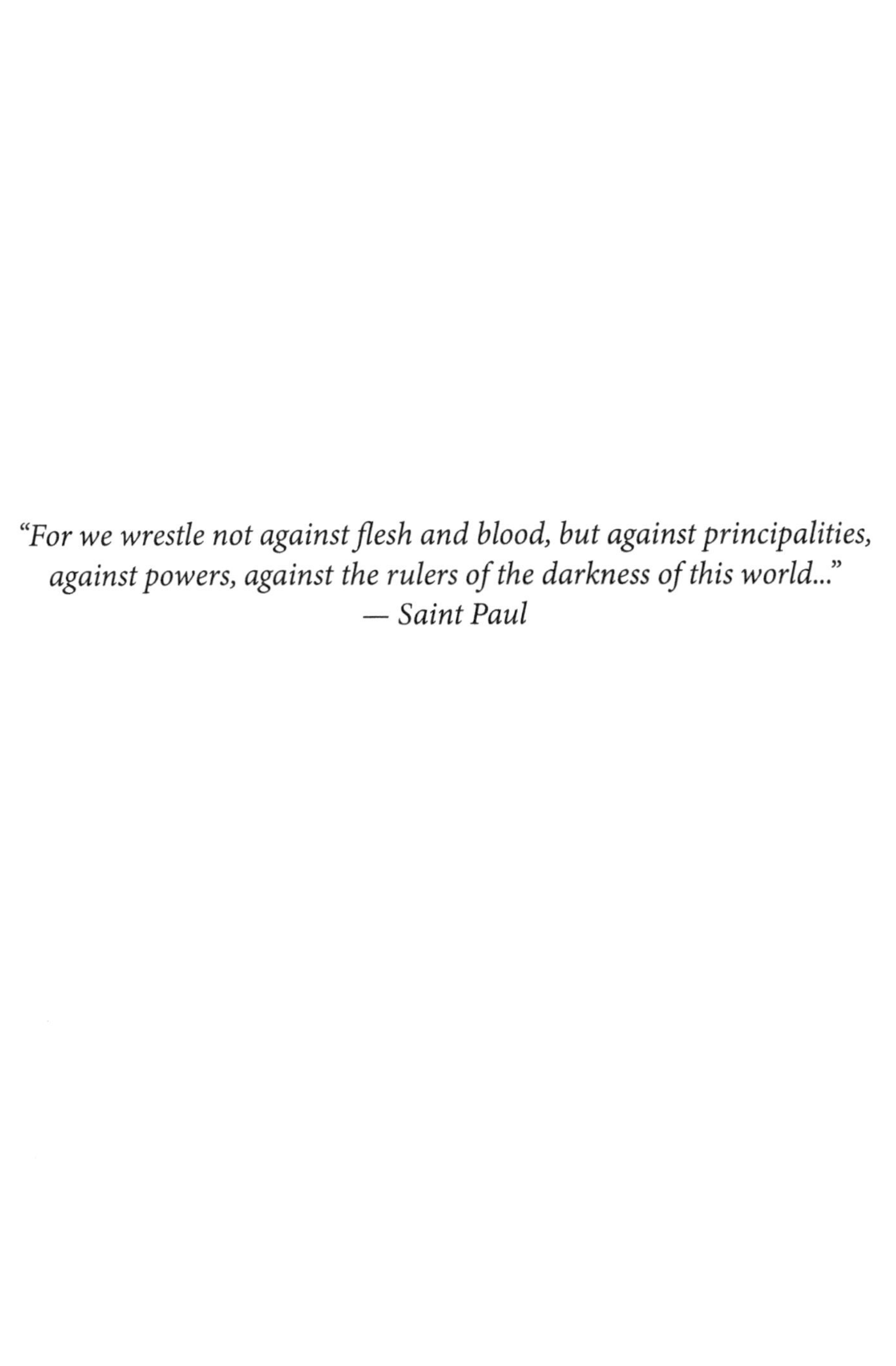

"For we wrestle not against flesh and blood, but against principalities, against powers, against the rulers of the darkness of this world..."
— Saint Paul

Editor's Note

As a child, I was given a steady diet of fire-and-brimstone sermons, which was topped with movies like *The Exorcist* and *Poltergeist*. I regularly watched Cleveland's horror lineup of "Hoolihan and Big Chuck" on a 13-inch black-and-white, then witnessed real-life church mothers cast out demons in midweek services. My exposure to horror actually scared me straight, and in many ways, I feel ghost stories have a cathartic quality.

Ghost tales are entertaining—fun around the campfire, thrilling in front of the Christmas tree, titillating when bored. But their true power lies in reminding us that there is a dimension of consciousness beyond the physical; there are spiritual beings that support, contend with, or even vex us. Nearly every indigenous culture embraces the spiritual world in its collective story—through its beliefs, art, and folklore. Folklore was a tool to inspire humanity towards goodness and light.

One of the great losses of colonization and Western dominance is the erasure of these stories and the avoidance of the spiritual realm altogether. The spiritual world has either been suffocated by organized religion or invalidated by the Age of Enlightenment and scientific discovery. While I am thankful for science, the spiritual domain will always elude its grasp. Science depends on measurable, repeatable data. The eternal world has no measure and reveals itself in random glimpses. Spiritual forces are rarely seen; their *presence* is sensed.

I like to think of the storytellers within this collection as scientists of the spiritual realm. They use their sixth sense and imagination to explore the unknowns of the paranormal, diving into an ethereal domain that can only be understood with the mind's eye. They tap into a stream of consciousness to—in many ways—give us a glimpse of this otherworldly plane, but within the safety of fiction—terrifyingly cathartic fiction.

— Monique Franz, Senior Editor

Part 1

Shadows

Part 2

Abyss

Part 1

Shadows

Shadows on the Frontier

Mir Aziz

Marri Country

Scorpions scurry through shifting sands, forging nests in the sun-bleached skeletons of creatures long dead. Jackals and hyenas patrol from the hills' ragged rocks, watching camels, cattle, and men slowly succumbing to the hounding heat and lack of water. The beasts stand ready to pounce and maul the stragglers struggling to keep up with the herd. Brown and barren brush are scattered throughout the desert terrain, their thorns tearing the skin of those foolish enough to seek refuge amongst them.

Marri country is carved out of high mountains, with rolling dunes, having clear maps of constellations in the dark, and picturesque deserts in the light. The sun itself is the greatest of tormentors; its relentless rays scald those unfortunate enough to be caught in the path of its awesome power. Buzzards, vultures, and dogs stalk the victims of the solar overlord, nipping and gnawing at the unfortunate souls whilst their breath remains. The day boils men alive, then the night freezes them where they lay.

The sun descends and the moon takes its place, giving no respite. The eyelids weld together, of man and beast alike, icicles binding eyelashes to flesh.

Tough countries breed tough men, and this place is no exception. The mountains to the north are home to the Kakar and Safi Pashtuns, accomplished tribesmen whose domains span from the edges of Kandahar to the hills of Quetta. To the east are the Kacchi tribes, home to the twin masters of the horse, the Dombki and Jatoi, whose hunting grounds encompass the whole of Sindh. To the south is nothing but sand—the same sand that destroyed the armies of Alexander the Great. In the hills towards the northeast live the Bugti, resilient hill men trained from birth in the art of slaving and sniping. The Bugti are the principal enemies of the natives of this country—the Marri. The Marris, like the others, are tough, ruthless men with an innate knowledge and expertise in the art of war. Yet they differ in one crucial sense. The Khans and tribes of the Indo-Afghan frontier were crushed, humbled, and resettled by the British war machine in Calcutta. Even the Emir of Kabul, Dost Mohammad, was deposed, Afghanistan pacified and humbled—but not the Marri. Their refusal to bend the knee became their greatest crime. John Keane led an army to punish them for this misdeed.

The Army Departs for Kahan

"Hard men, the Marri," the local guide said, pushing aside dead brush before descending the jagged rocks.

A thin column of sepoys, no more than fifteen, followed him, fumbling around stones and thicket, trying and failing to match the pace of the guide. Their bright red uniforms roasted them alive during the day, the dyed wool indistinguishable from their rashes and burnt skin. Their boots began falling apart, their khakis soiled with blood, faeces, and urine. They were initially part of a larger detachment but split up to cross the narrow mountain passes and hostile deserts. They brought with them three buffalo, a mule, two camels, and two horses. The buffalo were the first to go, falling as soon as the party entered Marri country. The horses did not do so well either, but the mule and camels were fine.

A White man turned back to face his war party; their obsidian eyes stared back. Swarthy, red-skinned Rohilla Pathans, stout and strong. They all wore piercings and facial hair. Some had long moustaches with no beards, some with long beards and no moustaches, others with both. Beige turbans wrapped tightly around the heads of long hair; pristine cloths sat above the hooked noses. The White man observed the sorry state of his men and their animals with little interest. His own trousers wore the grime of the wilderness, his hands and face now pink under the relentless sun rays.

"We have cracked alleged hard men before," the White man said. He then yawned, half covering his maw with the back of his large, pink hand.

"Not the Marri," the guide responded.

"We have conquered Pathans before," was the reply, as uninterested as before, this time staring off towards the never-ending rolling hills.

"Not Pathans, sir. We are Baluch," the guide said, his voice resolute and firm.

The White man stared at the Baluch, a quick flash of anger dissipating and giving way to a wide grin.

The Baluch was wiry and more sinewy than the Indians. He wore a long white tunic in the fashion of the frontiersmen, with loose-fitting trousers that seemed exceptionally baggy, even by local standards.

Wrapped over his shoulders was a black woollen shawl with various floral patterns sewn into it. The White man could not help but be fixated on the Baluch's face. Black and rough, the man had a large brow with one giant eyebrow covering it. His nose was large and aquiline and gave way to a long, bushy moustache that covered thin, parched lips. His cheekbones were high, sitting just above a peculiarly well-kept beard about a fist in length. The man's eyes were small and beady, yet prominent in their position, two parallel stars in a pitch-black night. His wild hair descended just past his shoulders, the top covered by a white turban, tied loosely with its end covering his neck. Slung over his shoulder was an old jezail, an ornate musket with calligraphy and flowers carved into its butt. A tightly wound sash along his waist carried an ancient flintlock pistol, a curved knife sheathed in a ruby case detailed in actual gold, and a large sword wrapped in cowhide. A grey donkey strolled at the Baluch's side, a tired and decrepit looking creature with joints protruding through tightly stretched skin.

"Not Pathans? Then what are they?" asked the White man.

"We are Baluch, sir."

The guide stood and observed the White man before him. The Bugti had come across white men before, but he had always objected to their designation as such. After all, they were mostly pink. But they were certainly sights to behold. The white men were tall and broad. The most miserable of them had great, sturdy statures; those only seen in the wealthiest of chiefs. The Baluch found them to be peculiar in appearance, for they never kept beards and rarely wore moustaches—attributes the Baluch understood to be the pride of a man. And they wore red, tight clothes that looked uncomfortable. The Baluch was certain the thick red coat the White man wore would not help him beat the sun, but they were imposing.

The white men were not of this land. They came from India, and they were not natives but came from far across the sea. The Baluch assumed they were excellent fighters, having conquered all of India. They recently conquered Kabul and were going to destroy the Marri. The Baluch observed the White man's long face—strong with stubble dotting his stone jaw. A neat crop of brown hair set about his ear lobes, a large scar running down his left cheek. His blue eyes stared without prominent eyelashes; a small nose turned upwards at its end. Even by white men's standards, the man was huge, standing a head taller than the Baluch. The size of his hands was comparable to bear paws. If anyone was going to defeat the Marri, he thought, it would probably be this man. He was less convinced of the hobble of Rohillas accompanying him. Some referred to them as 'Pathans', but they were unlike any Pashtuns he had seen before.

"We? These are your people?"

"No," the Baluch responded. "I am Bugti. You want to kill Marri. Bugti and Marri—we are Baluch. But we hate them. Only good Marri is a dead Marri."

The White man smirked, "It appears the company hates them, too. We will be glad to help you be rid of them."

The Bugti grunted. The White man detected disbelief, and so he began, "Bugti, do you see these men behind me?"

The Bugti grunted once again.

"Their forefathers were courageous Yusufzais who conquered India. Cruel and crude men, really. One could not fault them as warriors, but the mind struggles to think of any other achievements they attained. It was through the gift of British ethics and guiding principles that we have elevated these men. See how the Rohilla Pathans have become civilised, that they have careers in soldiering rather than raiding; that they now work the land and serve the state. We have saved these men—and we will save the Baluch, Marri and Bugti alike, too."

"Alright."

"Do you work any land, Bugti?"

"I am not a slave to grains."

"Do you work any land?"

"No."

"What do you do?"

"Herd goats—mostly. Place to place."

"Do you not envy the people of Sindh? How they can rely so regularly on harvest and plan accordingly? How they have land. Do you or your people not want that?"

"No."

The White man scoffed, "You do not know what you do not know. And in any case, you wanting one thing or another hardly matters."

The Bugti's face remained unchanged, and he continued through the rocks and paths, leading the company further into Marri country. The sun began to set; the sky became a flurry of purple and orange as the moon and stars emerged from their hides. The Bugti tightened his shawl around his face as the chill clawed at his head and hands. He halted, looking towards the White man, who nodded in turn.

"Here," the Bugti shouted.

The Rohillas halted the pack animals, unrolled and pitched the tents, set up a large fire in the centre of the makeshift camp, and prepared gruel, jerky, and tea. The Rohillas broke up into three different groups, chatting amongst themselves. They told occasional jokes, tearing at their rations with their incisors, sipping hot tea with cracked lips, joy etched in their faces. They kicked off their hard boots and reclined. Their turbans were placed on seats beside them, high off the floor. The men wrapped light cotton shawls around their shoulders, the cloth doing little against the chill.

The White man sat away from the soldiers, keeping his boots on. He stared at them, lighting his tobacco pipe. He took a long puff on it.

The Bugti came and sat next to him. The White man faced him, shifting away. The Bugti followed, carefully removing his hide sandals.

He unwrapped his turban, folding it eight times and resting it over his shawl-shrouded shoulder, a small brown cap resting on the back of his head. He took tobacco and chewed, chomping loudly.

"Would you rather not sit with the Pathans?"

"No," the Bugti responded, not meeting the White man's face, covering his own with his shawl.

The White man chuckled, rocked his head back and took another puff on his pipe. "How far are we from Kahan? I gather the distance is not too much more, with large climbs in latitude?"

"Yes. Kahan in five days. Maybe six. How hardy are your Pathans?" The Bugti cleared his throat and spat into the fire.

"Hard enough for the task ahead of us, without a doubt."

"How hardy are you?"

The White man choked a little on his pipe and chuckled a little more. "Hard enough for the task ahead of us," he replied, smiling. "And tell me, Bugti, how hardy are you?"

The Bugti shrugged and spat again.

The sky became black, and the light of the flame danced in the shadows of the White man, accentuating and exaggerating his brow and nose. The White man's grin seemed even larger, his cheekbones sharply angled, complete blackness below merging with the void, and a tainted orange glow above his protruding blue eyes.

The Bugti shuddered, and the White man's upturned mouth seemed to expand into infinity, his eyes projecting through eternity.

"You know this country well, I gather."

"Well enough to guide you."

"Yes, well. I was trying to make conversation with you. It's awfully chilly these nights."

"It is."

"You know, where I come from, it can get very cold too."

"Calcutta?"

The White man laughed at the Bugti and put his arm around his shoulders. He hooked his forearm so that he was almost choking him, "No, not Calcutta. England. Have you heard of England?"

"It is where the white men come from."

"It is indeed. And we came from there and conquered India and we elevated that country in ways the natives could not have ever imagined. And now we are here and will do the same."

"I heard you are here to kill Marris so that you can kill Afghans so that you can kill Russians."

The White man tightened his grip and laughed again, "Something like that, I suppose. But it's not just to kill. To kill will be an unfortunate necessity, but ultimately, as I told you before, you people will be made better. Willingly or not."

The White man released his grip, and the Bugti sat in silence.

"The winds are loud this night," the White man said as he turned to look over his shoulder.

"Yes."

"Why is that?"

"It is the wails of the wronged. Some nights it is louder than others."

"The wronged are especially talkative tonight," the White man said and chuckled.

The Bugti spat into the fire and said nothing.

The Raid

A horde of war horses neighed in rage and agony as they thundered across the cracked earth, kicking up storms of sand that marked their dreadful charge towards the unaware party. Atop them sat silent riders dressed in long robes, black turbans covering all but their eyes. They wore neck chains formed of human fingers and ears. Their belts were ropes decorated with decomposing heads.

The men rode bare upon their beasts, which were tattooed with three vertical dots between their eyes. Small cuts of hide served as saddles as the men's knees became the stirrups and bridles. They carried diverse archaic weapons: ornate sabres, lances, and flintlocks.

"Raiders," shouted one of the Rohillas. "Raiders!"

But it was too late. Already the sky erupted with the cracks of guns. The shrieks of war cries and chants pierced the waking ears of the camp.

One Rohilla with a long moustache and a bald head stood from the camp for a moment, folding down to his knees as a small hole appeared in the centre of his forehead. A crimson river flowed down his face, dripping into and being indistinguishable from his coat. The man's khakis turned red as a pool of viscera surrounded the collapsed body.

The White man rushed to his feet, cocked a pistol, and fired towards the horde. He missed. A raider slashed at and missed him three times, and so grabbed the sword with his hands and brought the hilt smashing atop the White man's skull. An ear-splitting crack was heard as he fell to the ground. Another raider thrust a lance down upon him, the spear splintering the forearm as the rider continued on.

More riders flooded the camp, cutting down the Rohillas where they stood. Swords and spears slashed and skewered; limbs and heads fell from their bodies with squelches, crunches, and thuds among a chaotic carnival of carnage. A gelatinous slosh of flesh, sinew, cartilage, marrow, and intestines flooded the ground as raiders commanded their blades as masterfully as an artist directs his brush.

And almost as soon as it started, it ended. The horsemen galloped off into the horizon, carrying with them animals, supplies, weapons, and an assortment of severed heads. Their presence seemed like a shooting star, gone in an instant, leaving a streaming tail of terror in their wake.

Gone with the wind, the turbaned reapers took the souls of most of the party with them, leaving but a single mule.

The Bugti crept up from behind a large rock. He looked around, his eyes narrowing as he placed a small brown cap on the back of his head. He dusted off the sleeves and drapes of his tunic, stepped up, and cupped his black, bony fingers around his eyes. The Bugti sighed, cleared his throat, and spat. Thirteen headless corpses littered the ground, almost floating in a sea of blood. The man heaved as the iron smell of gore and faeces tore at his nostrils. Looking up, he saw the White man's body twitch before he saw it rise, cradling its head in its huge paws. The Bugti ran over and threw the White man's shoulder over his, then struggled to his feet. The White man rose with him, laboured breaths filling the crisp dawn air.

A crimson stream ran down the White man's cheek, his eyes bloodshot red. He swished his tongue around his mouth, sure his teeth had been shattered. He spat on the ground as though searching for shards of molars and incisors, staring at the jelly of blood, phlegm, and maybe muscle tissue before him.

He lifted his eyes towards the camp, his men slain, headless, and lying in their own viscera. He raised his hands, staring at his dusty fingers before cupping them around his face. He sighed and looked down at the wiry native at his side and the intricacy of his hat. The yellow embroidery stitching and pattern stood out from its brown felt.

"You seem well," the White man started.

"I am."

"Well, I am glad that you are, at least."

"Raiders."

"What?"

"Raiders killed Indians."

"Well, yes, I can very much see that. Thank you," the White man retorted, sighing again. He crouched down, running his fingers through the red lake. He brought them back up to his face before wiping them against his jacket. "I meant to ask, who were they?"

"Raiders."

"Yes," the White man sighed again, more agitated. "And they are?"

"Desert men. Horsemen."

"And how did they find us?" An accusatory tone marked the question.

The native shrugged and grunted.

"How did they find us?"

"Sight. Tracks. Smell, maybe."

"You don't seem concerned, Bugti."

"I am alive."

"And many are not."

"I am."

"And my Pathans are not."

"Indians are dead. I am not. You are not."

"I can see that. I can see that very clearly."

The Bugti grunted.

A lone Pathan stood amongst the carnage, eyeing his dead comrades. More than dead. Destroyed. Their limbs twisted, their heads taken, their existence—their very presence—annihilated. He stared at contorted corpses, stoic and stern, assessing in a fashion alien to men who did not understand the path of a warrior. He turned his head to see a battered Britisher, blood coagulated across his muzzle. The tribesman next to him, turbanless and unscathed.

The Pathan dusted off the sleeves and breast of his red jacket, put his fingers into his mouth, and twirled his moustache. His hand fell from his shaven jaw down to his butt chin. He patted his thick head of hair, coughed, spat, and trudged through the organs and bodies of his fallen peers. As he reached the White man, he saluted.

"Sir," he said, his voice deep and coarse. As he brought his hand back to his side, he turned to face the tribesman and stared, and the tribesman stared back.

The Pathan saw an unkempt, primitive frontiersman. One who seemed to have no appreciation or sophistication of understanding to probably anything, besides stealing from civilised people, and possibly herding goats. The man might be capable of terrible acts of spontaneous violence, but such savages would not, could not, comprehend the arts of the martial sciences, tactics or high politics. The scene before him was plenty of evidence of this. And this wiry savage was likely behind it. So he stared, and continued to long after the tribesman faced away, his pupils piercing the man's skin.

A cool morning breeze glazed over them all, delivering the putrid smell of iron. The sun rose, prying away the faded, tainted dawn with its fingers. Buzzards circled overhead, while a vulture descended upon the dead Rohillas, picking at their flesh and organs. A pack of hyenas squabbled amongst themselves, hiding behind the rocks, watching the feast before them. Whining and barking, they hesitated to advance, peering at the surviving men.

A hulking beast emerged from the group. Its striped, tan body covered with a bristling mane that danced with the winds. The animal galloped down from the rocks, its eyes fixated on the men, snarling with cracked fangs, jeering as it advanced. It came to a corpse whose liver was being torn out by a vulture. The enormous bird with a grey, bald face stood its ground upon the body. A pulsating red tumor dangled from under its beak. It gawked at the hyena, lifting its great wings before its face twice. The hyena lunged forward, howling, and the vulture took flight in silence.

The four-legged animal took the corpse by the bicep and bit down. A thundering crunch. Then, the hyena walked backwards towards the rocks from which it emerged. Slowly. Its eyes fixated on the Pathan with a brown-skinned arm hanging from its mangled maw, now red and wet.

The vulture returned, perching on the same body to continue its dig at the liver. Then, more hyenas came, more vultures descended, all shovelling fresh meat from headless necks.

The men gawked at the horrid feast, their former colleagues now scavenger sustenance, eventually excrement. The White man broke the silence, wiping a sleeve across his cheek.

"How far is Kahan from here?"

"Less men. Less animals. Maybe three days and one half day."

"And how far back to Sindh?"

"Long."

"And how is the terrain till Kahan?"

"The same."

"It appears to me that it would be best to continue to advance," the Pathan spoke. "Keane should be there. We can rendezvous with the army, join their ranks, sir."

"I figure that would be a good plan, though I hesitate in advancing further into hostile territories, just you and I. And the Bugti."

"To head back would be longer in badlands, sir. That is, if the Bugti is truthful. If he is reliable."

"This is true. This. Is. True. Onward to Kahan, Bugti."

The Pathan led the mule by its ears, wading through the blood of his brothers as the four set off. The Bugti led, of course, and the White man fell towards the back with the Pathan and mule. He held his head in his hands, which he had wrapped with cloth to mask his wounds. The cloth grew soaked and red.

The White man said, in English, "If the tribesman looks even a smidge suspicious, blow his brains out."

"So now?"

The White man chuckled. "When we arrive in Kahan. But before, if necessary. I'm sorry to see the state of your people back there, Pathan."

"Yes, sir."

Tents

The men and the mule stood atop the face of a cliff. A camel skin tarp was visible upon the ravine's horizon, the silhouettes of camels around it. To ease the ache in their stomachs, the men descended the rocks.

Fire seemed to radiate from the ground through the men's boots, sweltering their legs and feet, but the cold air bit at their bones. The wind sang silently, toying with the hairs on the back of their necks. The land was cracked and barren apart from a small dry bush that the mule, who carried the White man, stopped to chew. Suddenly, its mount rose, throwing him off, grunting and moaning in pain. It bashed its head into the sides of the ravine, whimpering and whining. The beast dragged its head in circles, heaving and huffing as it staggered.

"Snake bite," the Bugti said, watching shiny scales slither into the cracks of the earth. Its colours were irregular.

The Pathan glared at him, a freshly lit pipe hanging from his mouth. He stretched to help the White man to his feet.

The mule rolled onto its side, tight leather expanding over cracked ribs. Its head swelled, the nose a cancerous balloon.

"Poor thing," the White man remarked, rubbing his now bruised bottom.

The Pathan brushed off his sleeves, puffed upon his tobacco, and restocked it in his mouth. He then loaded a pistol, aimed it at the beast, and pulled back the hammer.

"Stop," the Bugti said, right before the Pathan could pull the trigger. He gestured to the tents.

The Pathan pointed to ammunition on his belt. "Don't be worried for them. I have plenty more."

"They have more, maybe."

The Pathan ignored him and again raised his pistol until the White man spoke up. "Perhaps save it."

"Alright." The pistol went back into his belt, and instead, the Pathan pulled out his bayonet and grabbed the mule by the ear.

The mule resisted. As it saw the blade, it tried to move, whining and grovelling, but it was too weak and too late. As its throat was sawed apart, the wretched creature contested, meekly bleating, trying to retreat. As he cut the jugular, it became a sprinkler of red mist on the Pathan's face. He stood unmoved and unbothered, continuing to saw until the swollen head was in his hands. Holding it by its ears, the Pathan looked into the empty eyes and saw himself. He then threw it to the side, wiped his face on his sleeves and his hands on his khakis. He spat, then took his pipe with two fingers and exhaled. Smoke rose from his lips as he stashed his blade back in his belt. Another spit before he faced the Bugti, grinning.

The Bugti shuddered. "You enjoyed that?"

"It is not a question of enjoyment," the Pathan responded, cracking his knuckles. He took a long puff on his pipe. "In fact, there is no question to it at all. It is expression. I wanted to kill it and I saw a reason, so I did it."

The White man added, "More than that, it was the right thing to do. The poor creature was snake bitten. It needed to be disposed of."

"Necessary," the Bugti replied. "Not more than that."

"What a simple thing you are, Bugti," the Pathan said, baring his teeth, now red with mule's blood.

The Bugti grunted as the three of them moved onward.

The dark, unembellished tents sat upon the intricately woven red carpets, many decorated with plants formed from yellow and brown strings. A metal teapot sat in the centre, having mismatched earthen cups surrounding it. There was a straw plate filled with chunks of overcooked meat.

"Salaam," said the Bugti, announcing his presence to the camp.

"Walaikum salaam," a shrill voice responded. A small, hunched man wearing a loosely wrapped turban emerged from the tent. His eyebrows covered his eyes, and his beard reached his knees.

"We are tired and hungry, good sir. Could you spare us a little of your hospitality?" the Bugti asked.

"There is nothing more noble than caring for guests. Please, be comfortable," the elder responded.

The other two stared intensely, unable to speak or understand Baluchi.

"Enter," the Bugti said, pointing to the carpets.

Before they could, two veiled figures exited the space and hid themselves in a smaller adjoining tent.

Tattoos

The three men sat down, and the elder host laid out a selection of nuts and dry fruit. He took clay cups, wiped them with his shirt, and poured steaming green tea. The nuts and tea satisfied them. The sun was setting, and the night winds made themselves known. The men were, for the first time in a while, comfortable.

"How is the condition of India these days?" the elder asked in Hindustani.

"Things could not be better," the White man responded, a genuine smile on his face.

The elder nodded. "I hear the trade caravans gain far more wealth nowadays than they used to."

"Of course."

"But I have also heard of great wars. Of great hunger. Yes, I have heard some very miserable conditions."

"Yes, well, ruling a nation is a hard thing. So many little cogs and things could be better if the natives allowed it. Alas, their customs often interfere in efficient and good governance."

"And what customs of the Indians would want them to prefer starvation to nourishment?"

"The same customs that allow the conditions of the land to be as wretched as they were before our presence."

The elder chuckled, and the White man smiled back.

"To rule is harder than to conquer," the elder insisted. "And so, it befits a wise conqueror to know the worth of what he conquers. You are in an odd spot, I suppose. A company who rules the richest and most populous of countries, the authorities in your own country speak with merchants about governance and geopolitics."

"And for it, we have made much wealth in India, stopped much chaos, and tamed anarchy. We have crushed marauders, destroyed vagabonds and gifted sciences upon the people of India. God willing, we will continue to do so," the White man responded in a gentle tone, a smile still plastered across his face.

The elder nodded again, and faced the Pathan, who was working his hand around his pipe and wrapping his shawl around his shoulder. "So, things are better?"

The Pathan did not look up, and instead drew a long puff on his pipe. He then said simply, "God save the King."

The White man did not know if he was joking.

"God has cursed those who take the title 'king', did you know?" the elder said.

"Well then, it is good we do not have a king, but a queen," the White man responded.

"And a country run by women will never prosper."

"So, were all the kingdoms of India run by women, then?"

The elder laughed once again. "You White men have a funny wit about you."

The elder turned to the Bugti and spoke in Baluchi, "And where have you come from, my countryman?"

"Dera Bugti."

"Bugti, yes, yes. Why do you ride with the Indians?"

"They will help us kill many Marris."

The elder sighed and looked down into his cup. His cracked, black fingers wrapped around the edges of the clay. "You know, Bugti, this feud will be the end of both of you. You have your grievances, but do you not see what the White men are doing?"

"We are not stupid, sir. Of course we see."

"Then why do you go along with it?"

The Bugti shrugged. "Why does it matter? We allegedly are ruled by the Khan in Kalat, and before him, the Emir in Kabul. So, what if we then pay lip service to the King of Calcutta? Or Queen? The Marri have hurt me, and I will hurt them. You know what they have done to us."

As the men conversed, the Pathan rose and left the tent.

The Bugti continued, "I know you see it as wrong, sir. And it might be. But this violence, this war, is necessary for our survival. The Marri must be defanged."

The elder sighed, "And that is exactly what they will say about you when they take the Russians as friends."

"I know. But tell me, what do we do? The White man is here, and he is here to stay. We may well take what help we can. What else can we do?"

"Take the White men as friends, and then overlords, I suppose." He switched to Hindustani. "You should learn Baluchi, Britisher. It will make you beloved over here," he said, smiling towards the White man.

The Pathan burst back into the tent, his pipe in his mouth and pistol raised. He fired at the elder, piercing his chest, turning his white robes red. The old man gasped, staggering back. The Pathan raised his pistol again and shot the elder between the eyes, the shriek of the bullet shattering the night's silence. Confused screams came from the neighbouring tent.

"What have you done, Pathan?" asked the White man, his eyes wide, his mouth now agape at the scene before him.

"I was outside smoking and I inspected their livestock. I noticed their animals had tattoos of three vertical dots on their heads. These are the same people who attacked us," the Pathan said before he spat.

"How? It's an old man!" The Bugti shouted.

"Don't raise your voice at me, Bugti. They were of the same tribe, you know that. They have the same tattoos to mark their animals."

"Yes. But this man did not attack us."

The Pathan shrugged. "The tribes understand that when they attack us, any of theirs are fair game. Is that not frontier policy, sir?" he asked, turning to the White man.

"Yes…"

"In fact, is that not what makes a tribe a tribe? Collective responsibility for the acts of criminals?"

The White man once again agreed.

"And so there will be a need to reprimand."

"No."

"And there are two more to deal with. It's dark out. Best to camp here after. Isn't that right, sir?"

The Bugti and White man looked at each other solemnly, and after a pause, the White man said, "Yes."

"This is wrong," the Bugti said.

"This is law," the White man responded, his voice devoid of any enthusiasm.

And so the three exited the main tent.

The black cloak of night enshrouded them. The moon bestowed a cold glow, decorated by a sea of stars. The wind's chill could crack stone, and it plucked at the bare skin of the men; its claws raising their goosebumps. The White man and the Bugti again stared at each other, and then at the Pathan. Blowing his pipe, the Pathan looked back at them, drew his pistol, raised the hammer, and entered the tent once again.

There were screams, followed by a gunshot, and then there was only one scream. A muffled cry went on for minutes, then a wet squelch, followed by laboured breaths. The men outside sat in stunned silence.

The Pathan returned from the tent. The moon lit his face, now a collage of purples and reds, his moustache, an obsidian bar. He looked to his compatriots, who themselves eyed the Indian god of savagery. His sleeves rolled high; his hands and arms painted in gore.

"It is done," the god said. And he returned to the main tent, washing his face and hands in a water jug.

Dreams

The men woke with the sun, except the Bugti, who woke a little earlier to pray. The Bugti rubbed his eyes as he rose up, though before he could see, the stench of death assaulted his nose.

He turned to the murdered—no—killed elder. The old man still lay the same as he had following his execution. His mouth gaped open, a slimy black tongue dangling out of it. The eyes had rolled up, just the whites were visible. Blood continued to flow from his forehead and chest, his robes now entirely soaked, much of the carpet beneath was a sponge of gore.

The White man sighed and then gagged. *That smell. The damn smell.* He had smelt decomposing bodies before, but this odour was especially bad. Quite odd, given how little time had passed since the man's passing, and there was a surprising lack of scavengers. Not even a fly circled the man's body.

"Sorry, old fellow," the White man uttered under his breath before spitting on the ground. He rummaged through the chests in the tent and found cloth to redress his head wound. The Pathan joined them, finding a long black cloth neatly folded among weapons. He stashed a looted knife and pistol in his belt and lit a fire under the teapot. The Pathan then began what the White man considered a "cruel and odd custom." He sawed at the dead man's throat to prepare another trophy.

The White man gagged at the sight. "You didn't care to join the Bugti in prayers?"

"I don't care to pray nowadays," the Pathan said, his bloodied hands across the blade's handle, the severed head rolling into his arms.

"You don't believe?"

"I didn't say that," he responded, moving to fill the tea cup. He brought the hot drink to his lips, his eyes not leaving the earthen vessel.

The White man looked at his empty cup for a moment before filling it. "Then what do you mean?"

"Exactly what I said, sir."

"Which was?"

"That I don't care to pray nowadays."

"You've said that already."

"I did, and not anything else. That is exactly what I meant. It is exactly what I mean."

"So, you still believe."

"Believe what?"

"In religion?"

"Well, what is religion?"

"Oh, don't be difficult with me, Pathan."

"Well, what exactly do you want to know?"

"Do you believe in God?"

"Yes."

The White man sat, waiting for an elaboration. But there was none. "But you don't pray?"

"Nor do you."

"Well, I am not a Muslim."

"But you believe in God."

"Not in the same sense that you do."

"You don't know in what sense I do personally—" There was a pause. "—sir." And then a grin.

"So, in what sense do you believe?"

The Pathan threw his head back, swigging the tea. He lit his pipe and took a long puff. Finally, he turned his head to face the white man.

"I had a dream last night, sir."

"Alright."

"I was in a small village—something quite nondescript. Ordinary, in fact. An ordinary little rabble of mud huts. I don't know if you can smell in dreams, though I imagine you can. It probably smells like shit and animals. It is dark, and I hold a pole with a lantern. There's a red glow somewhere, and I walk towards it. And there she is. The most beautiful, alluring woman I have ever seen. Gorgeous. I stare at her, and she stares at me. I come close to her, and she takes my face in her hands, but they feel like fire, and my hands are bloodied. She smiles at me, her teeth red, and kisses me, her breath like iron."

"And she told me, go forth and do what you know you must. She is War. And I love her. I am devoted to her. She is the material. The medium. And I am her instrument. I am hers. And so I went forth, and I killed everyone in that village, a smile on my face, knowing why I do this. War is my mistress, Smith. I worship her. And that is why I believe in God. For the existence of War, that which encompasses all, permeates all natures, is the underlying truth of all. She necessitates the existence of God. But do you know what the worst sin is? It is to worship that other than God. And I worship War. And so, I know my pursuit of this, my devotion to her, my obsession with my art, will lead me to hell. In fact, I am already there. I am in hell. I am its agent. I am a mushrik. I am its devotee."

The White man's eyes sunk into his skull, and he had unintentionally shuffled backwards. "What an odd dream, Pathan," he said, his voice hoarse.

The Pathan grinned. "Oh, I have this dream every night, sir. And I awake with a smile on my lips."

"Why did you tell me that?"

"You asked about my beliefs, and so I answered."

The White man appeared uneasy, and so the Pathan continued smiling and said, "We all will be dead soon anyway, sir."

On the Way to Kahan Once Again

The group felt uneasy as the sun did not completely rise, waiting in a seemingly permanent state of twilight, its cloak of purple draped above them. Whispering were the morning winds, cursing them for what they had done. The stench of rotting flesh followed. The cold tugged at their flesh, seeming to tear it from their bones. There was no life, no insects, no birds, and no dogs but them.

They walked in silence, their mouths muzzled, their eyes vacant. The Bugti, at their lead, pulled two camels stolen from the camp. The Pathan sat upon one camel, having tied the turban of the dead man on his own head. From his skull was made a trophy with its eyes and tongue removed. A knot from the hair was tied to his belt.

The White man sat upon the other, his wound dressing wrapped into something that vaguely resembled a turban. All three were wrapped in black shawls decorated with red and yellow threads. The Bugti having his own shawl, and the other two wearing pieces looted from the camp. They walked. And walked. And walked. The ground, still cracked and miserable beneath them, the weather still bitter and spiteful.

Hours passed before the White man complained of stomach pain, potentially derived from hunger, dysentery, or both. And so the three stopped and unravelled a carpet before bringing the camels down and trying to tie their legs together, the beasts groaning in protest.

"Shhhh," the Bugti whispered to the creatures, patting their heads and stroking their necks.

The Pathan chuckled, "What are you doing, man?"

"Comforting it."

"It's an animal."

"I know."

"How are you comforting it?"

The Bugti looked at the Pathan, confused. "What?"

"How are you comforting it?"

"I stroke it, and I say all is well."

"So, you are lying to it?"

"It's an animal."

"Yes. I said that already. You're still lying to it," the Pathan said, sitting down to light his pipe.

"Lies are sometimes necessary."

"But the truth will always be apparent. Especially when that truth is violence."

The Bugti stared silently while the camels bleated.

The Pathan continued. "In that sense, you could say that violence is the ultimate arbiter of truth and so war is the ultimate test of reality. So, war is the ultimate form and expression of truth."

"What are you talking about?"

The Pathan spat and smiled, taking his pipe into his mouth again. He faced the Bugti. "I'm telling you the truth. War is all-encompassing. Violence is the basis of everything."

"Not true," the Bugti responded, clearing his throat and spitting by his feet.

"But it is."

"Well, what about love?"

"Love?"

"Yes. Love. How is that war?"

"Are you married?"

"We do not talk about such things."

"Are you married?"

"Do not—"

"Are you married?"

"—yes."

"Do you love her?"

"Yes."

"Does she love you?"

"Yes."

"Why?"

"Because I provide. Because I protect."

"Indeed. And what would you do if she was seen by another man?"

"What?" he whispered, anger in his voice.

"What would you do if she was seen by another man?"

"I would kill her and him."

"And so—" the Pathan said, taking another puff on his pipe, then waving it like a wand. "What underpins your love is violence. And the consequence of violating this love is also violence. Your love is still underpinned by violence, and conflict defines it."

The Bugti looked unconvinced. "No. You confuse an incidental aspect of love as defining it. Not underpinning it."

"Tell me how violence is merely an incidental aspect of love. For I have told you how it underpins it."

"The stories of the ancients," the Bugti said, sitting by the Pathan. By this point, Smith had finished redressing his head wounds and came to join them. "The ancient romances end in death. Yes. But these deaths are incidental. They do not form the basis of their love. Adam and Durkhani. Their love stemmed from a mastery of art."

The White man interjected. "And I would love to hear how you would define art as war, Pathan. Certainly, there are ways in which art, and martial prowess generally, can be artistic. But as art?"

The Pathan replied, "Well, Bugti, well, sir, what you say supports what I have stated. What is art?"

The White man responded, "An outward manifestation of inward expression."

"So tell me, what is a greater manifestation of expression than to force it upon those who stand in your way? By your definition, if I were to dislike a man, would not the most primal, the most expressive expression of this dislike be to remove his head from his shoulders and then take his wife as mine? If I detested a people, what more perfectly encapsulates a manifestation, the physical embodiment of my hatred, than to butcher the children, the elderly, the men, and to take the young women as slaves upon which further expressions of rage are to be enacted in various forms? I ask you two here and now, is there a more clear way that I have expressed myself than this example? War is the highest form of art. It is the pinnacle and purest form of any human emotion, of any human expression."

The head on the Pathan's belt gently swayed in the wind, as if nodding in agreement. The Bugti looked at the Pathan, disgust apparent in his scrunched brow.

"I am not a man of knowledge. I am not a city man. I ride with my flock. I camp with my family. I protect them, as I do now. And I know what you say is wrong."

"Wrong?"

"Yes."

"Wrong in what sense?"

"You know it is wrong to kill people for art."

"Well, whether it is wrong or right is beside the point. The point is, that it is art, the highest form of it, definitionally."

The White man interjected again. "Perhaps the specific act of violence itself can be artistic. I will concede that. But to claim that war, in and of itself, is artistic is absurd. War is a scientific contest between nations. It is a process by which the strong, the enlightened, conquer the weak and the backward, to then share knowledge to uplift the savages. It is to protect or expand the polity. A natural process of survival and determination between states. Now, we, as men of virtue, then use our initiative to bring virtue post-conquest to the defeated. But the process itself is a natural one, so then it cannot be art."

As the Pathan began his response, the Bugti interrupted. "What are you two even debating? Why is war one thing or why another? Must it be characterised instead of being just war?"

The Pathan repeated, "What a simple creature you are..." the Pathan repeated before he was made to be silent.

The men turned around as the winds struck from all directions, howling and screaming. The sky switched to dark; the stars smothered by an encompassing ethereal smog. The White man lit a torch and hung it on a pole, holding it out into the darkness. A gentle glow of the flicker of the flame seemed pathetic against the surrounding darkness.

And then it appeared.

Now

A silhouette appeared on the horizon, creeping towards the men. The winds stopped speaking; the silence pierced. Even the camels, tied and tired, ceased bleating. In that moment, nothing existed in the universe but the men and that which advanced towards them. It came towards them, staggering. And as it got closer, it visibly twisted with creaks, cracks, and snaps from bone and ligaments. A raspy breath paired with its pained gurgle; a low croak emanated from it.

"I-is that a woman?" The White man asked, crouched and squinting.

"Well, it is wearing a black burqa, so I suppose it is," the Pathan said, loading a pistol with his pipe still in his mouth.

"But why is she by herself?"

"I don't know what to tell you, Bugti," the Pathan said as he rose, bringing down the hammer. "God also blessed women with legs and, unfortunately, they sometimes use them to move." He chortled and aimed his pistol at the figure.

"Oh, for the love of God, Pathan!" the White man barked.

But it was too late. The crack of gunpowder shattered as though splitting the world into a thousand pieces. The Bugti jumped to his feet, trying to wrestle the gun away, but the Pathan grabbed his neck before throwing him to the ground. He then cocked the pistol twice, fired twice, all shots finding their mark. But the figure did not fall. Instead, it propelled forward in a twisted march of agony, walking with audible cracking and creaking of its disfigured limbs.

The White man stared at the thing, moving back, dropping his torch. "Shoot that thing again!" he said as he picked up a rifle, hastily reloading it.

The Pathan shot again, and again nothing happened other than the slow advance, the gurgled cry, its joints breaking under its own weight.

The White man fired. *Crack. Crack. Crack.*

Each shot dissipated into the void as she came into view. Her black burqa was decorated in crusted puddles of blood, torn in a way that left her ivory face and hair exposed. She stared at the men with large emerald eyes and heavy lashes. An aquiline nose gave way to full lips that rasped and gurgled as her auburn hair danced with the winds. Her throat resembled a delicate lily. A gaping gash slashed through it, the wound appeared to breathe on its own, pulsating with a crimson sludge oozing from it.

The Pathan gasped and froze when he saw her face. "Run."

"What?" the Bugti asked, loading his own weapon.

"Run."

And so, the men floundered around the camp, pushing things over as they flailed over one another. They slung rifles and swords over their shoulders, stuffed knives and pistols into their belts. The men ran into the abyss, panicking as the tormented figure advanced, creeping and cracking towards them.

Having Run Away

"How long to Kahan?"

"I do not know."

The Bugti's knees became like water, and he collapsed on the ground, dry heaving and rolling onto his back. His tunic and trousers browned by dust, the white now a rustic orange, his turban lopsided. He unravelled the whole thing and threw the cloth to the floor. The White man followed, similarly collapsing and panting. He tore off his jacket, revealing a red-stained undershirt. He unwrapped his head wrap, holding it to his chest. His face had become pink, his chin caked in dried blood. Then the Pathan arrived, staring back at where they came from; his boots crushing the turban on the ground.

"Did anyone bring supplies with them?" There was silence. "Do you know how we can find water, Bugti?"

"Not here. I do not know."

The sun emerged from across the horizon. The sea of sand before them was an endless desert, illuminated dimly by embers in the sky. No hills, no cliffs, no lakes, or streams. The desert dawn was cold. Cold enough to crack a man and send his soul to heaven or hell. The three men wrapped their shawls tightly, the Bugti also covering his face.

"Which way do we go?" the White man asked.

"Well, definitely not the way we came from, sir."

"This is not Marri country. This is no country I know," the Bugti responded.

"Alright. But again, which way do we go?"

"I do not know."

The three stood in silence, except for the irregular chorus of morning gusts.

"What was that? That thing?" the White man started again. There was silence again. After a few moments, he confronted the Pathan. "You did this. This is because of you."

"How could it be because of me?"

"Oh, don't be coy, Pathan!" the White man shouted, jumping up in frustration. "You did this. What did you do in that tent?"

"What did that thing have to do with the tent?"

"I saw how you looked at her. You knew her, didn't you?" the White man asked, taking steps closer. "Was she in the tent? What did you do to her?"

Standing tall, the Pathan replied, "I conquered and acted according to the rights of the conqueror."

"You bastard."

"There is nothing bastardly about it. These are the rules of war, and I acted in accordance with them. Rules fully endorsed and known by you, your company, and its directors."

The White man charged at the Pathan, howling, grabbing for his legs, but the Pathan sprawled atop him. The two grappled on the ground before they came to their feet, using each other as support. The White man hooked his fist into the Pathan's jaw.

The Pathan grunted and stumbled a bit before pouncing back and clenching the White man tightly, squeezing his forearms into his neck and grinding his chin into his eye socket. He disengaged for a second and threw his elbow into the White man's forehead, constricting him again. He smashed his elbow into the White man three more times, splitting his forehead open, the blood now a stream down his face as he fell again to his knees. The blood splattered upon the sand. As he heaved and panted, the Pathan kicked him in his ribs. He spat blood. The Pathan looked to the Bugti and stared blankly. The Bugti stared back at him, a great Indian god of death.

The maroon silhouette, lord of the horizon, stood tall ahead of the dawn. His sculpted face, an idol carved from sandstone. The Bugti shuddered, turning to face the White man on the ground. He took a step towards him, but stepped back at the great avatar of destruction before him.

The White man slowly rose to his knees, coughing red mist. He wiped his face and then held his hands before him and shuddered.

"You're a dead man when we reach Kahan."

There was no response. Instead, the Pathan looked off to the horizon and cracked his knuckles into his palms. He turned again to the Bugti. "You don't know where we are."

"No."

"Alright."

The Pathan squatted down and removed the trophy head from his belt. He looked into its eye sockets, now empty galaxies, cold and unfeeling. The Bugti watched for what seemed like an eternity before the Pathan tied the head back to his belt and stood up.

With the sunrise, the dunes became visible before them, a small formation of red cliffs far off into the distance.

"Do you see those?"

"I do."

"Do you know them?"

"I do not."

"It would be a better place to be."

"It would. But it will get hot."

"Hmm?"

"Very hot. Midday desert sun."

"Alright."

"And we have no water."

"I am aware. So let's get this over with."

The Bugti grunted and spat on the ground, green jelly pulsating on the sands.

"What of the White man?"

"He can come. But I am going to kill him before we rendezvous with the Indian army."

"Kill him?"

"Yes."

"Why?"

"Because he will have you and I killed. But, more importantly, because I can, and I want to." The Pathan smiled.

"You do not know if he will because it has not happened. And you cannot kill a man just because you want to."

"Actually, I can."

"No,"

"It has been the case so far. And who will stop me from killing the White man? You?"

"Yes."

The Pathan chuckled. "Just like you stopped me from killing that old man and his women?"

The Bugti said nothing as the two stared at each other. Then, the Bugti withdrew his pistol from his belt and aimed it at the Pathan's forehead.

"Go on," the Pathan urged.

The Bugti stood still. He shivered, and he did not know if it was because of a sudden gust or if it had come from inside him. Time froze. He could hear the thumping of his heart, the rhythmic drumbeat of his breaths. He lowered the weapon, returning it to his belt.

"You've never killed a man before," the Pathan remarked, his eyes narrow, his face blank. Again, the Bugti remained silent, lowering his gaze.

"Funny," he continued. "The white men often think you hill tribes are fierce killers, but I know better. Certainly, tribal groups are capable of awe-inspiring violence. But you are too stupid to realise that war and violence are art. And by 'you', I mean you individually and your people as a collective. I explained this to you, how the greatest form of expression is art and the most complete, dominating manifestation of expression is war, but you didn't understand. Even now, you don't."

The Bugti looked despondent.

"On we go," the Pathan commanded, grabbing the pistol from the Bugti's hand, throwing it into the sand.

The Bugti stood in silence for a bit before helping the White man to his feet, taking his arm over his shoulder.

"Quickly—before that thing comes back."

The three slowly marched across the sands as the sun, at its zenith, beat down, roasting the men's flesh, caking their blood and scars. The Pathan re-wrapped his turban to cover his entire face, and effortlessly crushed sand beneath his boots. Besides the Bugti's little brown cap, he and the White man bore naked heads. Their skin began to blacken and crack under the celestial oven. Their throats tightened as pools of phlegm coagulated in the back of their throats, but none dared to spit.

They grew weaker as they summited hills of sand, crossing destitute oases. Beads of sweat fell like rosary beads from their brows and noses. The men passed the skeleton of a beast. Its colossal, bleached bones, an ancient megalith erect since time immemorial. They marched through its ribs; giant vertebrae casting shadows. Its dark cavern provided brief respite from the sun.

"What is this thing?" the Pathan asked.

"I don't know."

"Okay."

"Have you come across them before?" asked the White man, who was now walking properly; the gash in his head welded shut by the sun.

"Yes."

"Have you asked anyone about them?"

"No."

The White man sighed loudly. "You Orientals are a lazy, idiotic bunch. For God's sake! You have a great mystery in front of you and you have not the slightest interest in solving it."

"Why should I?"

"Don't you want to know?"

"No. Why would I?"

"Because knowledge is something one should aspire to gain."

"I know what I need to."

"But you could know more."

The Pathan's face snarled. "Why would he need to know more? He lives in some God forsaken hill in the middle of nowhere. His only experience of life prior to this was probably herding sheep. Tell me, Britisher. Tell me why he needs to know this, and what this was. Your preoccupation with knowing has done nothing for us. You 'know' and it means nothing. You're still stuck with him, running from something you will never understand."

"You and your kind would never understand. You can shoot guns and that's about it. That's all you are and all you'll ever be good for, and you will never understand the sense of curiosity and desire to attain knowledge that propels men to greatness."

"Yes, and your greatness in knowing things has helped you on this expedition. The entire column was wiped out. Your entire column was wiped out. And now look where we are. What do you even know? What did you know about those raiders? What did you know about any of this country?"

"Well, Pathan, I know it is wrong to murder innocent people."

The Pathan laughed. "On whose behalf do the Indians kill?" he asked, leaning on a rib. The bone's shadow cast itself over him, enveloping the warrior in a black cloak. The whites of his eyes pierced through the darkness, his high cheekbones and jaw stressed by his thick moustache.

"The Indians kill because that is the only thing they know. I have tried to civilise you and your people and God willing, we will continue to do so. But at present, in history and for the foreseeable future, you are and will be savages. You kill because you can. You are creatures of impulse, and that is all there is to it. We may be at war with the Afghans, or the Russians, or the Punjabis, and you will fight—not because you care—but because you can."

The Pathan's teeth penetrated the shadows, curling into another smile.

Then the Bugti stood up. "Horror is here. Even so, you two speak much and say nothing."

"Well, what would you like us to say?"

"Nothing."

"Nothing? Fine then. Bugti, you speak. What was that thing? That woman who chased us?"

"Ask him," the Bugti said, pointing to the Pathan.

"How would I know what it was?" he said.

"She was in the tent. Wasn't she?"

The Pathan hesitated for a moment. "Someone who looked like her was in the tent, but you're not seriously asking me to believe that they are the same?"

"Not a question of belief. It is."

"How can that be? I killed her, Bugti. I did what I wished with her and I slit her throat with my own hands. I sawed her head halfway off with my bayonet and saw the white of her vertebrae as I cut her flesh. How is she alive? And if she is alive, how did she not die after being shot? There is no way it is her. People are not like that."

"She is no longer people," the Bugti said.

"What are you talking about?"

The White man interrupted, "No, I remember reading of something like this. Collective delusions. I can't remember too much of the specifics, but multiple people who are in a stressful situation can fall prey to a kind of shared hysteria. That must be it. The Pathan is right. People cannot survive their throats being slit, let alone being shot multiple times."

The Bugti sighed. "You asked me on knowing about it. Well now, I tell you what I know. That is her. That is who you killed."

"If I killed her, how does she live?"

"Because she is no longer people."

"Yes, exactly," the Pathan said, his dark figure slowly approaching. "It's a figment of our fatigue."

The Bugti sat with his legs tucked under his body, and he once again sighed a long, laboured breath.

Koh-i-Chiltan

"This is an ancient country. Older than white men or Indians know. Old forces live here. Old forces that I do not understand. No one understands. But this place—it does things. I do not know what it does. But the country can do things to people. To animals. Not good things. I think Satan must do it. Because he torments the dead. The living too. But the dying and the dead especially.

"The elders tell us about the ancients. In one account was a very poor man and his wife, who lived high in the mountains. Neither could have children. They searched for a saint to intercede for them, to help them conceive, but each one told the couple that their plight was what God had written. This was their test, but they did not listen.

"One day, a wanderer arrived, dressed in all black, his face wrapped tightly in a turban. They could only see his eyes—empty, red eyes. He told the couple, 'I am the Saint of a realm you do not know. I will give you children if you only do what I ask.' So, the couple agreed, participating in dark rituals. They desecrated the book and word of God, mocked His messengers and apostles, and disparaged and associated partners with His power.

"Then the wanderer disappeared and the woman fell pregnant and gave birth. And then she fell pregnant again, and she gave birth again. And again. And again. And again—until there were too many children.

"The youngest child was normal. The rest were all deformed in some way. Some with eyes that were totally black. Some had stubs on their heads—horns. Some even had cloven feet. But the woman loved them all as a mother would love her children. But they could not afford them. So, one winter, the man gathered all of his children, except the youngest. He led them up the mountain and told them to wait at the summit; he left them there as he descended for home.

"The woman found out, and she cried and cried, trying to reach the top, but the snow made it impossible. A few years passed, and the youngest was now a healthy, beautiful boy with an interest in exploring. He wanted to climb the mountain on a fine spring day, so his mother took him. When they reached the top, they heard laughter and saw the abandoned children. The children were as peculiar as they had once been.

"They called out, 'Our mother, our mother, we are here!' The woman cried in joy to be reunited, responding with, 'My loves, I am here.' And they said to her, 'Mother, close your eyes. We want to play with our brother. Close your eyes, then try to find us!' So she closed her eyes and smiled.

"She opened her eyes, and no one was there. The youngest child, gone too."

"Why did you tell us that, Bugti?"

"Don't know. Maybe I thought if I told you, you would understand. You would comprehend what this country is, what happens here, that sometimes what is apparent is true, and that what is true isn't always logical, especially when it is evident."

"Your ghost story means nothing, Bugti. And it does not explain that thing we saw. It was a collective hysteric episode. That is all. We need to get to Kahan, and we will survive and be fine."

"Yes. It must have been a collective delusion. It is a coincidence it bore resemblance to the woman of that tent. I can't believe it to be real."

"Again. It is not belief. It is truth and it is evident."

"If you say so, Bugti, but we must leave and we must get out."

The men left the respite of the cavernous carrion. The sun dipped low, and the winds and sands grew cool. The North Star emerged in the purple sky, reminding them of the night to come.

"From the location you remember last, where was Kahan in relation to true north?" the Pathan asked, staring at the star.

"Southeast."

"Then that is the best way to go. In any case, it is where the cliffs are."

"We have no idea if we are still in a location to which Kahan remains in the southeast. And we have tried to reach those cliffs for a day with no food, and it seems we will not reach there before we die of dehydration," the White man said.

"Perhaps. But we have no other options," replied the Pathan, sifting sand between his fingers. "Clearly, we three are delirious, suffering from collective hysteria. And it seems we either move southeast, or we stay and die of madness and dehydration."

In response, the White man nodded in agreement, so they proceeded. The Bugti scanned the landscape and scrunched his brow.

"What's wrong, Bugti?" the Pathan asked.

"Blood."

"Yes. It's from when I cut the White man."

"I know."

"Then what's the issue?"

"No hyenas. No birds."

"Well, the night is setting."

"None earlier, either."

"Isn't that a good thing? We don't have many bullets between us," the White man said.

"Not normal," he said, turning back and pulling his shawl tightly over his face.

Traversing the Night

The Pathan headed the group and drearily marched the men through the frigid sands. The tail of his turban wrapped around his face, his shawl over his head and body as he gripped its corners tightly. They followed the North Star, the brilliant diamond among the dull pearls. The moon, a lamp over the celestial treasure chest. Winds once again sang their solemn shanty, frost and chill piercing every note. The dry freeze pained like an ice pick lodged in their parched throats. They shivered, their teeth chattering violently.

The White man and the Bugti walked back a few paces, shuddering as they plodded along. The White man's hair fluttered in the wind, whilst the Bugti's locks were kept tightly wound in his shawl.

"He's going to kill us, you know," the White man whispered.

"Maybe," replied the Bugti, his face sternly forward.

"Not a maybe. He will."

"He said that you said to kill me when I take you to Kahan."

"Maybe I did, Bugti. But it was immediately after my men were slaughtered by those other Baloch. And besides, that hardly matters now, does it? You've seen what he does, what he's capable of. He'll do it to us."

The Bugti grunted. "He may, but he is your man."

"Hmm. He is *our* man. Or rather, *was* our man. We need to dispatch him before he rids us."

The Bugti snorted audibly as the Pathan glanced behind at them. "You lost control of your Indian," the Bugti said.

"Lost control of my Indian? You can never control Indians."

"Sure, you can."

"Before this, had you ever met Indians?"

"Yes. Merchants and slaves."

"And did you ever meet a good Indian?"

"Only good Indian I ever met were dead Indians."

"And why do you say that?"

"Well, now I've met a free Indian. And he scares me."

"So, you know what we have to deal with?"

"Yes, but the White men are behind the Indians."

"No, no, no. Listen here, Bugti. I tell you here and now that, living amongst the Indians, I am more qualified than any to speak on them. I am telling you that no one can control them. They are wild, beastly people who have descended from ancient glories to hedonism and degeneracy.

"You know India was a land of murder, banditry, and anarchy and that the changes in circumstances were solely due to us. We used politics and violence as a tool to educate them. To show them the wonders of the natural sciences, the rational, the empirically true. But the Indian spirit is built on millennia of casteism and deference to authority. Those unfamiliar with the Indians may incorrectly assume they are a people submissive and easy to control, and that may be true on a group level, but individual Indians are often violent, deranged criminals.

"Tell me of a place on earth with anything comparable to the thuggees or the roving rohillas. You can't, because the Indian is uniquely savage. The Indian is a simple creature whose entire being is about violently asserting authority upon the feeble to be rewarded by the ruler. And when there is no firm ruler, there is anarchy and violence. To rule Indians is to enforce consequence on a race that wishes to exist in constant predation of their inferiors. There is nothing noble about them. They plan faux philosophies, justifying their depraved nonsense as esoteric or artistic, but they are savages, a wretched race. They need a hard stick to bring them to heel. He needs to be brought to heel."

The Bugti remained silent.

The White man continued, "You said it yourself, that the only good Indian is a dead Indian, and we can make a good Indian right here."

"Are you two planning to kill me?"

The White man froze in his tracks and so did the Bugti. "No, don't be stupid, Pathan."

"Well, you're hardly back there whispering, discussing how to throw me a party," the Pathan responded. His obsidian eyes sliced through the night to the White man, who lowered his face to the ground. The Bugti looked at the Pathan, whose usual maroon skin appeared blue and black under the sky's lamps.

"It's quite alright," the Pathan continued. "It's only natural you would, and so I don't resent you for it. Both of you seem to have developed a dislike for me, especially this White man who failed to get the better of me. If I were you, I would probably do the same."

"We weren't planning anything," the White man reiterated.

"I find there to be a natural prohibition amongst Englishmen telling the truth. I'm not sure if this is something you agree on as a society or if it is genetically predisposed. But it is evident that everything an Englishman says is either a lie or a statement to be broken. Perhaps that is unfair to say this about Englishmen. I am sure Scots or the Welsh are scarcely better, but I've never seen a White man's word to be true."

"And Indians are the paragon of truth and virtue? Remind me of the state of the land before we arrived."

"Indians may not speak in truth, and an Indian's word is never to be trusted, if I am to say so myself. But I must say that Indians act in a way more apparently truthful than an Englishman could ever imagine. The Indian deals in violence and fear, these two being the key considerations informing the fact of life—survival. In a way, Indians are the most truthful men on earth. White men write in abstracts about esoteric assumptions or conclusions of nature. The Indian speaks and behaves as is apparent in the reality around him."

"There were Indian philosophers and English idiots. Neither is entirely one nor the other," the Bugti remarked.

"Thank you, Bugti," said the Pathan. "Obviously, not every Englishman is one way and not every Indian is one way. That is not what I was saying. Rather, in general, this is the rule that describes the attributes of Indians and White men."

"Take the rule. It is evidently wrong on so many occasions. So, what is the point of the rule?"

"To describe in broad strokes the traits and qualities of these people, as I have said."

The Bugti grunted. "Hmm. The White Man says you are one thing, because he knows Indians are like that. And you say he must be another thing because you know English men are like that. But you can be neither nor both."

The Pathan laughed and looked towards the Bugti, his face like carved granite glistening in the lunar rays. "You see Bugti, as with art, I—"

His laughter turned to instant dread. The winds stopped singing, transforming into screeching banshees speeding through the sky. The stars and moon faded.

"What is this?"

"I don't know."

"What is this!"

"I don't know."

"This isn't a delusion."

"No. Yes. It must be. It can't be. It must be."

"She's here."

"No, no, no."

"She is here."

The shadowy figure staggered towards them, with vicious winds surrounding her. The ghastly chorus reached a crescendo, screaming in pain and regret. The sands rose with her; their grains swept up from the dunes, grounding her every step. The men's breathing became heavy and laboured. The White man panted hysterically, falling to his knees.

"It's not real. It's a figment of our imagination!"

"For God's sake, it's the same thing as before! How can it then be a delusion?" the Pathan shouted.

"We—we haven't had water for two days. We're crazy. It's not real."

"Alright," the Pathan said as he backed away with the Bugti. "It's not real."

"Yes, I said it's not real. I'm dehydrated. I'm hungry. I'm stressed. This isn't anything but my mind."

"Yes, alright. Yes, you're right," the Pathan said as he and the Bugti slipped into the night.

The woman continued to advance, slowly, cricks and cracks audible with her every movement. Her body staggered towards the White man.

The White Man

In the all-encompassing darkness stood the White man and a woman—perhaps even a girl—with no name. The winds, the chill, and sands ceased to exist. In this moment, the only things apparent were him and her. The White man studied the woman, her ivory skin replacing the moon in radiance. Her plump, cherry lips wore a line of blood running to her jaw, slowly dripping from her chin. She licked her lips, wiping her cheeks with her long, pointed tongue. Her high cheekbones cast a shadow across the rest of her face and her sapphire eyes shone like stars in the darkness, a captivating eminence that froze the White man in place. As she exhaled, a hiss came from the gash in her delicate throat, only to be replaced by a wretched croak as she inhaled. Flesh, blood, and plasma oozed and pulsated like a gory jelly. Inside the sliced throat sat a black carrion bird, barely the size of a man's thumb. It picked and tore at the wound, nibbling on black and green pus around its new nest. Her eyes fixed on him, and he could do little but stare back with eyes wide and mouth gaped.

"You're not real. You're not."

The woman raised her arms slowly, her black cloak retreating from white wrists. Spindly fingers appeared as spider limbs and scorpion tails, wiry and edged with jagged claws for nails. She placed those nails on his face as he insisted that he was in a dream. Perhaps he knew it was not, for her flesh on his was white hot, a fire never experienced before.

She hissed and gasped, rubbing her palms across his cheeks and brow before setting them just above his eyes. She stabbed them with her thumbs, skewering them upon the digits. He let out a blood-curdling scream, grasping her arms, trying desperately to move her hands. But every time he tried to grab her; her flesh burnt through him. He screamed in pain, wailing like a stray dog being torn asunder and eaten alive by wild hyenas. Her thumbs remained in his sockets, and she pulled and pulled, the internal breaks and fractures of his face splitting into two. His skull tore apart from the inside, his eye sockets, then his maxilla, then mandible, and then the frontal lobe cracked apart. Blood and brain fluid poured from his facial orifices.

The woman stood in the desert, slowly bringing her prize to her. The clumps of crumpled flesh, bone, hair, and viscera in each of her hands. She threw them on the sands, next to the collapsed corpse, now in a pool of its own blood. Most of the brain remained intact on the ground and she stomped on it, pounding it into nothingness. She then turned her green gaze to the two brown men across the dunes who began running. And she followed.

Scaling Cliffs

The Bugti and the Pathan ran into the great black void, directionless and lost. The Pathan's boots were worn through. One of them lost a sole, so he ran on his bare sock. The Bugti had lost both sandals some time ago, and his feet were cut on jagged stones, but he did not realise it, because they now felt like frozen stubs, devoid of feeling.

The two looked back and saw a trail of their own blood following them. They escaped the nightmare for now, if only temporarily. The sun rose again, turning the black into purple. It was cold, but still warmer than the night, and so their nerves slowly returned to their limbs and digits.

The Bugti and Pathan started to dry heave. Both yelling from pain and exhaustion, staring at paths of their own viscera in the sands. The Bugti fell to the floor, and the Pathan squatted down by him.

"We need water," the Pathan said.

"I know."

"Where do we get it?"

"I don't know."

"It's been two days."

"Yes."

"If we can't find water, I'm going to kill you and drink your blood."

The Bugti said nothing and stared at the ground. Then he spoke again, "You see. She is not just in our imagination."

It was the Pathan's turn to be silent and to stare at the sand. He stood up and pointed weakly towards the cliffs. "There must be vegetation up there. We can wring them out for water and try to eat them for nutrition."

"She's coming."

"From the cliffs we can then scout out where we will advance to, still southeast I believe, towards Kahan."

"She is coming for you."

The Pathan sighed and readjusted his turban, the black cloth still tightly wound despite all the exertion. "How do you know it is coming for me?"

The Bugti pointed to the head tied to his hips.

"This?"

"Yes."

"It wants the head?"

"Maybe. Maybe revenge for her father. Or herself. But it wants you."

"You don't know that for certain."

"No. But you have a head on your belt. And you killed her."

"How did I kill her if she is clearly alive and walking?"

"The White man tried to argue with reality. Look what happened. You're next, Indian."

"How do I stop it?"

"I don't know."

The Pathan grabbed the old man's head and removed it from his belt. The thing barely stayed in his grip, its flesh now grey. Slimy clumps of fat and skin fell into his palms. The hair had fallen out, but there was no smell and no flies. He looked into its empty eye sockets, black voids that contained the endless depth of space and time within them. He faced back to the Bugti. "I will give her this."

"Okay."

"Will she accept it?"

"I don't know."

The two stood silently for a few moments, the cold gusts soon replaced by the lashings of the sun. The men looked towards the cliffs they intended to scale and cupped their eyes. For the first time in a long time, they saw an animal along it. It was too distant to make out what exactly it was.

"There must be vegetation; something is living off of it," the Pathan remarked.

"Might be a predator. A hyena," the Bugti retorted.

"Even better. A predator means prey, and prey means plants, and plants mean water."

The Bugti grunted in agreement.

"I figure we could get up there in less than half a day."

"I agree. If there are no distractions."

"Oh, I intend for there to be none, Bugti."

"Neither did the White man intend for one."

"Yes, well," the Pathan began as he and the Bugti ventured across the dunes towards the cliff. "White men generally don't intend for many of the consequences they bring upon themselves."

"But you killed her."

"Yes. But why am I here?"

"Because you chose to be."

The Pathan scoffed and then chuckled, smiling for the first time in a while. "And so did you."

"I did what I had to do for my people."

"And I for mine. But the difference between you and me, Bugti, is that I am cut out for this. I have told you before. War is art and I am its greatest student, but you don't understand, and you never will. You're just some man who thought he could gain a few rupees. You're not a killer, but I am. And I have done what I needed to do, and enjoyed what rights my mastery over this art has bought me. But you can't and you won't."

"Maybe. But I do not need your words and your philosophy to convince me. Killing an innocent man and raping his women is wrong."

The Pathan laughed again and put his arm around the Bugti's shoulders. "I see. You know it is wrong for me to kill men and enjoy women, and then kill them too, because you're a man of principles. But it is not wrong for you to bring me to them?"

"I did not know you would do that."

"What is it you suppose a conquering army does, Bugti? Do they coddle the men they conquer? Do they treat the women as their mothers and raise the children as their own? No, you idiot. You know the rules of the art as well as I do, even if you pretend to be ignorant of them. We kill every man. We kill all the elderly. We kill the children, the babies, and the women carrying them in their arms or wombs. We spare only the young women unburdened by offspring and we take them as our slaves, and even then, if we so desire, we may kill some of them for sport as well. This is the ultimate form of expression, the peak of art. To assert complete domination, to the point of death, upon your rival, to slit the throats of his children, and to take his women as prizes. This is war. This is what you brought us to do."

"No. No. This is what you have done."

"And I could only have done it thanks to you," the Pathan said, grinning, still hugging the Bugti under his arm.

"So, see the retribution your action has brought upon you."

The Pathan scowled. "Upon us."

"Upon you."

"How are you so uncertain that it wants nothing to do with you and everything to do with me?"

"Again. Who killed her?"

"Hmm. And who bought us into her father's tents as guests? Who disarmed him, pretending to be a native friend. I've said it before and I will say it again, Bugti, you're a fool. You know the policy of the company and you know the nature of war, and you still claim to be ignorant. Actually, you are not a fool. You're a coward. You know reality and your culpability in it, but you close your eyes and pretend to be ignorant."

"I know what is evident, and that actions rest with those who commit them."

The Pathan laughed and said, "She is coming for you, Bugti. She is coming for you, too."

"If she comes, give her the head."

"Well, hopefully we will have worked our way out of this by then."

"You can't outrun her."

"We already have, twice."

"These things play with us. She could have killed us both by now. Appease her with the head when she returns."

"You think it will work?"

"I don't know."

"Alright. Well, we don't have much else to work with now, do we?"

"No."

"We need to scale that cliff?"

"Yes."

Under the burning heat marched the two brown men, stumbling, thirsty, and hungry. They became dumb, unwilling to dry their throats with parched words. The sand cooked the leather of their boots and the skin of their feet, boiling the blood that dripped on its wretched grains.

The Bugti fell by a large black rock. He hugged it and pulled himself atop of it; the thing cooking his limbs through his tunic. "I cannot go on."

"Okay," remarked the Pathan, who squatted for a bit, coughing, before he walked again.

"You will not wait for me?"

"Why would I?"

"I would wait for you."

"Well, I'm not you."

"That is clear."

"Then why try to force an equivalence?"

"Maybe you would change."

"I would not. Certainly not for you."

"I can't go any further," the Bugti said. He lifted his feet, mangled and bloodied like a freshly slaughtered lamb. The white undersides of his feet had become bright red, fried by the scorching sands.

The Pathan looked at the Bugti's stumps and sighed. He drew his pistol from his belt and examined the chamber.

"You will shoot me?" asked the Bugti.

"It would be a mercy. But no," said the Pathan. He fiddled around with the thing, emptying the chamber into his hand, counting the single bullet and carefully placing it back.

"Then what?"

"Leave you here, I suppose."

"I will die."

"I know."

"Why?"

"Why what?"

"Why will you leave me to die?"

The Pathan sighed and wiped his face with his hands. He came to the side of the Bugti's stone and crouched down beside him, his knees audibly cracking as he did so. He wiped yellow mucus from the edge of his eyes and sighed once more.

"Alright Bugti, there are four options here. One is that I wait here with you. Look at the condition of your feet. You won't ever leave here on your own accord. You will die of dehydration, or that woman will come back here. In such a case, I also die, either through the woman or water. Second, I can try to carry you with me to the cliff. What will I do with you when we arrive and we need to scale it? I can't carry you, and you can't climb. So again, you will die through any number of ways, and so will I. Besides, Bugti, you know I am also thirsty. I can't take you there. Third, I shoot you. That would be best for you, but I may well need this bullet, and I cannot waste it on you. So, that leaves us with the fourth option. I will leave you here whilst I go to the cliffs."

The two sat in silence for a moment.

"Do you understand?" the Pathan asked.

"Yes." And they remained in silence for some time more. "I cannot be bait for her if she wants to kill you."

"Of course you can. You'll be here, and she's no doubt following us."

"These things don't work like that."

"Work like what?"

"Not how you think."

"What?"

"It's out for revenge. It will get you."

"Perhaps," the Pathan said, strapping his boots and raising the pistol to his face once more. He caressed its barrel and wooden handle, his maroon hand blending into the mahogany hilt that gave way to ornately decorated iron. "But before it does, it will get you."

The Pathan walked away, but the abandoned meat behind him called out.

"You speak of war and philosophy and art and morals, but you will leave me here to die."

"War has no time for mercy for the meek."

"You're a sick man."

"You're a dead one."

"You're scared."

"I'm terrified."

And for the first time in a long time, the Bugti saw the Pathan as he really was. The great Indian god of war had become mortal, fear clear in his actions and face. "All that complex philosophy. Questioning me and my morals. Speaking of art. Speaking of war. But you're just like me. A man. Just a man."

"Well, that was never a doubt in my mind," the Pathan said. He stopped again, crossing his legs on the sand. He removed his open, torn red coat. "He who lives by the sword must appreciate that man is mortal. And no one is more familiar with this than soldiers. And what is an Indian good for but soldiering? Not much, in all honesty. Myself, those Rohillas who came with us, and many other men understand, or understood, this.

"I know, I'm a man. I know I'm mortal. And it's that mortality, that fact that I am just a man, that brings me joy when I slaughter apes like yourself. I enjoy snuffing out the flickering candles of life from those who are in my way. I told you, I worship war, and these are my sacrifices to her. I am just a man—one dedicated to war. So, I am a killer of men.

A killer of women. A killer of children. And as a man dedicated to war, I always knew that one day, something would do the same to me. Something would come to me, related to war, and snuff out my existence in the same way I have done to countless others.

"This may well be my end. Gone. The very act of my death, a final spectacle of devotion in the endless violence that is prayer. But I don't want that. At least, not now. Not before you. I'm not sure ever.

"So, I will save myself, Bugti. I'm not sorry that I won't put you out of your misery. You're between me and it, and I'd rather you buy me time to drink and leave. I promise you, when I arrive at Kahan, I will join the largest army the White men have ever assembled from India, and we will march into these forsaken mountains and deserts and kill every single one of your wretched race. We will slaughter your men and elderly and children and rape your young women and bring them back to India as slaves, where we will rape them all again in full view of the entire country."

The Pathan picked up the skull from his belt and raised it, staring into its sockets. "You have my word."

"An ugly oath."

"I intended it to be." The Pathan stood up and rolled his jacket up under his sleeve. He hesitated and unrolled it, removing a brass pin and throwing it at the Bugti. It landed squarely in the lap of his tunic. "I have one mercy for you. Split your arteries and veins with it if you want."

The Bugti picked it up in silence and clasped it between both of his black hands, resting it on his stomach.

The Desert

The Pathan wandered through the sands, struggling through the beige inferno in his undershirt, khakis, broken boots, and his red jacket under his armpit. In his belt, he carried a pistol with a single shot, a bayonet, and the decapitated head swaying from his belt. The black turban was now wrapped across his face and neck. He stopped for a bit, huffing, and wiped the bridge of his nose on his sleeve. There was no sweat, and he knew what that meant. All the while, the cliffs appeared no closer. In fact, they seemed further. He wondered if there were any hills at all, let alone ones containing any semblance of life.

He replayed what he saw on the cliff again and again in his head, trying to discern if the shadows of creatures resembled the shape of any animal he knew of, or if it was a mirage induced through dehydration. But if it was his imagination, then how did the Bugti see it? Clearly through the phenomenon explained by that poor White man. *Collective hysteria.* His mind wandered for a second, contemplating if the word "hysteria" had to mean what he assumed it meant, a crazy reaction to something imagined—or if one seeing a mirage would similarly satisfy its definition. If it did, then what was the difference between one's imagination and one's hysteria?

His head snapped back to his present circumstance, ceasing to contemplate on the meanings of English words. Instead, he pondered his situation. There were two possibilities: the cliff was real, or it was not. And there were two possible conditions of that cliff: that it sustained life, or it did not. So, the Pathan sat and calculated that, given his state, there was perhaps an equal chance of delusion as there was of the cliff being real. Any life he witnessed may have also been a hallucination; the second was dependent on the first. He would most likely die here, but if he kept pushing, there was a slim chance he might save himself.

He rose to his feet once more, his boots now feeling like thin wraps of leather bandages around his battered feet. His joints cracked under each step; his head ached in sharp jolts in ways he did not know the head could produce. He tried to control his breathing. He rubbed his hands; the skin became like paper, crumpling and folding under the pressure, but it did not revert to its original state. Looking towards the impossible cliffs, he lifted off again. The beating sun, only a slight relief as it descended from its zenith. Every few steps, he stopped to catch his breath. His vision clouded with black spots. The Pathan staggered and stopped, staggered and stopped, and continued like this.

The cliffs appeared no closer. The beige wastelands did not cease in any direction. The Pathan contemplated for a moment, deciding to wait for the cool night to continue, and lay in the sands. He unbuttoned his khakis; the metal stinging his fingers with conducted heat, and removed his undershirt. He tied the garments together to form a makeshift blanket, which he wrapped around his body. He unwrapped the turban, the fabric cooking in his hands, and placed it to his side. The Pathan unrolled his jacket, laid it onto the sand, sat upon it, and untied what remained of his boots. Lying down, he then took a loose sleeve from his blanket and wrapped it around his head, creating an insular void in the face of the screaming sun. He roasted in the sand as the heat radiated through his jacket, but this was better than lying directly on the sand, being flash-fried alive.

Despite the mental and physical difficulty, the Pathan eventually drifted into a bleak abyss, empty voids encapsulating him. He slowly succumbed to sleep, its absence of conciseness, an eternity in nothing. But the Pathan woke again, his brain screaming in pain, his eyes heavy, his limbs dead. He untied the sleeve from his face and looked around at his unchanged circumstance. The sun had not moved, the sands still scorched, and the cliffs were still far.

The Pathan closed his eyes, picked at their lids, plucking away the mucus with his fingernails. He gagged, trying to hold his throat firm, for he knew he could not risk losing more moisture. But he could not help it and spat out a green, pulsating blob into the sand. It burrowed into the ground. The Pathan stared at where his spit had once been, deciding he had gone insane. He then felt the sand, something wet in it, and disputed if he really had lost his sanity or if something else was happening. Or both.

He removed the head from his belt, tried to split it open with his bayonet, but it had become jerky under the sun. So, he sliced a piece of the cheek and chewed on it. It was dry, sucking more moisture from his parched tongue than it provided. The Pathan gagged again. He scraped the crushed flesh from his tongue and threw it onto the sand where it sizzled for a few moments. He hooked at remnants of flesh from between his incisors and pulled at that which was stuck in the gaps of his molars, but he could not reach it all, leaving remnants pinched in his gums.

The Pathan untied his makeshift blanket, put on his undershirt, and rolled up his sleeves to his elbows. He buttoned up his khakis, wrapped what was left of his boots around his feet, and rolled his jacket under his shoulder before throwing the turban loosely around his head and shoulders. He attached the head to his belt, struggling up to continue his fruitless advance. He could now hardly stand, and every few steps he fell again to his knees.

An endless ocean of beige surrounded the Pathan. Dunes rolled on forever, rippling into innumerable infinities; the great sand plains expanded into eternity. The sky was a brilliant blue, the kind men admired as the sun shone brightly, not a cloud in sight. Except this was torture. The lack of clouds meant no respite and no rain. The perfect sky offered no protection from the cosmic torment that drained him physically and emotionally. The Pathan dragged himself atop a dune and cupped his hands over his eyes, observing the boundless expanse before him. He noted the innumerable particles of microscopic sand comprising the desert. If he was a bit more put together, he would have something profound to say, but philosophising escaped his mind. He refocused on the cliffs, continuing his traverse through the wastelands.

A little wind emerged across the sand peaks. At first, it was barely noticeable, like a child gently tugging at the ends of a tunic. And after some time, it was a nuisance—hot wind hitting hot skin. But then the Pathan was blasted by scorching winds carrying millions of shards of sand, tearing at his eyes and nose. He tried in vain to tie his turban over his face, but it was too late. He could no longer see. Wetness formed under his nose and ears. The blood did not run, for he was so lacking in body water that it congealed almost instantly. The wind continued its assault, now a full sandstorm enveloping the Pathan. He could see nothing, but grains carried by the shifting winds. He crawled into a foetal position, struggling to cover his head in cloth, but almost as soon as the storm started, it finished. The winds were no more.

The Pathan arose, coughing out sand, his face bloodied. An oasis stood before him, an impossible pool of water, clear and bright, a mirror to the sky. Around it were trees of all varieties; robust date and coconut trees, mango shrubs barely taller than him, carrying bountiful, ripe fruits, ready to be plucked by hands.

"God is great," muttered the Pathan, approaching the place. He walked under the date trees, and for the first time in a long time, he received respite from the heat. He sat in the shade of the great leaves, in shadows of bliss and serenity. After a few moments, he rose and plucked a handful of dates from the tree. He rolled the yellow fruits between his fingers, their waxy skin soft and pleasant against his cracked skin. He moved to the edge of the pool and sat down, the cool breeze serenading him. The Pathan waded his hand through the water, the chill radiating through him, soothing his flesh and soul. He cupped the same hand and scooped the water to his face. He closed his eyes, bringing the water to his parched, crusty lips. He gulped and spat it out immediately. A heavy taste of iron and salt repulsed him. The Pathan gagged heavily, choking on the thick liquid that ran red down his chin. He heaved and spat on the ground again and again and again. The dates in his other hand began to wiggle, becoming maggots and cockroaches; their wretched forms bursting out of the yellow flesh. He threw them to the ground, stomping them violently into the sand.

He now stood in a deep crimson pool. Severed arms and legs and torsos bobbed up and down in the gory pond; bone, muscle, limbs, and corpses. The Pathan hyperventilated as the trees turned black. The hanging fruits transformed to rotting flesh swarmed by flies, their incessant buzzing drilling into his eardrums, worms and grubs crawled in and out of their fleshy burrows.

The skull on the Pathan's belt started to rattle. He took it in his hands and a viper slithered between its eye sockets before it retreated into its brain cavity. The Pathan screamed, throwing it on the ground. He kicked it, screamed again, and scrunched his eyes shut.

The Pathan opened his eyes after a few seconds. He saw nothing but an all-encompassing black void. He shuffled around, trying desperately to find traces of the trees and pool that had been there, the taste of salt and iron still in his throat. The cool that, a moment ago, had been a relief, had twisted into a biting chill, slicing his skin and hair in icy malice. The winds began to speak—hushed ugly whispers that remarked of his mortality and predicament.

You are but a man—and all men die.

The Pathan

The sun disappeared; no moon emerged to take its place. Instead, an obsidian cloak forced itself on to the world, distorting the earth it displaced. The whispers became screams. The Pathan's ears oozed blood as the never-ending screeches of torment thundered through his sanity, stabbing like an ice pick.

Then all became silent.

She appeared on the horizon, her twisted, demented figure creaked and cracked its way to him. He saw her and rose to his feet. All pain and trauma left his body instantly. He leapt to position, loading the final round into the chamber of the pistol. His hand squeezed the stock, the cold metal now burning his hand. He did not care and could not feel. He raised his thumb and pulled down the hammer, aiming directly at her head. His finger squeezed.

A thundering crack shattered the silence. A flash of orange tore through the abyss.

The woman still advanced. Unfettered. Undeterred. Unwavering.

He could see her limbs twist, convulsing through her robes, her ivory skin protruding through parts of her black burqa, her bones splintering through rancid flesh. Her raspy call became audible, each breath resonating a thousand times between his ears. Her green eyes burned his soul, balls of smokeless fire singeing themselves into his being. He stood in silence, his arm grew limp, and the pistol slipped from his fingers.

She continued towards him, and he was powerless to resist her. His arms were stone, unmoving at his side. The Pathan's legs were petrified, frozen like a sculpture of ice. His mouth gaped; his breath, a pale smoke wafting before his face.

The air performed a macabre dance around the approaching figure. Her auburn hair waded through the black night, her ruby lips uttering ancient curses, her eyes fixated on the object of despair. She approached with dilated pupils, a kind of ethereal glow above her so that every ghastly and visceral detail of her wretched state was apparent to him. The Pathan's eyes were forced into place by some unknown force. There before him was a testament to his sins. There before him stood the living, or dead, or undead canvas upon which the art of war had been expressed. There before him stood the manifestation of his desires and actions. And it stared back at him, her eyes perfectly parallel with his, the two seeing each other candidly. The Pathan saw a hurt soul, a humiliated soul, a soul that desired vengeance. And she saw fear.

They said and did nothing for what seemed like forever until the Pathan let out a sharp breath and reached for his belt. He took the head with the nonexistent eyes—the trophy—between his palms. He turned the thing around, knelt on one knee, his eyes fixated on her, and raised the grisly thing. She continued to walk, each crack in her bones piercing through the void until she was but three steps ahead of him. And she stopped. She looked at him and his offering and shot out her white arms, the sleeves of her burqa rolled up. She grabbed the head and examined it. He didn't know what she was doing with it, but she seemed to remember at least a few things about what it was. She gently caressed its decayed features, then threw it behind her into the nothingness. The Pathan grabbed his bayonet, holding it ahead of him with two hands, shivering and shuddering with every laboured breath.

She stepped towards him.

Crunch again. Crack again.

She was there.

The Pathan lunged forward, but she caught his arm in an icy grip. He screamed and let go of the knife. She squeezed his arm, which seared from the freeze of her touch. He continued to wail, trying desperately to pry himself from her grip with his other hand, but it was no use. Her jagged fingernails pierced his flesh, hoisting her prey into place. Blood emerged, but he was so devoid of liquid that it coagulated into a crimson gelatine mess. His eyes widened at the torn state of his arm. He wanted to scream again, but his neck throbbed in pain. Each ululation felt like a thousand knives in his throat. He convulsed, and again tried to pry her grip from him, but she did not waver, instead she took his throat in her other hand and dug into his sun-cracked flesh. She pulled his head down as he flailed in fruitless resistance, bringing him closer. He was taken to his knees, and she kneeled down too, having his face in both of her hands. He felt the ice pierce through his cheeks and his skull chatter within her grip.

They stared into each other's eyes for a moment, and she let go of his face, moving her arms and hands down to his waist to embrace him, pressing her head against his chest. Then she began to weep and wail, but without sound. Then, a stifled cry followed by an audible inhale, her tears wet on his body. He brought his hands down to the back of her head and across her shoulder, and with all the strength he could muster, uttered a quiet 'shush'.

She pulled away from him and again looked at his face. For what seemed like an eternity, the two did only that. He became lost in the somber beauty of her eyes, those precious stones becoming enticing snares. He was astounded by her shapely lips, the plumpness of cherry curves. The definition of her jaw and the rise in her cheekbones humbled him. Her neck was so delicate, so precious. The throbbing gash seemed to accentuate the enchanting fragility of her throat. He knew it was not the first time he had fallen in love with her. He remembered how he had taken her beauty in his hands before, trying to dispose of it when he was finished with it. And now she was here. She had returned and there was no disposing of her now. There she stood, all her features and beauty somehow so apparent despite the black stage surrounding them. And there she stood, bearing the consequences of his desire for them.

She took his head in her hands once more, gently caressing him, her coarse broken fingers striking each thick strand of black hair. She wept again. He sat motionless, listening as each tear conveyed part of a short story of hardship, grief, and violence in which he was the most pivotal character.

But he was not moved. He knew in his heart that he acted in accordance with the law of the conqueror and so he lowered his gaze to look into nothing and he thought nothing of the consequences of his previous actions, beyond the fact that he was now the conquered, and whatever happened now was merely the final act of worship to war. To live by the sword was to die by the sword, and he had danced upon its edge since before he could walk.

The woman forced her fingers into the Pathan's mouth, tearing through his crusty lips, slicing his gums. He tried to bite them in resistance but lost all strength. She grabbed onto his lower jaw, hooking her digits under his teeth, pulling and burrowing through his dental roots. Puddles of viscera pooled through the gory holes in his face. She pulled down, loud cracks piercing the silence until his jaw came off. A bloody mess of mandible and flesh in her hands. She swung it into his skull, a loud crack thundering louder than any pistol. She did it again and again and again until he fell over and there was nothing left of his face but a ruined coagulation of brain, sinew, organs, and a single eyeball amongst the carnage.

The Lone Survivor

The Bugti began to feel his feet, agony across a million nerves, each synapse-marked pain more intense than the last. Escaping from here would entail potential amputation of both feet, but the more immediate question related to leaving this place first.

He hoisted himself off of his rock, his arms, two blackened swings. He threw himself up and crumpled into the sands' unrelenting furnace, each grain aflame. He couldn't move and lay grunting, roasting alive. He finally forced himself upright and tore off his tunic, which he placed beneath him. The blood from his gashes solidified like a gory cement around his feet and legs, but he still could not move them.

The Bugti took the brass pin from his trousers, using all his might to pry apart the sleeves from his tunic. He wrapped them around his feet, the white cotton becoming carmine stained bandages. He put his elbows on the rock, heaving in pain as he lifted himself, trying to walk. He stumbled a few steps and then stood motionless, panting and cursing. His head ached, his kidneys and liver were also in pain. His vision went in and out of black before he fell to the ground. When he came to again, the beige dunes and blue sky somehow merged into the sandy horizon. He sat up with his legs crossed, falling in and out of consciousness; his insides writhing from its lack of nourishment.

Some time later, the sun set, and the moon rose; their celestial lights intersected into a magenta sky with yellow accents and orange highlights. But all this was lost on the Bugti, who could no longer distinguish the hues. All he knew was that night was coming, and with that came the cold, and he was without a shirt. He contemplated whether it would be better to die of dehydration, of exposure to the icy winds, or to simply split open his arteries.

After some time, the Bugti held the pin in his hand tightly, his fingers trembling as the world turned black. He stabbed into his wrists and closed his eyes, and slowly drifted away into the realm of dreams.

He saw a black ram with twisted, knobby horns. Its sides were bare of wool and skin. Instead, it bore red, tender flesh, marbled with whirls of pink fat. It sat in silence as a small flock of carrion birds flew around it, cawing at each other as they flew atop the creature. They pecked at its sides alternately before flying off. The Bugti looked to the right, where he saw a mountain of dead lambs, each white and pristine, save for their eyes and tongues that were removed with surgical precision. Each had a cavity in their chests from where their lungs had been pulled out.

He approached the corpses and felt around them; fresh blood covered his fingers. Then each of the heads on the mountain of death twisted to face him and bleated. Slowly at first—meekly. The bleating gradually raised in tempo and volume until the Bugti could hear nothing but the desperate pleas of the savaged animals, each call like ghastly talons clawing at his eardrums.

The Bugti opened his eyes, his breathing heavy, and his brow thick with sweat. His fingers were wet and though he did not know where the liquid had come from or what it was, his parched tongue greedily lapped at it. There was nothing before him but the silhouettes of the dunes now made black and purple under the ethereal shade of the moon and the stars.

He examined his wrists and saw how the blood immediately congealed on exit. He sighed in both frustration and relief, realising that one of his three grisly options was not possible given his condition. He raised himself off the remains of his tunic and slid it back over him. He tried to walk and advance, slowly and steadily, until he realised that the air had gone from cold to a searing freeze that bit his exposed flesh. There were no more silhouettes, no celestial bodies. In fact, he could not even tell where the earth ended and the sky began. There began the subtle chorus of the winds, their harrowing notes delivering their song of despair. He knew what was going to happen. He knew what had to happen.

From the void came the woman, her burqa tattered, her face as battered as he had remembered. As she staggered towards him, he tried to get up, and for a second, he did. He hobbled a few steps on shredded feet before tumbling down into a loud thud. He smacked into inky, invisible ground. Flat on his rear, he tried to crawl backwards on the palms of his hands, barely dragging the rest of his body with him. He heaved as she came closer, knowing his retreat could not save him. He became a pathetic grovel in the face of her methodical pursuit. She cornered him like the disloyal dog he knew he was. A raspy breath exhaled through her mouth, her gash pulsing a demented beat, a monotonous pounding juxtaposed by the screeching winds.

When she was a few feet away, all went silent. For there were just the two of them in that moment, an enclave of spite hidden from all else. The two stared at each other, anticipating what the other would do.

"Tell me, dear," the Bugti said in Baluchi, his voice tense. "Why have you come here? Why have you come for me?"

She stood in silence, but the gash in her throat spoke, pulsating and undulating with each breath. Her face stood fixated on his, holding a judgmental scowl.

"I'm an innocent man. I did you no wrong."

The plea fell on deaf ears; her face remained unchanged as she inched closer on broken ankles and toes.

He ceased crawling backwards, the futility of escape now clear. "Leave me be. Return to the desert."

But she did not leave him, and she did not return to anything. She stood—tall and firm.

"I have a wife, dear. You would not make her a widow, would you?" She continued.

"I have children. You would not make them orphans. Would you?" She continued.

As the woman approached, the Bugti crossed one arm around his face and stuck his other in front of him to defend the attack. She grabbed the outstretched limb in her jagged claws and pulled, long gashes being torn through his sun-jerkied arm. He screeched in pain, pulling his body backwards, trying to free his arm, but as he retreated, her nails deepened within him until they cut through capillaries and veins.

She pulled, and he came tumbling towards her feet. She finally released him. He grovelled before her, whimpering in pain and fear. But there was no use. She descended to her knees, forcibly hooking her fingers into his sides, and hoisted him to his feet. The Bugti screamed in anguish. She then felt around his bare chest until her freezing fingertips happened upon his centre. She gently tapped and then dug at the ribs until she burrowed into his chest cavity. The man howled a primal scream. Once she grasped a pair of ribs, she pulled outwards until they snapped and shattered through the other side of his body. She then dug deeper, grabbing hold of a throbbing organ and pulled it out. The man's last conscious moment was the vision of the woman holding his beating heart.

The Bugti slumped to the ground, his cavernous wound leaking heaps of gore.

In the End

In the end, Marri country was never conquered by the Company, nor the Empire after it. Kearney's men were defeated as they marched on Kahan. It became a boast that the Marri alone, among the Rajas of India and Khans of Afghanistan, defeated the British and the Indians in battle. Soon after, the White man would lose Kabul as Afghan warriors crushed their imperial ambitions beneath their boots in the snows of Hindu Kush.

This story of the sands and mountains and plains repeated time and time again, the essence of man etched into the fabric of the landscape through abandoned castles, tents, and towns. But people remain, as they always have and always will. The impression of ancestors recent and long gone embedded into the genetic and cultural legacy of a nomad girl, their features carved into her face, their stories, fears, hopes, and aspiration inscribed into her consciousness. They manifest in her memory as she tends to her father, her mother, and camels in a small encampment where strangers arrive, beg as guests, having their true nature unknown, yet the duty of hospitality is incumbent upon them. This has happened a million times before, and it will happen a million times again.

In the Grip

Mei Davis

’ve told Jenny a thousand times if I’ve told her once the front door won’t open anymore, but does she listen? No, she goes to the front door, knocks three times, crosses her arms, and presses her lips like she can barely contain what a hellhole she thinks the house has become, and I know she goes to the front door on purpose just to get at me.

Someone’s always trying to get at me.

“The back door!” I yell from my bedroom window. “You know that door won’t open!”

“You said you would clear everything out.”

“The hell I did! Why are you here, anyway?”

She waves her phone. “You tell me. I woke up in the middle of the night to a message—largely incoherent, I should add—rambling about someone breaking into the house?” She pushes her sunglasses to the top of her head, as if showing off her red, puffy eyes will prove she would rather be anywhere other than visiting her own mother. “Have you been drinking again?”

"I'm an adult. I'll do what I please, and if you don't like it, then go home!"

"Is someone really breaking into the house?"

I jut out my chin. "Come inside and see, if you don't believe me." A challenge if there ever was one.

Little Miss Prim and Proper hasn't come inside the house for years. Says she won't do it anymore, that it's not good for her health, blah blah blah. A germaphobe, that's what she is. Even as a child, she was always after me to throw this out or clean that up, like I was her maid. Like I wasn't working double shifts just to keep food on the table. Like I didn't have it hard enough raising the brat by myself, but no, I had to be Martha Stewart while I did it!

"Fine," she mutters. "But just for a minute, and because I'm worried."

She walks to the side gate and circles around to the back of the house. The sliding glass door shattered a few years ago, but the screen is in good shape and keeps the worst of the bugs and critters out.

"If you're worried about burglars, you should get that door replaced," she says.

"You come here just to nag me to death?" She knows I don't have money for repairs but has to rub it in my face every chance she gets.

"The only reason I ever come here is to help you." She slides the screen open and steps inside, pressing her handbag against her body as she squeezes between the piles of my things flanking either side of the door. She won't say it, but she's afraid her expensive leather will get contaminated if it touches anything in the house, and isn't it just like her to care more about her handbag than her own mother?

"Forget burglars, I'll be dead of old age by the time you finally get in here!"

"You don't need to be a contortionist to get into my house, so forgive me if I'm a little out of practice."

Of course, she'd say that, even though the living room is something I can be proud of. I'll own that the rest of the house could use some tidying, but in the living room I've piled up everything carefully, made a nice path from the back door to the kitchen, and another one to the bedrooms. But what does Jenny do? Tiptoes into the room like she's walking through a minefield, halting at an itty-bitty pile of old magazines like she's at the foot of the Himalayas.

"Just step over it!" I say. "It's not hard!"

"These are covered in mold," she says. "Why are you keeping them?"

"Because I haven't read them!"

"Throw them out. They're disgusting! This whole house is disgusting, and I hate it!" She clenches her fists. Her mouth trembles, and it's on the tip of her tongue to tell me that she hates me too, but she won't say it. No, she'd never stoop so low, crawl through the muck and mire like her disgusting mother

"You think I'm disgusting, don't you? Well, I think you're an ungrateful brat, and I wouldn't care if you never came here again!"

"Forget it, Mom. Forget what I said and show me what you're talking about so I can get out of here."

I lead her down the hall to my bedroom. "Just take a look at that!"

"What? It's a roomful of garbage, the same as it always is."

"Garbage?" There she goes again. Trying to spite me, when she knows full well I have tens of thousands of dollars gathered into this room, a priceless collection of imported kimonos that I've arranged in several stacks from floor to ceiling. "This is my retirement. I tell you that all the time, but you call it garbage!"

She sighs, rubs her forehead like she's got a headache, like I'm the biggest pain in her life that no amount of pills will cure. "Just tell me what's missing."

"My purple *kosode*, with the *yabane* pattern. My most valuable, and I can't find it! I've gone through my pile of silks and my pile of cottons, even went through the full-sleeved kimonos, but it's not anywhere!"

Jenny points to the crammed, overflowing closet. "Maybe it's in there?"

"It wouldn't be in there!"

"How do you know?"

I want to shout, *the same way you know your milk isn't in your oven!* Instead, I say, "Because I would never put it there. That pile's for regular clothes. The ones I buy on sale at the outlets to sell later online."

"There's a Tupperware of old toothbrushes in that pile. I can see it from here."

Why did I even call her? I knew she wouldn't be any help, would only come here to put me down. "Someone's coming into this house at night and stealing my kimonos, stealing them right from under my nose, and you don't care! Think I'm just a disgusting liar, don't you?"

"Mom, please stop crying. Look, I'm sorry. Can you tell me what this person looks like? Have you seen them?"

I calm somewhat, wipe my nose with the back of my hand. "Just their hands." I look down at my own hands—ugly and spotted, glistening with snot. "White hands. Stark white, like they're dead. Pale, dead hands reaching out from the sleeves of my kimonos."

"If you're really concerned, we should call the police. But if you have no proof…" She shrugs, walks out the way she came in, tiptoeing around landmines, clutching her bag like a lifeline. Even though I got her back inside the house, after she said she never would again. When she slides into her car without another word or glance, it doesn't feel much like victory.

"Serves you right if they strangle me in my sleep!" I yell out the window as her car pulls away.

I search through my pile of silks, then my pile of cottons. No purple *kosode*, but there's a few nibbling mice that I shoo away. They've eaten into some hems, nothing that can't be repaired, though Jenny complains about them. As if her own home doesn't have a squeaker or two. Every home does. The pesky things can fit through a hole the size of a bean! But Jenny has to make me feel bad for having a few dozen or so in the house, even if I don't clean up their droppings as often as I should. Once I get the place cleaned up, I'm getting a new carpet, so what does it matter?

Afternoon turns to dusk. I still haven't found my purple *kosode,* but with the light fading, I can't work anymore. I've only got the one lamp in the living room, so I head to the bathroom to get ready for bed. The shower drain's been clogged up for a while, but the faucet works just fine. I use it to brush my teeth and mop myself with a rag, since the sink is filled up with my toiletries. They're really nice toiletries: scented shampoos and creamy soaps I get as free samples from a neighbor. Jenny tells me to throw them out. Free—and she wants me to throw them out! That's how I know she's spoiled rotten and doesn't understand hardship. People who understand hardship don't throw free things away, things you can use. And I will use them. I'll use all of them, eventually, once I fix up the clogged drain and clean out the stagnant water in the tub and fix the toilet. It's been busted for years, the whole thing rusted and fallen over, so I have to relieve myself in the big orange bucket I got from the hardware store. Even though I empty the bucket every week or so, Jenny threatens to call social services. Tells me it's a health hazard, as if I enjoy going in a big orange bucket. Of course I don't! But how can I get the toilet fixed or the shower cleaned out or the sink emptied when no one ever helps me?

Twilight dims to night. I settle into the cozy crawl space I've carved out by the vent, right behind my piles of kimonos, where I keep my pillow and a little flask that helps me get to sleep. Jenny says I should have a blanket, but I don't need one, not when I've got my kimonos looking down on me, keeping me tucked in and warm. They remind me of Obachan, my old grandma who emigrated from Japan and gave me that purple *kosode*, my very first kimono, when I came to live with her and Ojisan. Before bed, she'd lay the kimono beside me, tell me dark tales about white hands reaching out from the sleeves, the ghosts of the women who once wore them. She told me that if I ever felt hands trying to get me at night, sneaking in my room and snaking up my blanket, that they were just the hands of ghosts.

"So don't ever tell anyone about them," she told me in harsh whispers as Ojisan stood silent by my bedroom door, hidden by shadows. "Not your teachers or your friends. The hands are just ghosts, and no one will believe you!"

Just like Jenny doesn't believe me when I tell her someone's coming into the house, stealing my kimonos and trying to get at me.

Someone's always trying to get at me.

I wake up to Jenny banging my car window. "Mom? Mom, are you okay?"

I roll down the tinted window, squinting at the sharp sunlight, because I guess I've slept in the car. "Why are you here, Jenny?"

"Are you serious?" You'd think she'd look sympathetic, knowing there's a thief in my house and that I had to sleep in the car. But she just looks tired. "You left ten messages last night. You said someone was in the house and that you had to run for your life!"

"What else am I supposed to do when someone's sneaking into my house, stealing my kimonos and trying to get at me!" I jab my head out the window. "Someone's always trying to get me!"

"Of course they are." She lifts up a grocery bag. "I bought some new light bulbs. If you're going to keep running away from invisible people in the middle of the night, then we need to get your lighting sorted out. It's not safe for you to trip around in the dark."

She spends the whole day clearing paths to the outlets, installing new lamps and bulbs. She never says a word, but her silence speaks volumes. *Disgusting. Dirty. Gross.*

Liar.

I already know I'm all those things without her saying it, or not saying it. I know that I live in a pile of garbage, that I'm no better than garbage myself, and while she works, I sit on my folding chair and sort through a few piles in the living room to make me feel better. I dig out an old cookie tin shaped like a teddy bear that I bought New Years of '89, a limited edition, which is why I had to keep it. "Remember this, Jenny?"

She glances at it. "No."

"You used to keep barrettes in it." I open it up. There's still a few of her old hair things rattling inside, and some pretty marbles, too. "You want it for Clara?"

"Clara doesn't need thirty-year-old junk."

My granddaughter's just as spoiled and ungrateful as my daughter. But some other little girl will like it, so I put it aside and keep rummaging. Jenny never liked sorting, but I could spend all day getting lost in my things. Tubes of half-used lipstick. Discolored baby toys. Frayed straw hats and a stained shirt that no longer fits me but could be cut up for a sewing project. Like an endless Christmas morning, every second recovering an old treasure, that little thrill of knowing it's mine, and no one can take it away from me.

The sun's starting to set by the time Jenny installs the last bulb and flicks on all the lights. "What do you think, Mom?"

"Not bright enough. If you cared about me at all, you'd have bought forty watts instead of whatever energy-saving crap this is."

This is where she usually cries. A small whimper at first, before she lets loose the fat tears to try and make me feel guilty.

She stares at me with hard, dry eyes. "What made you this way?"

What can I do but snort? Only answer she deserves after a question like that.

"Angry, selfish, bitter, rude," she continues. "I love you. I've tried for decades to get this place cleaned up and just... *livable,* but you won't listen to me—or anyone!" She strides to the front door. I've told her a thousand times, if I've told her once, that it won't open, but she goes there anyway, starts tearing down the piles blocking the way. "I hope someone does steal your kimonos and everything else in this wretched house!"

"Stop it!" I shout. "You'll ruin my things!"

She doesn't listen. With a scream, she pushes them all down, and my lovely things come crashing to the ground in a swell of angry dust.

Jenny yanks at the knob until the door cracks open. "Don't ever call me again!"

With Jenny's new lights, I can spend the whole night restacking the piles she knocked over, getting them just right. All my precious things are spread out and jumbled up like they've been spit out by a tornado, and I cry as I try to piece them back together. "What has she done to you?"

By the time I finish, it's too late to wash myself up or brush my teeth. I'm too tired to turn off all those lights, so they stay on, shining like a thousand candles as I collapse into the little space by the vent, nestled behind the kimonos, where I keep my pillow and flask.

I take sip after sip. The sleep starts to come on, that hazy pull I know so well. I've almost dropped off completely when something brushes against my leg, and I bolt upright.

I look down at my legs. Nothing. I look up at the piles that surround me—my wall of stacked kimonos. Once upon a time, they kept me tucked in and warm. A barrier that kept away all the things trying to get at me. But now someone's stealing them, stealing them right from under my nose. I first noticed it one night when I couldn't sleep, when I couldn't drown myself to oblivion no matter how much I sipped at my flask. I laid awake for hours, in pin-drop silence, until—

The rustle of fabric. The weight of breath against my face. And there, in the darkness, a pair of white hands reaching out from the sleeves of my purple *kosode*.

I screamed for help, screamed and screamed until I thought my lungs would burst. But Jenny was gone. She hadn't come into the house for years. No one was around to hear me or help me, and they wouldn't believe me anyway. So, I yanked the *kosode* out of the pile, took it outside and burned it. When I came back, the stack of kimonos had changed. Instead of guarding me, they loomed over me as I sipped my flask. They sent their ghostly white hands after me every time I nodded off.

A finger slides down my leg, and I scramble to my knees with a scream. "Get off me! Get off me!"

Hands, hands, a hundred white hands emerge from the sleeves, reaching for me, trying to get at me. Why are they always trying to get at me? I tried being a good girl. I tried being a bad girl. Finally, I covered myself in garbage and filth and hoped they'd leave me alone. But they didn't. After all these years, the hands are still reaching for me, sneaking into my room, snaking up my blanket, tickles of cold flesh crawling up and down my body.

I heave out of my little sleeping space and lurch out of the bedroom. I slam the door behind me and lean against it, because I'll be safe out here. Like Obachan said, the hands only come out of the kimonos, and they can't get me if I stay away from them. They can't get me if they're in there, and I'm out here. Tomorrow, I'll burn every one of them.

Then I see it. A hand. Two hands. A pair of dead, white hands. They creep from under the lid of an ancient board game, fingers cracked and grasping. Another pair dangles from an old vase perched at the top of a nearby pile. Another appears, then another, because they've escaped from the kimonos. Like the mice, they've infested everything: a thousand white hands reaching out from countless piles, out of old plastic cups and desiccated cereal boxes, between the tines of a broken blender, and the folds of old, moldering magazines.

I shoot to my feet and try to make a run for it. But I can't run in this house. All my things are piled up every which-where, and even with Jenny's lights blazing the room into a hot, white glow, I knock into every one of them. My whole life crashes to the floor in a cloud of dust and shame, but I don't care. All I want is to get out of this house, leave it all behind.

I climb over the shambles of my broken life, white hands reaching for me as I make a break for the front door. But it won't open. No, that door doesn't open anymore, no matter how much I pull and yank and bang and scream. My piles and piles of things block any way of escape, and before long, one white hand clamps onto me, then another. A thousand pale fingers drag me back under the mire I've created. They thread their fingers through my matted hair, grab my unwashed arms and legs. My decades of belongings swarm on top of me as their cold touch sneaks under my clothes, snakes into my nose and mouth and everywhere else. They wrap around my neck, and squeeze, and I know it won't be long. I'm in their grip, and maybe I always have been.

But there's one thing I can do before they take me away for good.

I dial Jenny's number.

"The hands," I say to the message recorder, gasping for air. "I never told anyone about the hands, because Grandma told me not to. But I'm telling you now, Jenny. I'm telling you that the hands have finally got me.

They'd sneak into my room, snake up my blanket. They used to come only in the darkness, but now they're here in the light, too. Because they're *my* hands, Jenny. At first, they were someone else's hands trying to get me, turning me into something worse than garbage. But now they've become my own. My very own hands.

"But don't you worry. I'll get rid of them. I'll destroy them before they can get you, too. Because I love you more than anything in the world, more than anything in this house."

One of my own hands breaks free. It may be wrinkled and spotted, but at least it's alive. With struggling breath, I knock over the nearest lamp, the lamp that Jenny got for me. It falls onto the sea of all the things that have drowned me alive, and I stare at the white heat of the bulb. For hours or days, who knows how long, I watch as it slowly smolders a yellowed newspaper, and the newspaper crackles into a spreading pool of flames. I grin as the hands that have been after me my whole life shrink from the orange tongues of fire, shriek with pain, and burn to blackened bones.

Grey smoke creeps into every crevice, choking the air away. But for the first time in decades, I can breathe. The hands are gone, and at long last, I'm finally freed from it.

Freed from the grip.

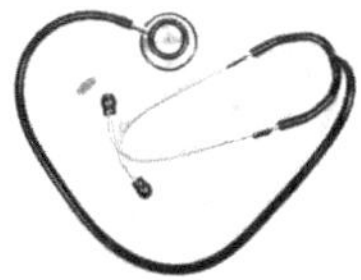

The Spirit Board
Jonathan Brònico

apá says he's glad for our house's ghost stories because we wouldn't have been able to afford our new home otherwise, but Mamá disagrees so loudly that I can hear it all from the living room.

"How could you keep a secret like this from me, Hector?" she says. "What good is a big house in the country if we have to share it with El Diablo?"

"The devil has nothing to do with this," Papá says in that voice of his that's usually paired with an eye roll. "People think they see someone standing in the window sometimes. It's just a trick of the eyes."

"You'll think differently when he steals our children's souls."

A door slams upstairs followed by the kind of silence that I hate to be the first one to break. My little sister, however, isn't old enough to have that kind of concern. She stops playing doctor, removing her toy stethoscope from her doll just long enough to ask a question.

"Carlos, what are Mamá and Papá talking about?" She's only five, and she doesn't understand how adults talk yet.

"I think our house is haunted, Evie," I reply.

"What does 'haunted' mean?"

Footsteps march down the stairs. "It means we're moving out as soon as we can," Mamá says. She's carrying our baby brother, Miguel. He's crying his eyes out and clawing at Mamá's wooden crucifix, its golden-brown oak all but disappearing against her neck.

Another set of footsteps follows her. "Lucía," Papá says, "we're staying *here*. This neighborhood is safer for the *hijos*, and the local middle school is better for Carlos. Besides, where would we get the money from?"

Mamá purses her lips and storms off into the kitchen. Papá, rather than pressing his luck any further, simply shrugs and returns upstairs.

Evelyn tugs on my shirt and lowers her voice to a whisper. "What are Mamá and Papá angry about?"

"I think it's the ghost."

Every day, Mamá continues her protest, but Papá dismisses her. Truth be told, Evie and I want to see the ghost, but nothing spooky ever happens.

Soon, it's the start of a new school year, and I have the *absolute pleasure* of being the new kid. I keep mostly to myself until lunch, when another kid joins me at my otherwise empty table. His wild, copper-red hair juts out from his baseball cap, and determination covers his rosy pink face.

He takes the seat next to mine. "I hear you just moved into the old Beckett house. Have you seen him yet?"

I'm still in shock that someone dared to talk to the new kid. "What?"

"The ghost," he says, his eyes burning with curiosity. "I've never seen him myself, but my cousin, Eddie, said one time he saw a guy dressed all in white walk by the window while the house was for sale. Said it *had* to be Beckett's ghost."

"Who are you talking about?"

I take a bite of my sandwich as my new friend shares his story.

"He was a scientist that did all kinds of experiments on people many, many years ago."

My eyes grow wide. "Like what?"

The kid shifts in his chair. "Like... all kinds of stuff."

I narrow my eyes. "You don't really know, do you?"

He sighs. "Okay, you got me." He leans even closer, his eager eyes even brighter than before. "But I always wanted to find out, though. Any chance I can come over?"

I size the kid up. He's basically a stranger, and he wants me to invite him over. On the other hand, he's the only person who's bothered to talk to me today.

After a long pause, I say, "I'll ask. What's your name?"

The friendly stranger beams a wide, goofy grin. "Steve."

I smile. "Carlos."

Weekends come and go, and Steve is a regular at my house by the time the fall air grows crisp and Halloween decorations dot the neighbors' porches. But neither of us has seen anything close to a ghost. Everything changes the first time Steve sleeps over. Late at night, when my family thinks Steve and I are asleep, Steve turns on his flashlight and pulls a strange wooden board from his backpack.

I wipe the sleep from my eyes. "Steve, what is this?"

"It's a spirit board."

My eyes bug out; I'm completely awake now. "Steve, my mom will kill us if she finds that. She says those things are for contacting the devil."

Steve props up his flashlight to illuminate the board. "Don't worry, she's asleep." He digs into his backpack and pulls out the little slidy-pointer-thing that always comes with the board in the movies. Steve looks at me with a hopeful grin.

I stare at the board like I'm peering into the gates of hell itself. "I don't know."

"You want to see the ghost or not?"

I'm torn as I look from my friend to the board. Mamá would ground me if she found out... but if I let Steve down, I wouldn't have any friends to hang out with anyway.

I sit on the floor. "How does it work?"

Steve launches into an explanation, but I'm too busy looking at the board to listen. Every letter of the alphabet and numbers zero through nine are etched into the wooden board. The only words carved onto the board are *yes*, *no*, and *goodbye*.

I return my attention to Steve as he finishes his explanation.

"—and we put our fingers on the pointer and the ghost moves it around to answer our questions." He pauses. "Want to give it a try?"

I don't, but if not trying means losing my only friend, then I guess I have no choice. I place my fingers on the pointer. "But Mamá *can't* find out."

Steve places his fingers on the other side of the pointer. "She won't." He takes a deep breath. "Mr. Beckett, are you here?"

Then the pointer begins to move. It slides across the board. It lands on the word *yes*, and we look at one another. Steve's eyes brim with excitement, but I can't imagine mine are filled with anything but fear.

Steve whispers his next question. "Were you really a mad scientist?"

The pointer slides onto *no*.

A disappointed look crosses Steve's face. "That's not what I heard."

"Maybe you were told the wrong thing," I say. With curiosity displacing some of my fear, I lean closer to the board. "What *did* you used to do?"

The pointer moves again, slowly highlighting several letters: D-O-C-T-O-R.

Steve's face lights up again. "Did you ever operate on people?

The pointer slides back to *yes*.

"I knew it," Steve says. "Did you ever kill anyone after cutting them open?"

The pointer slides with incredible speed to the word *goodbye*.

Next week, Halloween arrives. All the other kids on the street march up and down, trick-or-treating, but of course, Mamá won't let me go. At least she agreed to let Steve come over for another sleepover. As I watch the street for Steve's parents' car, my sister's voice calls from the upstairs nursery.

"Mamá, Miguel is crying!"

I don't think anything of it at first. Miguel cries every day. But when I overhear snippets of my parents' conversation, I start becoming as concerned as they sound.

"He doesn't want his bottle," Papá says, confused, "and his diaper is clean. What's wrong?"

"Evie said that he cried when she touched his stomach," Mamá replies. "Normally he likes that. I think he's sick. Do you think we should take him to the hospital?"

As I climb the stairs, their voices become more clear.

Papá sighs. "It'll take a day or two for me to scrape together enough money to pay the insurance bill. We're behind on our payments."

"What should we do?" Mamá asks.

"Wait a day or two and see if it passes. It's probably just gas."

I poke my head in the nursery. Mamá and Papá are standing over Miguel's crib in the cramped room. The floor creaks under Papá's feet as he bounces Miguel back and forth to cheer him up.

"Is everything okay?" I ask.

"Your little brother isn't feeling well," Papá says. "Nothing for you to worry about."

I bite my lip. "Can Steve still stay over tonight? Mamá promised."

Papá shrugs. "I don't see why not."

A light shines in my face, and I slowly pry my eyes open.

"Wake up," Steve whispers. "It's almost midnight on the spookiest night of the year. We won't get a better chance to talk to the ghost."

He pulls the board from his backpack and sets it up on the floor. The floor creaks as he walks.

"Quiet, we'll wake up my parents."

"They've been asleep for hours. Now, do you want to talk to the ghost or not?"

I drag myself out of bed and join him on the floor. We place our fingers on the pointer, and Steve begins.

"Hello, Dr. Beckett. Are you there?"

The pointer creeps from the center of the board onto *yes*.

I lean closer to the board. "How did you die?"

The pointer shifts around the board, spelling out N-O-T-I-M-E.

My little brother's cries suddenly pierce the silence of the night.

My hand flies off the pointer. "Steve, we've got to stop."

The glow of the flashlight catches his mischievous smile. "What's the matter? Scared?"

I switch off the light. "My parents are coming."

As the words leave my mouth, my parents' footsteps pound up the stairs. They pass my door, and thump into the nursery in the next room.

Steve grabs the flashlight from me and flicks it back on. "Sounds to me like they have other things to deal with." He places his fingers on the pointer. "Now, are you with me or not?"

"You don't get it, Steve. If my Mamá catches us with this board, I'll be grounded until Christmas—the one *next year.*"

Steve shrugs. "Just do what I do: say you didn't know any better and pretend you're really sorry. Works every time." He nods to the board. "Are you going to let me do this by myself? I thought you were my friend."

I listen carefully to my parents' voices in the nursery. They *do* sound concerned. They probably won't think of checking in on us for a while.

I place my fingers on the pointer. "Let's be quick."

Steve clears his throat. "Dr. Beckett, are you still here?"

The floorboards creak outside my door, and the doorknob turns with a muted rattle. Our hands fly off the board, and Steve points the flashlight at my door. It creaks open, and Evie walks in.

"Is everything okay with Miguel?" she asks. As she approaches, she spots the board between Steve and me. "What's that?"

My moment of relief turns into an opportunity for a new terror. I race to the door and close it again. "You can't say anything about it, Evie. Okay?"

She cocks her head. "Is that a ghost board?"

How does she...? She's not old enough to see the kinds of movies that these things are in, but everyone's old enough to watch the commercials for them, I guess. "Evie, why don't you go back to sleep?"

But Evie is nothing if not persistent. "Have you talked to the ghost yet?"

I'm stunned into silence, but Steve sees an opportunity. "Yeah, would you like to talk to him too?"

Evie taps her chin. "Is he friendly?"

Before I can answer, Steve jumps in. "'Course he's friendly." He slides over to make room for my sister. "Just put your fingers on the pointer, and ask a question."

"Wait," I say. "I can't let Evie do this."

Steve gives me a look out of the corner of his eye. "Should I call my parents and ask them to pick me up?"

I march over to the board and put my fingers next to my sister's. "Let's get this over with."

Steve begins again. "Are you still there, Dr. Beckett?"

The pointer slides to *yes*. It's moving faster this time.

My turn. "Do you always stay inside this house?"

The slider circles around *yes* before coming to a stop.

Evie speaks up. "Carlos, give the ghost a chance to speak. He's a person too." She looks up at the ceiling. "Mr. Ghost, is there anything you'd like to say?"

The slider circles around *yes* once more. Steve and I exchange glances.

"What is it?" Evie says.

The pointer begins spelling.

The wooden piece crosses the *M* before looping around to the *I* followed by the *G*. When it finishes spelling, Evie calls out with excitement.

"Miguel!" she says.

Cold sweat erupts over my forehead. I don't like where this is going.

"Do you have a message for my brother?" Evie says. She sounds like she's talking to the next-door neighbor instead of a creepy, dead doctor. She's too young to understand that none of this is normal.

The pointer begins its trek over the board: H-E-N-E-E-D-S-H-E-L-P.

I jump in. "But Mamá and Papá are already helping him."

The pointer crawls over the board again: H-E-L-P-H-I-M-N-O-W.

Evie leans closer. "What's wrong with him?"

The pointer moves even faster: A-P-P-E-N-D-I-X.

"Oh, man," Steve says. "My cousin Eddie had his appendix taken out last year. He said the doctors needed to get it out before it burst. Otherwise, he could've died."

The pointer jolts over to the word *yes*, dragging our arms along for the ride.

I remove my hand. "Maybe we should stop."

Evie looks at me with her puppy-dog eyes. "Carlos, is Miguel going to be alright?"

"Of course he is," I say. "I'm just going to tell Mamá and Papá that they should take him to the hospital. You stay here." I turn to Steve. "And *you* put that thing away. I'll be right back."

I inch open the door and slip into the hall. I'm not sure if the ghost is telling the truth, but either way, it's probably a good idea to get Miguel out of the house. I peek into the nursery in the next room. Mamá and Papá are comforting my brother as best as they can, but he's still crying so loud that I'm surprised we're not getting calls from the neighbors. It's either now or never.

I summon the courage to knock. "Mamá?"

My father turns instead, leaving Mamá to hold my brother. "Carlos, you should be asleep."

"Is Miguel going to have to go to the hospital?"

Papá kneels to look me straight in the eyes. "Your brother will be fine. Now go back to your room, and get some sleep."

"But Papá, what if he needs to go to the hospital right now, but he can't tell you?"

Mamá places Miguel in his crib. "We'll take care of him, Carlos. Good night." She kisses Papá on the head. "You too. You have a long day tomorrow."

Papá drags himself downstairs, and I return to my room. But instead of finding my sister gone and Steve asleep, they're both still using the board. I shut the door and run over to them just as the pointer guides their hands to the letter *P*.

"What did I tell you two?" I hiss, trying to yell and whisper at the same time. "Put that thing away."

"But the ghost says he can help," Evie says. "He used to be a doctor."

I look at Steve. "We need to talk."

I pull him over to the other side of my bedroom, away from my sister. "I don't think that this is a good idea. Didn't you hear that this guy used to do experiments on people?"

"We just wanted to know how we could help your brother," Steve says, gesturing wildly. "That's all. I promise."

"What did he say? What did he say *exactly*?"

"He said that he could do the operation."

"*What?*" I slap my hand over my own mouth, in a weak attempt to control my volume. I lower my voice. "The ghost is *not* going to operate on my brother. You told him that, right?"

Steve takes a deep breath. "Don't worry. He said that he needed a few things to do the surgery. As long as we don't give him what he needs, he can't do the operation, right?"

I take a deep breath. "We still need to convince my Mamá to take Miguel to the hospital now." I pause. "What kind of things would a ghost need to operate with anyway?"

"I don't know," Steve replies. "He said he'd tell us in just a…" He looks around the room as his voice trails off. "Hey, Carlos, where'd your sister go?"

My heart quickens, and I spin around. Evie is nowhere to be seen. My eyes dart to the board, sitting in the puddle of light cast by my flashlight. My heart sinks when I notice that the pointer has been shifted onto *E*.

"Steve," I say, trying to remain calm, "did you ever say goodbye to the ghost before I came in?"

"No."

The lump that forms in my throat is so large, I'm convinced that I'll never swallow again. "I think that Evie's helping the ghost. We have to find her." I turn to Steve. "What did Beckett need?"

Steve shrugs. "You pulled me away from the board before he said."

I roll my eyes. "Evie plays doctor downstairs. Let's check there first."

Steve and I creep out of the room, picking up our pace with each step down the stairs.

"Evie," I call out, barely louder than a whisper. "Evie, where are you?" I meet Steve's eyes. "We have to find her before my parents do. I'll see if she's hiding in the living room; you check the kitchen."

Steve and I split up right as my brother's wails blare like an annoying car alarm. How does he have the energy to keep this up? As I poke around the living room, I summon the courage to raise my voice.

"Evie, where are you? I need to talk with you."

After checking the narrow space behind the couch, Steve calls from the kitchen.

"Hey, Carlos?"

I rush in, and my eyes follow the direction of his index finger. The silverware drawer has been pulled almost all the way out, and it's tilting toward the ground.

"Where's Evie?" I ask.

"Isn't she the only one short enough to need to tilt a drawer down to see into it?"

"Okay...." I reply, marching over to the drawer, "but where's she now?"

Steve shrugs. "She wasn't in the living room?"

I try shoving the drawer back into place, but it's stuck, wedged in at a weird angle. "I barely had time to check because you called me in here."

I shove the drawer again, but it wobbles when I push, dipping down instead of up. The drawer slams onto the floor, and the silverware crashes like a thousand clanging cymbals as it scatters across the wood.

I look at Steve. He looks at me. We're both frozen in our spots as footsteps descend the stairs, away from my brother's cries in the nursery. Mamá hustles into the kitchen, and Papá sleepwalks in from his bedroom. They look at the floor, then at each other, and Papá returns to the bedroom, still not fully awake.

Mamá folds her arms over her crucifix. "What happened here?"

I look at Steve. "We were... looking for Evie. We thought she was in the kitchen."

Mamá stares at me, confused. "Why were you looking for Evie?"

I turn to Steve, who looks like he's counting the number of boards on the floor. Looks like I have to speak for both of us.

"She was scared with all of Miguel's crying," I say, "and she came into my room." As I look up, Evie emerges from the living room. "Evie!" I rush over to my sister. "Are you okay?"

She smiles. "I was helping Miguel."

My heart sinks.

Mamá kneels to her eye level. "What do you mean, Evie?"

"I was playing doctor for real."

Mamá takes Evie by the shoulders. "What do you mean, *hija*? Did you take his temperature?"

Evie shakes her head. "I was getting things for the doctor."

Mamá tilts her head. "What doctor?"

My stomach starts to turn, and I rush into the living room and up the stairs. I don't bother with my room—I'm probably grounded already. I blitz straight to the nursery, finding the door closed. I try the knob: locked. Miguel's crying inside, but he's gotten even louder, if that's possible.

"Carlos!" The next thing I know, Mamá is at the top of the stairs, looking into my bedroom. Her face contorts in disgust, and she crosses her heart as she storms inside. A second later, she emerges with the spirit board.

"Carlos, what have you done? This is the work of El Diablo. You and your friend have invited him into this house." She turns as Steve makes his way upstairs. "*You*. You take this *thing*"—she tosses the board down the stairs—"and wait outside until I call for your parents."

"Yes, Mrs. Gonzalez." Steve takes the board, and the front door slams a few seconds later.

Mamá brushes me aside and tries the door to the nursery. The knob rattles in her hand, but the door doesn't budge. In between bouts of my brother's wailing, footsteps march upstairs. I turn to find Evie leading Papá to the nursery.

"What's going on?" Papá asks, bleary-eyed and ready for more sleep.

"I was helping Miguel," Evie announces proudly.

Mamá grabs her by the shoulders. "Evie, tell me what you did, honey." She turns to Papá. "I need the nursery door open *now*."

Papá sighs. "Lucía..."

She slams her hand against the wall and points at the nursery door. "I told you El Diablo would steal our children's souls, and this is the proof. Open it."

Papá tries the doorknob—unsuccessfully—while Mamá looks Evie in the eye.

Evie's voice is almost a squeak. "Am I in trouble, Mamá?"

"No, *hija*," she says. She turns to flash me a fiery stare. "But your *brother* is." She returns her attention to Evie. "Tell me what you did for the doctor."

Evie twists her pajamas in her hands as she tells the story. "I asked the doctor what he needed, and he said a needle and thread, so I put them on a tray and gave it to him because the doctor said Miguel was sick."

Papá still can't open the door. "Hija, if your brother is sick, what's needle and thread going to do?"

My heart beats so hard that I can feel my pulse in my neck. "Evie, if you were looking for a needle and thread, why did you go into the silverware drawer?"

Evie smiles. "The doctor needed a knife."

Mamá's brown face goes as ashen as I've ever seen it. Papá's eyes grow large. And we all gasp as the screech of metal grinding on metal squeals from within the nursery.

Papá throws his weight against the door, ramming his shoulder repeatedly into the wood, but the old oak door is solid and unyielding. Miguel's cries grow louder and contorted into garbled, guttural sounds that twist my stomach into knots. Mamá grabs her crucifix, crosses herself, and prays every prayer she was ever taught. Evie and I look at each other, wondering what the two of us had done.

"Miguel!" Papá cries. He slams against the door, but it doesn't budge. He storms off down the stairs. "I need an ax."

And then Miguel stops crying. Dead silence... until the nursery door creaks open with the soft moan of unoiled hinges.

We exchange horrified glances. The silence grows more painful with each noiseless moment that we stare at the door. But since I'm the closest—and because I'm responsible—I'm the first to make a move.

"*Hijo*," Mamá barks, "get back here."

But I don't listen. I push open the door, and rush into the nursery. The crib sits in the corner, and inside it, my baby brother's little chest rises and falls. He's sound asleep, sucking his thumb.

As I move closer, a thin line of purple stands out against his brown stomach. I look at the tray that Evie had left behind for the ghost. On it, I spot purple thread, a needle, a bloody knife, and my brother's appendix.

After my parents return from the hospital, they reduce my punishment to being grounded for only one week, and Mamá apologizes for losing her temper. The doctors—the living ones—said that Miguel's appendix could've burst anytime that night. He's lucky it was removed when it was.

And the next time I talk to Steve, he tells me that his uncle knew Doctor Beckett back in the day. Beckett never experimented on people— he was simply a doctor who died after losing a patient—a baby—in an operation. Funny how only the bad parts of a story are the ones that get repeated.

We never heard from Doctor Beckett after the incident. Maybe saving a life put his spirit to rest.

A Bridge of Bones

Justin Alcala

innigan O'Neill would be dead in a week. There were signs everywhere, but no one in County Kerry ever complimented the sedulously scrappy old man for his intuition. Leaves fell rotten, the weather chilled, and the night blackened a shade conceived in tombs. On this frigid Monday night, a cardinal even flew up the O'Neill chimney and dropped lifelessly into the ash. So as Finnigan downed his last pint of the night, as he did with his best friend Liam each evening except Sundays at the Barley Crow Pub, he became oblivious to what fate held in store for him.

"Same time tomorrow?" asked Liam.

"For the last forty years," said Finnigan, nose smudged with soot.

"How's Éilís?"

"Spooked about a dead bird in our chimney."

"Not a cardinal, was it?"

"Why else would she be spooked if it wasn't a cardinal?"

"Bad omen, is all."

"What a superstitious lot I surround myself with."

"Just be careful walking home," said the ever-anodyne Liam. "I'll say no more."

"Yes, of course. Now, let's get home before the wives send out a search party."

"We should be so lucky."

The pair laughed themselves out of the Barley Crow Pub. Finnigan and Liam collected their out-of-date lanterns from the covered porch, lit them, and split direction along the public grassland road as they did every night for four decades. Finnigan's breath hung in the air as he trudged the mile back to his cottage, climbing atop of St. Joseph's Hill. Though his eyesight often failed him, a pinprick of light below crossed the distant creek's bridge. It struck him as odd seeing that the stone overpass led solely to his property. Finnigan presumed it was his wife, but when he returned to the cottage to a sleeping Éilís, he wrote it off as a trick of bad eyes and moonlight.

"Same time tomorrow?" asked Liam.

"For the last forty years," Finnigan burped, car grease on his fingers.

On Tuesday night, Liam and Finnigan left out the Barley Crow Pub, collected their lanterns, and went to the road. Finnigan stared down his path, hesitant.

"What ales you?" asked Liam.

"Strangest thing," said Finnigan. "I could have sworn I saw a lantern crossing my bridge last night."

"Éilís?"

"No, she was sound asleep."

"Need me to walk you home, big guy?" Liam asked.

"Come off it," Finnigan laughed.

Finnigan journeyed the road to the O'Neill cottage, traversing countryside, and climbing a hill. When he neared the bend along the creek, a lantern light glinted once more. Only this time, the flame trailed alongside the last of the public road, stopped, and turned onto Finnigan's bridge. Finnigan pushed to catch up to the flame's keeper, but his old legs resigned to a walk, and he lost sight amidst the wall of trees encompassing his garden. Upon entering his house, Finnigan found his wife asleep.

"Your boyfriend sneaking about?" Finnigan asked, kicking off his boots.

"Finnigan O'Neill," said Éilís, eyes still closed. "What on earth are you talking about?"

"Saw the lantern light on our bridge."

"If I keep two lovers, at least one knows to tread lightly. Now, come to bed, I'm freezing."

Finnigan did as told, and instead of considering firelight, fell straight to sleep.

"Same time tomorrow?" asked Liam on Wednesday night.

"For the last forty years," Finnigan sighed.

"Why the long face?" asked Liam.

"That's two nights now that I saw someone with a lantern cross my bridge. The wife says she has nothing to do with it."

"Old Thomas?"

"He's supposed to be in Dublin."

"Maybe...no, forget it."

"Come out with it, Liam."

"Well, my father used to talk of will-o'-the-wisps."

"I ain't got time for fairies and ghosts."

"Then what do you think it is?"

"Not sure. I'll uncover the truth tonight."

"Have a plan, do you?"

"I'm going to call it out."

"Good luck. Remember, you're not the bruiser you were."

"What's that supposed to mean?"

"You're more likely to hurt your back than an intruder."

"I'll hurt you," Finnigan grinned, holding out his liver-spotted fist.

The pair departed the Barley Crow Pub, collected and lit their lanterns, then divided along the road. The night drew wintrier than days past, but it didn't stop Finnigan from his hectic pace. He huffed halfway home to the peak of St. Joseph's Hill, where, to his consternation, the mysterious lantern keeper drew even closer than yesterday, traveling at the foot of the knoll. The lantern keeper's obscure silhouette, comparable in height to Finnigan, raised the lantern over their head.

"Oye," shouted Finnigan. "Old Thomas, that you?"

The lantern keeper remained steadfast, carrying to the bend.

"Stay where you are," said Finnigan. The lantern keeper proceeded to the fork where Finnigan's bridge split from the public road. "Don't you dare cross that bridge, you hear me?"

Finnigan descended St. Joseph's Hill, but halfway down a rock bit his boot, and he rolled to the bottom. Lightning scrambled up Finnigan's knees, and his cheek stung from scraping it on the cruelty of shrill weeds. By the time Finnigan gathered his wits and ensured no parts were broken, his bridge trespasser vanished. Finnigan limped the rest of the way home, distracted by pain. He entered his cottage with the grace of a spooked horse, shuffling through kitchen cabinets in search of the first aid kit.

"What on Earth happened to you?" asked Éilís.

"Fell down St. Joseph," said Finnigan.

"You need to slow down. You're not a young man anymore."

Finnigan winced, pressing an ointment on his cheek. "Nonsense. I'm as healthy as on our wedding night."

"Well, care to repeat that evening?"

"Oh?" Finnigan raised a brow.

"First get into bed," smirked Éilís. "Then pass out five minutes before anything interesting happens."

"You're the devil," Finnigan said, but he followed his wife's instructions and melted into bed.

"Same time tomorrow?" asked Liam on Thursday.

"Say, what are you doing tonight?" Finnigan asked, red paint on his shirt.

"The usual—letting out Toby when I get home, watching the telly next to Maggie until I fall asleep."

"Want to help me catch a trespasser?"

"No luck last night?"

"I took a tumble."

"That explains your cheek."

"Yes or no?"

"What do you have in mind?"

"Your legs are healthier than mine, so you'll cut through the bend once we spot them and lead them back to me. Then I'll nab the intruder."

"This is a horrible plan. I'm in."

It didn't take long for the pair to reach St. Joseph's Hill. The peak loomed over the countryside towards Finnigan's cottage. A keening lamented through the land as they waited for their trespasser. Finnigan and Liam lingered in the blackness, one-minute giving way to two, then ten, then thirty. When the Church of Immaculate Conception's sepulchral bells rang at midnight, Liam cleared his throat.

"You must've spooked them last night," said Liam. "Mission accomplished."

"I'm supposing you're right. Well, sorry to bother you."

"Anything for a friend. I better let the dog out. See you tomorrow."

"For the last forty years."

Finnigan and Liam collected their kerosene lanterns, kindled them, and split direction along the hill. Finnigan reached the base, startled by a flicker from a lamp ahead. The mysterious trespasser raised their lantern high at the edge of the bridge. This time, however, they lingered at the overpass. Finnigan rushed to the bridge, fist balled

"Who are you?" asked Finnigan.

He approached the last fifty steps to the mute trespasser. Finnigan's weak eyes caught the intruder's clothes, frayed and tattered, but his lamp would not color in any details. Finnigan wavered as the air went awry. Whispers tangled in the breeze, and although there was only one person before him, a jarring sense of an unseen gathering upturned the hairs on his neck.

"Eager for a right hand?" asked Finnigan. A cruel wind picked up strength, and his instincts cautioned him on this intruder's predatorial nature. Finnigan back-stepped, eyes locked on the intruder.

"Step on my property again, and it'll be the last time," said Finnigan.

He returned up the hill, took a detour to Tallulah Bridge, and arrived at his cottage from behind. Finnigan felt relief as he entered the warm cottage. After kissing his sleeping wife, Finnigan watched out his front door. The trespasser disappeared from the bridge but left a stain of terror. For the rest of nightfall, Finnigan's heart failed to settle as he stared out the window for signs of the trespasser. None came.

"Same time tomorrow?" asked Liam.

"Have I been acting different?" Finnigan asked on Friday, a yard leaf in his flat cap.

"Whatever do you mean?"

"I saw the lantern again after your departure."

"Your prowler?"

"Aye, that's the one."

"Can't be. Just you and me, not a living soul in sight."

"What if they ain't living?"

"What do you mean?"

"Tell me about the spooks again?"

"The will-o'-the-wisps?"

"Aye."

"You serious?"

Finnigan hung his head.

"Some say it's lights of unbaptized spirits, others call it fairy fire, and a few claim say it's the Grim Reaper herself, using soul fire to light her way towards her next victim."

"What do you believe?"

"Why are you asking such strangeness?"

"I need to know if I'm losing my mind or if I'm seeing this phantom?"

"Finnigan, the autumn plays tricks on people, especially tired geezers like me and you. You've stretched yourself too thin is all. Time to stop and smell the roses."

"What do you mean?"

"Slow down. Skip your chores and relax by taking Éilís to the village. Get some supper, go to bed early, and enjoy a long weekend."

"I suppose you're right."

"That a boy."

"See you Monday then?"

Liam smiled. "For the last forty years.

Finnigan and Liam walked themselves out of the Barley Crow Pub, gathered their lanterns, and split along the road. Finnigan didn't want to admit that each step to the bridge shrunk his courage. He walked the grassland path, over St. Joseph's Hill, and down to the bend with an unsettling buzz in his chest. All the while, Finnigan searched desperately through ominous fog rolling over the landscape for his lantern keeper. To his relief, no spectral flames, ragged trespassers, or portentous sensations mounted. When Finnigan reached the threshold to his bridge, only the creek's whir and a distant owl made their presence known.

"Autum playing tricks on me," said Finnigan, out of breath Finnigan's tender arm ached, so he lowered his lamp and took in the drape of midnight over his home. The fireplace glowed through the cottage windows, washing the tops of Éilís freshly pruned geranium bushes in orange. Finnigan's leaf pile, waiting to be bagged, stood as tall as his hatchback in the side yard. The drawn back curtains over his recently painted windowsill in the sitting room told Finnigan his wife expected his arrival. Finnigan smiled, gathered his lantern, and started to cross the bridge.

"Roses," he said to himself.

But as Finnigan took to the center of the overpass, an icy hand clasped fiercely over his shoulder. Alarmed, Finnigan twisted around to a macabre sight. A figure in threadbare robes upthrust its fireless lantern over Finnigan. Petrified, Finnigan watched as the lamp ignited independently. The intruder released Finnigan's shoulder and lowered their hood with a spidery hand. Finnigan stared at his own distorted reflection, eyes sunken in with maggots and gray skin painted over his bones. Finnigan clutched his chest as pain painted his face. He staggered, then his vision flooded black.

"Same time tomorrow?" asked Liam.

He raised the remnants of his glass to a picture of Finnigan framed behind the bar and drank. Liam withdrew from the inn, collected his out-of-date lantern from the covered porch, lit it, and left for home as he did every night for four decades. He followed the grassland road, the wind biting his back, past the old graveyard. When he reached his yard, Liam's wife, Maggie, waited for him at the door, and his dog, Toby, hurried to meet him at his white-fence which needed painting. As Liam made it through his uncut lawn, an eerie sensation like an unseen gathering raised the hairs on the back of Liam's neck. He turned to the road whence he came and spotted a pinprick of light near the graveyard's lich gate. Liam stared at the light until it extinguished itself with another draw of wind.

"Everything alright, darling?" asked Maggie.

"Aye," said Liam. "You know what. Why don't we make a quiet weekend for ourselves?"

"Oh? That'd be nice. What's the occasion?"

"Eh, I'm not a young man anymore. It's good to stop and smell the roses."

The Guardian

Alishia Dauterive

lack didn't scare Maya.

Black was her hair braided down when she needed a break. Black was her wig with slick strands hugging the slimness in her face on a night out. Black was her mascara. Black was her car, although the paint peeled. Black was her dress for the club, her headphones for the gym. Black was her skin to some people, depending on what was expected of her. So, it wasn't the black that scared her. It was the white.

They never blinked—the white, ominous, orb-like eyes embedded at the top of the thin shadow in the corner of her room. Its shape spread as an ethereal wallpaper. If Maya squinted hard enough in the right kind of light, its flat chest expanded with air, caved, expanded, and caved. And although there was no mouth, she felt its heated breath; although there was no nose, she heard its whistling; and although there were no ears, she knew it heard the life of her house—the laughter on game nights, the TV on movie nights, and the drunken mayhem on barbecue nights.

It perched in her window during the last family gathering. Maya saw it from the backyard. Her uncle blocked her view, having a stench of malt liquor coating his words. He asked her again what college she was going off to. She told him, and he nodded, said he heard good things about that place, knowing he never had, knowing he'd been the only one not to go, knowing he regretted it, but not enough to start anew.

The next day, the shadow spread across the backseat of her Accord, the white orbs a headlight glinting in her rearview mirror. It judged her hard braking, her choice of tunes, and her check engine light.

Maya told her cousin Neisha about the shadow. They sat in the quad of the university, Neisha's current school, Maya's future school. Neisha's brow scrunched and the corner of her lip raised, and she whipped her braids from her shoulder the way she did when something didn't make sense. They knocked against her back. Her sparkling teeth scraped against her bottom lip; her school's health insurance kept them white. She always told Maya to take more than these schools wanted to give, because what they *wanted* to give wasn't all they *had* to give. Neisha spoke in riddles like her mom, thinking it made her sound grown and wise. But she'd barely turned twenty, and all the aunties warned her life hadn't shown her nothing yet. Life had shown her the shadow, though.

"I'm just not sleeping enough." Neisha rubbed her arms. "Exams and all that. But you seen it too?"

"It follows me."

"Maybe we just tired. Mass hysteria or something."

Maya glanced at her Accord. The shadow sat patiently in the backseat.

"It won't talk. But it breathes. And hears."

Neisha shifted uncomfortably. She hated things she didn't understand. "You think other people see it?"

"No one noticed when I was driving."

Neisha surveyed the barren quad. Summer break. Only true nerds were here, taking accelerated classes and reading books in their free time. They'd graduate a year before everyone and think that meant something. Neisha was one of them. Ren was another.

He said he hated his full name—Reginald—and he didn't like the nickname Reg, which made him think of 'veg,' like a lazy person, or 'dredge,' like the muck dug up on the ocean floor, or 'ledge,' like the thing lost people cried on. So, he introduced himself to everyone as Ren. He stepped across the grass with his head buried in his cell phone, a pant leg dragging against the concrete. The other snagged by the lip of his sock. He'd draped himself in his typical long T-Shirt, purple for the royalty of the morning, always a crisp cool rush before the heat and humidity came.

He had his head in thoughts, not thoughts in his head, Neisha always said. She thought maybe his brain was woven throughout his locs, tied up like a blooming flower, protected and tight atop his head. People were only thoughts, he told Neisha one day, and thoughts were the translation of spirit. He talked like that a lot. All mystical and stuff, as Neisha mocked, but his ideas were attractive to her. They dripped smoothly from his mouth as if they didn't have to get past his big teeth.

She'd never tell him that though. She liked being the shy type for once. And what would everyone think, her bringing home this space case of a young man who wouldn't keep eye contact longer than five seconds if the conversation wasn't interesting enough. But he was dark and bold and smart; he wore his confidence like cologne. Neisha knew he'd know about the shadow.

Ren heard her flat-footed clown shoe steps slap the concrete, the patented Neisha shuffle. He spun quickly to startle her. She stumbled. He laughed with his tongue against the roof of his mouth, so it sounded like he'd taken a spoonful of peanut butter.

He knew she wouldn't be asking what he saw if there wasn't something to see. But there wasn't anything other than the same rusted hubcap on the same spare tire Maya had been riding for a month. Duct tape held a corner of her bumper against the back fender.

"You don't see it." Neisha dropped her shoulders in disappointment, then yelled, "Maya, he don't see it!"

"See what?" Ren demanded. "Her beat up car? I never miss it. Nobody on this whole campus ever miss it."

Neisha broke into a feverish description about the feeling she got when the shadow looked at her, like it saw every person she'd ever be, hoped to be, and had been. Maya stood at her side while both girls talked over each other, fighting for Ren's attention, as though they couldn't let his eyes wander.

Ren's backpack slid down his shoulder and he shrugged it back up, looped his free arm through the other strap. These girls were always yapping about something, usually drama on the internet. Ren thought maybe that's what this was; they'd read a scary post and were trying to convince him it was real. But Neisha's edges lifted slightly from her sweat alone, and she used the strongest edge control and a lot of it. Maya bit her tongue talking so quickly. They seemed truly afraid, and *that* interested Ren.

The three of them stood at the side of Maya's car. Ren pressed his face to the back window. He spotted a crumpled sweater and empty granola wrapper.

"What you say it look like again?" he asked.

They talked over each other.

"Can one of ya'll talk at a time? I only got two ears and you talking like you four people."

Maya pointed at the concrete. Her shadow.

"Like that," she said. "But thick. Dark. The eyes are white. *Just* white."

Ren scratched between his locs. He only had one question. "Does it speak?"

The girls shook their heads.

"Come to my uncle's store," he said.

Ren's uncle Ferris wasn't his uncle, just a man who knew his father from the time they were youngsters tossing cigarettes out a Chevy Caprice window, hollering at girls on the sidewalk, trying to sweet-talk them like they were from a different part of town. Ren had a lot of uncles that weren't his uncles, and while each of them had distinct laughs, smiles, and jokes, they all swung their arm across Ren's shoulder in the same way, making sure he knew they were there.

Ferris owned a bookstore on the east side of town known for dollar sales and community barbeques on Sundays, weather permitting. His wife's son, Trevion, helped him set the block up every week. He heaved out boxes of kids' books and used Black American fiction; he set out white fold-up tables and stacked paper plates for a buffet line. Standing out in the hundred-degree summer was worth it for Ferris, seeing the kids excited to read, and watching folks happy enough with the food and company to offer a donation—at least until his handkerchief got too damp from his sweat and the ribs ran out. Then, he put the young buck out there, Trevion, to man the money and learn some discipline.

Trev spotted Maya's beat up car. He could hear her bearings a mile out. As she pulled behind Ferris' sedan, Trev rolled up the bottom of his shirt, swiped it across his forehead. It wasn't blazing yet, but anticipating the heat made him break a sweat. Whenever Neisha's fine self came around, he liked showing off the body Ren didn't have. Neisha was too fiery for Ren, Trev knew. She needed someone who matched her flame, not some head-in-the-clouds-type-fool reading Manga on the back of a bus.

"Oh, you not going to say nothing?" Trev said cooly as Ren led the girls into the shop. Only Maya glanced back, having never met Trev. She almost felt rude for passing him without saying hello, but Neisha gave her the eyes that said "don't."

Trev waved at their backs with a defeated flap of his hand. "Man, whatever. Come grab some of these boxes and help for once! Always coming around here grabbing a plate!"

Neisha had been here once or twice, when Ren helped her with biology, but Maya had never seen the towers of books, used and new and vintage and rare and torn and stained, stacked and shelved and boxed, cluttered but organized by author last name, genre, and quality. Outside, the building sort of caved in on itself, but inside was an explosion of archives, hallways thin and deep, shelves to the ceiling, and the dust particles in the air seemed to come from between the pages, traveling through time with the stories.

"Don't be scared," Ren said.

"We're not scared of no books." Neisha laughed.

Ren dropped his backpack behind the shop counter, stacked a few books Ferris must have been indexing, or reading. "No. The shadows you seeing. You don't need to be scared. They got purpose. Come on."

Ren glided sideways between the looming shelves so his long arms didn't knock over the stacks of floor books. Those weren't intended for shelving; they were overflow. Ferris said every book he came into, he came into for a reason. Someone from somewhere would walk into his shop and stub their big toe on one, or knock a shoulder into another sticking out from a shelf. People didn't find books, books *called* to people.

Neisha stepped quickly, keeping up with Ren's stride. His mind looked something like this, a house of histories, facts, stories, realities, ripe to pluck when the right person came along for the right piece of knowledge. This was his element.

Ren and the girls emerged from the end of the walkway. Neisha flushed, and Maya dazed, having breathed in so much dust. They hopped up three stairs to the second level, an open office tucked in the back of the store, which Ferris reserved for children's book groups, closed shop events, and any meetings he had with the heavy-hitting donors. The décor was confused, although Ferris wouldn't know it. A fuzzy, textured blue carpet lay beneath furry seat pillows for the kids, two black loveseats, fold-out chairs stacked against the wall for shop events, and two executive office chairs pushed by the desk for when the donors came.

The man behind the desk wasn't Ferris. He held a cigarillo, but it wasn't tobacco. The skunky scent crept into their noses and wove into the fibers of their clothes. Silvery smoke spindled across the ceiling, lower at this level than the last, and the man didn't notice ashes falling beside his open book or that his thick dreads swished their ends through it all when his shoulders bobbed in a silent laugh. He'd been smoking and reading for a while now, judging by the redness in his eyes and the dryness of his lips. Canyons carved roughly through the skin of his face, eroded land from the salty waters of his life. They never looked like wrinkles to Ren, though, or old age—just proof of a life full of learning. Sip was another uncle.

"Hey Sip," Ren said.

Sip's eyes worked their way to Ren. It was hard switching between worlds sometimes. Sip's canyons cracked in his smile.

"Brother Ren. What can I do for you?"

"Ferris around?"

"He stepped out. Left me in charge of that boy out there." He didn't seem enthused. "Ferris will be back. Who you got here?"

Ren gestured to both girls respectively. "This Neisha, and this Maya. We were looking for Ferris 'cause . . . well, maybe you know. They seeing some guardians, I think."

Sip didn't hear at first. Words had to weave through the air and bounce off his dreads before wiggling into his ear. He closed his book slowly.

"What got you thinking like that?"

Ren shared the description the girls had given. They jumped in too, talking over each other again—Neisha stroking her braids nervously, Maya with her hands crossed in front of her like a schoolgirl with top grades, both of their lips flapping at lightning speed. Sip caught each word.

"I told 'em to not worry," Ren said, looking for assurance. Sip couldn't give him that exactly.

"Don't speak so quick, Ren." He smiled. "They're not dangerous. If you listen. But things can *get* dangerous, if you don't. You all know the story?"

The three shook their heads.

Sip leaned back in Ferris' desk chair with his hands folded on his pudge of a stomach. He'd taken to drinking beer these last few weeks, and it showed in his physique. Not as young as he once was—it reminded him. He shifted to put his palms flat on the desk, looked between the girls, then at Ren, then at all three simultaneously, his vision spread.

"I'll tell you if you all agree not to tell Ferris was smoking in here again."

They all nodded. Sip smiled.

"They guard stories," he said.

Maya sat in a plastic folding chair, the first to do so. Sip felt as if he told the story only to her. She was the one willing to receive it.

They didn't show themselves to everyone, he shared. They came when the clouds bunched in the right spot, vibrated with the right amount of precipitation, cast the right shadows, and when the sun flared with just the right spike of radiation, when the right car ran the right red light in the right part of town and narrowly missed hitting the right person. They came with an eternal mission, fueled by grief and hope and maybe a bit of obsession, but mostly obligation. If they didn't save our stories, who would?

That's how the book had described it. Sip didn't have the copy on him, but he could recite every page he'd read since his boyhood, all five hundred and sixty-five, every word, every feeling. There was no author, he said. Authorship rarely mattered in situations like these.

Neisha fixated on Sip's dry lips, the hair of his chin, slightly greyed since last summer, bobbing with his jaw, his tongue flicking quickly in the corners of his mouth. It was all she could do, she felt, to not float from her seat. Ren seemed so engrossed in the story, Maya too, and she suddenly felt stupid. She'd trusted Ren to bring them to someone with some sense. Ferris had sense. This guy, Sip or Zip or whatever his name was, smoked too much.

"Stories are living and breathing memory," he said. "Guardians hold them tenderly for that reason, with the promise that if we were willing to listen and learn, they were willing to record and save."

"What's that mean?" Neisha demanded. Perspiration bubbled along her forehead, and she patted make-up back into her skin. She brushed a trembling finger along her swirls of baby hairs, cute and defined this morning, but now a physical representation of her disbelief.

She didn't appreciate Sip's thinning lips. His eyes cut to Maya, as still and absorbent as a kitchen sponge. Her gaze left a snail trail across the carpet that only Neisha could see. Maya was like this, though—did what people told her, believed what people told her. Neisha had to save her in fourth grade, when the older kids told her stinging nettles would stop her from getting sick that winter. She had to save Maya again in seventh grade, again freshman year, and junior year. This was Maya's senior year now, and she needed saving yet again. Neisha's leg jiggled furiously. Ren's hand was a gentle pressure on her shoulder, which she whisked away.

"When mine came to me," Sip started, but Neisha rose abruptly.

"Ain't nothing came to you. You smoke too much weed, that's the damn problem. Maya, let's go. I told you we just need some sleep."

"You been tired?" Sip asked. "I got tired too, when mine came. It's a side-effect."

"Maya, *let's go.*" Neisha gripped her upper arm. Maya wriggled loose.

"What do we do? You said if we don't listen, they could get dangerous. How do we listen if they don't talk?" Maya asked.

"Maya, we're *leaving*!"

"You go!" Maya whipped her head toward her cousin, pointed toward the front of the store. "Go on! I'm tired of you telling me what to do!"

Neisha's rage stiffened her. The tension settled in the room with the grace of a feather. Sip cleared his throat and smashed the lit end of his blunt against the underside of the desk.

"They do talk," Sip said. "That rage in your friend right here—"

"She's my cousin."

"Some of that rage is them speaking. She's feeling stories, and she don't know it yet."

"You a damn kook," Neisha barked. "Maya, you coming or not?"

Maya ignored her.

Ren clicked his tongue. "How will you get home, Neisha? Just hear him out. Why you being like this? I thought you wanted my help?"

"This ain't help, Ren, this some crazy man talking out the side of his neck. I don't got time for this, I got Chem homework. I'll get a ride from Trev."

They watched her hop down the three steps and slither between the bookshelves. Maya kept her head down. Her toes sweat in her shoes and her fingertips burned like the tears in the corners of her eyes.

"Don't worry about her," Sip said softly. "I was like that, too. Wouldn't believe nothing other folks tried telling me."

"You got one?"

Sip nodded. "You haven't been sleeping much either?"

"No."

"And something feel off, don't it? Things are shifting."

Maya wiped a tear. Ren grabbed a folding chair and sat beside her, hunched, elbows on his knees. His mouth rested against his hands.

"It's nothing to cry about," Sip laughed, although Maya didn't find it funny. "Your guardian is learning your story. Saving it with the ones that came before yours, the ones you got to listen to. The world will look different soon, too, the more you listen. Your cousin may be feeling that already, she just don't know it." He seemed to nod at the skepticism creeping in her face. "Trust me. Just listen and feel."

Maya and Ren drove with silence between them. Ren didn't lift his head the whole ride. She watched him walk across the parking lot toward the dormitories, his backpack slung halfway off his shoulder, his pant legs dragging dirt. Thoughts really did swarm in his locs. Maya could almost see their lightning plaiting through his hair.

She knew her guardian sat in the backseat. Sip told her she would feel it in her blood, taste it on the back of her tongue, feel it looking through her eyes. It needed every sensation of her—good, bad, and ugly. It'd feel her stress, her joy, her fear, and anything in between, recording it in the buzzing of atoms. An eternal library, he said, and the point of listening to them was to learn from that library. In return, she'd feel different, see different, be different. She'd feel herself in the skin of it, behind its eyes.

Neisha didn't pick up the phone. The third time it went straight to voicemail.

Maya lay on her left side in her room, let the setting sun grip her ankles and feet from underneath her window blinds. Behind her, she felt the guardian, tried not to hate its hovering. It brought a weight with it, not strong enough to crush, but firm enough to keep her attention from wandering. If she closed her eyes, it throbbed along the passage of her sinuses, sucked air in her lungs, dilated her arteries, soothed her blood. She opened her eyes, twisted toward her guardian. The white orbs were baseballs nearly, bulging and hard. If Maya stared long enough, she saw swirls of color entangled within them, flashes of people's lives, the essence of their stories, the buzzing of atoms.

She agreed to listen and learn, if it agreed to stop hovering over her bed. "It's like when people walk real close to you on the sidewalk instead of going around. They breathe right on your neck," she told it. "Know what I mean? It's like, back off. Give me space."

It knew what she meant. The orbs seemed to blink, and the guardian smashed itself against the wall.

"You don't need to be *that* far."

The guardian pulled forward an inch.

"A little more."

Another inch.

"Perfect. Arm's length, at least." Maya put her arm out to test the distance and nodded. The guardian's blob of a head leaned forward slowly, an imitation of her action, and Maya's heart thumped hard in her chest. It'd been thumping hard for weeks. But she was ready to listen.

She took a deep breath. So did her guardian.

The Sweetest Fruit

John Sieber

I often come to the café that sits across from the park, a small chunk of adolescent memory. But today, something dreadful in the cluster of tree branches steals my gaze along with my will to look away. I'm taken back to a time brimming with the wondrous youthful gifts, a time when he, too, was part of my life. We spent countless hours of our youth in that park, he and I. Sometimes, we were so caught up in whatever we were doing that the sudden appearance of stars wasn't enough reason to leave.

On nights like those, we'd sit close together on the bench, under one of the only cherry trees—the one on the abandoned side of the property—and discuss things we couldn't have told anyone else, until our heavy eyelids allowed us to speak no more. Each day after school, we'd wander somewhere under the arms of the oak and elm, never knowing what the rest of the day had in store. But he had a way of making the place memorable.

Like scenes from a movie, memories beyond my imagination project before me. For a second, the world blurs, and I see myself running through the shady brush with him. Our sneakers play cat and mouse, kicking up dust along the loose gravel paths that wind between broken branches and tulip patches. Our careless laughter echoed beyond the *Quiet Zone* signs nailed to the tree trunks. I forget why we were running. We were always stirring up trouble.

On some of our braver nights, we'd sneak into one of our parents' liquor cellars with empty water bottles, picking and choosing which drink to take just enough of so that they wouldn't notice. On nights like those—the ones I was sober enough to remember—we climbed the trees and street lamps as high as we could, dodging the cops more than a few times, and only getting caught twice. But that would only heighten the moment. Having evaded the police, we'd wake up the next morning somewhere unfamiliar with scrapes and bruises on our legs and arms. We'd spend the day patching each other up, trying to piece together our misadventures. Those days are probably some of the best memories I have. I think about them often.

"Are you ready to order?"

I look up, noticing the newly employed waiter above me, pen in hand, annoyance lacing his words.

"Oh, no, I'm just..." My voice trickles over itself, "... waiting on a friend." I try my best not to irritate him any more than I must have already. He stares at me a bit longer than I think he should—as if he is inspecting me.

"The same friend that was supposed to come yesterday and the day before that?" He's annoyed that I'm here, that I'm just taking up space.

"He's coming," I say, avoiding eye contact.

We're quiet for a few seconds.

"I'll come to check on you in a bit." He dismisses himself back into the restaurant, leaving the bottom half of a creaky Dutch door swaying behind him.

I watch through the open top of the door as the flustered waiter speaks with the owner, glaring at me. "Well, he'll just be back tomorrow, wasting my time!"

The older man puts his hand on his shoulder, pats it a few times, and whispers something in his ear. The waiter pauses for a moment, glances back with an almost apologetic look, then walks away into the kitchen. The boss smiles, gives me a wave, and follows the waiter back.

I twine the corner of the tablecloth between my fingers, wiping beads of sweat from my forehead. I can't tell if they're from nerves or the strangely hot April afternoon. Sometimes I come to this café to reflect on a time when he and I still spoke to each other—or at least when he still spoke to me. Back when we could look each other in the eye and have real, deep conversations. I think we both played a part in ruining any chance of that happening again.

Sometimes, I still hear our laughter—the jokes we told each other, the stories we made up about strangers we thought were too far away to hear us. I can still feel the wet gravel clinging to the soles of my sneakers after a rainstorm as we stumbled down the paths, acting stupid, like teenage boys do. The reek of the algae-covered pond still lingers in my nose from the times we'd go down to the shoreline, trying to catch one of the ducks.There was that one time when we actually managed to snag a young duckling by the tail feathers. Its mother was already paddling away, thinking her baby was right behind her. Then she turned around and charged at us. We released the bird, falling to the ground, adrenaline surging through our veins. The duckling paddled back to its mother, who no longer seemed interested in attacking. We looked at each other in disbelief and started one of those laughs that begins to sound like relief; the kind that builds into a roar of rib pains and teary eyes. We must've laughed for hours that day. It happened so long ago, it almost feels as though it never took place.

"Careful thoughts can have dangerous consequences, you know."

A familiar hand falls on my shoulder. My body jolts back to reality, but I recognize the man before me. The beaming smile on olive skin is just as I always remembered it. Before I have time to take in more, he tugs my shoulder, urging me to stand, and pulls me into a hug. I'm pressed against the scraggly woolen turtleneck draped over his shoulders. When he doesn't feel my arms around his back, he draws me back, taking his turn to look me up and down, flashing me one of his signature grins.

"Are you feeling okay?" He tilts his head ever so slightly to the left. His voice rings in my ear like an old song I'd forgotten I loved. The thought makes me smile a little.

I force a crooked grin. "Yeah." He flashes his teeth at me again, just as bright as I remembered. "Why wouldn't I be?"

We take our seats from across one another, basking in the silence. We took our place more as strangers than old friends; neither of us knowing what to do or what to say, neither of us knowing anything about each other anymore, both of us probably trying to remember what it is we are even doing here in the first place.

"So, how have you been?" I ask, unsure of how to start.

"Same old, I suppose. Yourself?" He leans into the conversation. His hair keeps its shape as it bounces in the breeze.

"I've been alright." Silence slips between our lips again and steals whatever words we feel are right to say.

"It's funny, I honestly don't know what to talk about." I let out a nervous laugh. I don't want to come right out about everything. I don't want him to feel as though it was all his fault. But at the same time, I don't really want to feel like it was mine either. Even though I think this was mostly my doing, my therapist told me that I needed to stop blaming myself for things that happened in the past.

"Mom doesn't visit anymore. She used to a lot, but not anymore." I notice he has lent his eyes to the park. I let mine follow. I wonder if he remembers the same things I do about the place, about the night he left.

"I see her sometimes. Not often, but she's doing fine." I lie. I haven't seen her in years. She couldn't bear to look at me after everything. On the rare occasion that both of us leave our houses, I will sometimes run into her at the grocery store. I usually watch her from afar, avoiding a conversation that neither of us were ready to have. I can't help thinking that she blames me for ruining *her* life too.

"What are you looking at?" I ask, noticing he hasn't broken focus from across the road. I keep my eyes on him.

He's entranced by the trees. "Remember when those guys from school saw us there?"

How could I forget? We decided to work on our math homework one day, when the not-so-uncommon urge to fill our time with other things fell over us. We had gone to the library before they closed and grabbed a random poetry collection to read instead.

We already knew the perfect spot to go. The tree limbs in the park were always cut high because of kids like us getting into places we weren't supposed to. Perhaps we helped create this policy. A while back, in the emptier part of the grounds, we found a bench built next to a cherry tree, which we used to climb to the highest branch we could. It has been known to us as 'our spot' from then on.

We went down to the abandoned part of the park, we climbed our tree and read. We sat up there for the entire afternoon. I pressed close into the woolen sweater he wore, reading the old words aloud; he spoke only to point out his favorite stanzas and lines.

Sometime around the last moments of sunlight, a group of boys from our school made their way toward us—the type of boys who slammed baseball bats into the sides of mailboxes, got drunk on cheap beer in the grocery store parking lot, and made crude gestures at the girls who walked past them. We knew guys like them, but the fear that coursed through my veins didn't compare to the previous time they threatened us.

"No, no, you do it. Here, take it." We heard a few of them cackling. From behind a few branches and leaves, I saw one boy handing something over to another, and before we knew what was happening, something hurled our way, busting a piece of bark clean off the trunk. It was only an inch or so from my forehead.

"Damn it! I missed."

They were no longer trying to be quiet. A chilling panic swept over me, as rage flooded over him.

"You fuckers better start running!" Before I knew it, he was no longer sitting between my legs. He had already made it halfway down the tree.

The boys took off, their laughter in their hasted breath. "Fucking faggots!" The words flew with another rock aimed toward him.

Faggots. The word shot like a bullet. My arms shook so much that I could hardly pull myself up off the branch and keep hold of the book at the same time. By the time I got down, his face was buried in the dirt, his back heaving up and down.

He was down there like that until the stars came out, all the while wrapped in my arms. I didn't ask what made him so upset, why his rage so quickly burned into despair. I didn't know if the words hurt worse than the stone; if he hurt the same as I did. I never found the chance to ask him about it.

"Yes." The pain is suffocating. "I remember." My heart still pounds with the beat of the memory.

"Would you like to go over there?" he asks, as if he doesn't recall the story the way I do. His eyes now seem to carry a dullness, as if they've changed in seconds from a lively chocolate color to water-damaged mahogany. They're widened now, glued eagerly to the dancing tree limbs.

I take no time to respond. "No, not really."

His cheeks hold a yellowish hue I hadn't noticed before, even in the sunlight. All of a sudden, he's wearing the wrinkles of a smoker twice our age, and yet he looks as if he hasn't aged a day since I last saw him.

He keeps silent. That isn't an answer he'll accept. I take in a sharp breath. I know why I asked him to meet me here. Part of me thinks he knows too. We have to face the problem head on. I'll never forgive myself if we don't.

"Okay," I rise, scraping the chair legs against the floor. "Let's go." I'm as still as the air around us. Perhaps even more so. "Do you want to go over there?" My question comes out more like a demand than anything else.

"Yes." His eyes look as if they are about to rot and fall into the bags that now drape beneath them. "We need to. We've put it off for too long."

Without hesitation, he slowly rises across from me, pushing himself up with bony hands which bear his slim fingers and brittle nails. I throw some money onto the table, even though our waiter never came back.

We make our way across the slow road, over to the park that haunts me. As we approach, the oak and elm trees appear to be taller than redwoods. The crowds of rustling leaves welcome us with the sounds of late spring. The pollen from the cherry blossoms wisps past my nose, adding sweetness to the breeze. The picture almost makes me smile, but a dreaded feeling cracks the back of my head, as if an icepick burrowed its way into my skull. Suddenly, I am reminded of the evil it holds.

The soles of our shoes remember the dusty gravel they tread across, retracing the path to the bench beneath one of the many cherry trees—*our tree*. As I watch him from behind, his shoulders hang low, as if they barely fit into their sockets. Suddenly, I no longer feel the peculiar heat that April offered.

"It really is a beautiful tree." His voice is soft and raspy.

I twist my head toward him, startled by his sudden change of tone, and find his foggy eyes looking upward. The tree branch hovering above us holds only a few leaves clinging to it, with a handful of new blossoms making up for its mostly barren twigs.

I want my words to reduce the tree to nothing but a distant memory. My glare curses the blossoms with words my mouth can't think of. If looks could kill, they would burn—they would engulf this whole forest in hellfire until nothing remained. Until the ash mixed with the dirt and gravel below, so much so that no one would remember it was ever there—an erasure from time itself.

"And what makes it so beautiful?" I let my voice sink somberly.

"It's just so full of life."

"That's a funny way of putting it." The irony makes me chuckle a bit, though it feels inappropriate to do so.

He dropped his weightless head onto my shoulder. Even though it's a scorching day for April, his body's chill swallows me like winter, as if I were left alone in an abandoned, hollowed-out Alaskan cabin in a blizzard.

My ears fill with the periodic rustle of leaves and the faint sounds of children running somewhere far off, transporting me back to our adolescent years.

The last time I saw him was in this park. I was in his bed that night after the boys threw stones and slurs at us. It didn't feel right to leave him alone after the episode we had. I sent my parents a text, letting them know where I would be, and I took him home under my arm. We cleaned ourselves up, stripped off our clothes, and climbed into bed. Neither of us wanted to fall asleep.

We lay next to each other, staring at the ceiling, before he broke the silence.

"What if what they said was true?" I felt his body turn to face me.

I met him with mine. "What are you talking about?" I pretended not to understand. I didn't want to be the one to bring it up. I didn't want to be the first one to admit it. But if neither of us said a word, I felt that my heart's beating in my throat might choke me, and that we might never speak of this again.

"What they called us."

I felt a shame in his voice, as if he felt guilty about something he had done. Or something he was about to do.

I opened my mouth, but before anything came out, I felt his lips press into mine. I did not push him away. Instead, he pulled back, and I wondered if he found regret in what he had just done. His eyes sought for an answer that I could not give. I let him pull me in again to find another kiss from me.

That night was an adventure all its own. It brought a sense of euphoria I had never felt before, and I remember thinking there was no one else in the world I would rather share that feeling with than him.

Something woke me later that night, a void where he should have been. I threw a drowsy hand over to find him, but it came back with a piece of paper crumpled between the fingers. I flicked on the lamp on the nightstand to find my name scribbled sloppily on the face of the note. Something was very wrong.

My eyes didn't get far past the words *I'm sorry* before my hands were grabbing my clothes and my feet were rushing down the hallway. He was nowhere in the house.

It wasn't until I noticed his shoes missing that I went out to the only place I could think to find him. The sun had not yet risen when I wandered into the sea of trees. With only the glow of the dimmed street lamps, I wandered around looking for him. He wasn't running around on the gravel paths. I would have seen him by then. He wasn't bothering any ducks by the pond. I would have heard the squawking amongst his signature laughter.

My sneakers carried my weary legs to the abandoned part of the gardens. Busted lamp posts painted the area black; the treetops so thick that not even moonlight could cast upon the road ahead. But my feet felt the familiar ground and did not fail me. I came up to our spot, finding the bench we always treated as a step ladder. Finding nobody, I sat on the damp wood of the bench under the cherry tree, *our* tree, where we would spend hours laughing with one another. The tree where we read poetry instead of raising our math grades, talking about insignificant, philosophical things.

It wasn't until I felt a crumble of dried mud from the bottom of his shoe roll down my shoulder that I looked up. He swayed in the tree that we called ours, back and forth with the early morning breeze that carried down browning blossoms.

I stared into his barren eyes. His jaw swung low, just past a snapped neck. His throat bloodied and bruised from his woolen turtleneck sweater. My screams thrashed through my throat but rang empty in my ears.

Someone must've heard my desperate and futile cries for help. Not long after—or maybe after forever—the wails of the sirens drowned out my own.

I watched the paramedics as they cut down the sweetest fruit that hung from the cherry branches.

The rest of that day, and all of the days that followed were a blur. Nothing else after that made much sense.

I sit up from the bench and open my eyes. Suddenly dawn turns into day, and I'm back in reality. I hope I'm back in reality.

"I think I'm just going to go home." My trembling breath drips the words out of my mouth. "I don't really want to be here anymore."

I speak softly, tears clotting my words, but nobody is around to hear it.

Part 2

Abyss

Sugar Cake Lady
Franka Zeph

harlene knocked on the door and was greeted with silence. The loop of house keys rattled in her hand while she searched for the right one. Her palms were cold and sweaty as she pressed and turned the metal in the lock. It didn't give, so she tried another. She was certain that if her mother-in-law was in there she would have responded by now. This was her house after all, and she had the right to enter if she felt it was justified. That was the response she would give if she came face to face with the old woman.

The door purred open, and a rank odor escaped that reminded her of the dead cockroaches she used to find when cleaning her room in Trinidad. Their desiccated corpses smelled like stinky toes, and she had to cover her nose with a handkerchief as she swept them into the dustpan. She repeated the gesture with the sleeve of her pajama top to block out that awful scent and flipped the light switch on. Elsie's sweaters were neatly folded and stacked atop a large woven straw hamper. A leather-bound Bible rested on the night table beside a glass of water. Pink bedroom slippers with bunny ears lay in front of the bed that was neatly made up, the duvet pulled tight across the covers.

Everything was in order, except Elsie was gone.

A cool draft of autumn night air caressed her face from the open window. What if her crazy suspicions turned out to be true? In all likelihood, she was wrong—a dotish victim of old wives' tales. She truly hoped she was mistaken. Lives were at stake, and it was time for the search to begin.

"So, what do you think, darling? About Mom coming up to spend some time with us?" Dexter sipped his espresso. It was 6:16 AM and their final moments of early morning intimacy were slipping away.

"Sure, that sounds good." Sharlene savored her caffeine-free café au lait. "It would give her a chance to get to know her grandchildren."

"She not doing so well. Last time we had our video chat, she looked so skinny, like she's not eating properly. I think she's lonely. She needs to get out of that place for a while."

"I can imagine it's hard to live alone at her age."

"None of my brothers does check for her. Wendy swings by once a week to drop off groceries. Apart from that, she don't really have company."

"Oh, that's so sad! To be abandoned like that by your children."

"It's not that we abandoned her," he replied, defensiveness creeping into his voice. "It's just that everybody have their own life now, and where she living, all the way behind God's back in the countryside... there's not much going on there."

"Well, I could use the extra help." As if on cue, Sorel squealed in her crib upstairs.

Dexter patted Sharlene's lap. "So glad to know you're on board with this. I'll get started with the paperwork. If all goes well, she'll be with us by fourth of July weekend."

"Mommy!" Yunia screamed. Footsteps pounded the floor above them as her twin brother chased her around their room.

"I'm looking forward to it." Sharlene drained her cup. "Love my boos, but boy, they are a handful!"

"You think you know what's best for Mammy?" Marlon shouted at his brother. "I telling you she good right where she is!"

Dexter paced the floor of his home office while Sharlene nursed Sorel and listened on speaker phone. "Three months ain't long. She'll be back before you know it and besides, she never visited the States before. This trip will be good for her."

"Mom don't like trips. The last trip she took was to Tobago twenty-five years ago. What the ass make you think she want to hop on a plane now?"

"When last you pass by and see her, eh?" Dexter responded. "You doh even spend time with your mother and now you criticizing me?"

"Alright, Mr. Bigshot! You in your big house in America feel you better than me!"

"You can't even answer my question! Mom not doing so well. She get small-small, and none of all yuh doing a damn thing for her except Wendy."

"You acting like we doh care about Mammy. Trust me she okay, she doh complain about nothing. And you want to bring her out to America at her age? I say leave her be!"

"I want her to meet her grandchildren."

"Why you don't bring the grands down here to see her? You 'fraid dem might have to use ah outhouse? Wipe dey ass with gazette paper when she run out of toilet paper?"

"I don't see you doing anything to better her situation. She's my mother, and I have the right to bring her out here if I want to."

"Fine!" Marlon yelled. "I is Mr. Backward and you is Mr. Bigshot. Do what the hell you like!"

"Bye, brother." Dexter hung up and looked at his wife. "He's always been the jealous type, but he'll get over it."

"It'll be alright. Every family has disagreements—it's normal."

"I don't understand what his problem is." Dexter shook his head with disbelief. "I doing something nice for our mother, and he thinks I'm trying to steal her away or something."

Sorel began to whimper and fuss. Sharlene disengaged her nipple, placed the baby against her shoulder and rubbed her back. "I think it's great what you're doing for her."

"Good to know you've got my back, honey. I love you."

The baby burped as her stomach settled down. "I love you too," Sharlene said.

Two days before her mother-in-law's arrival, Sharlene was in the basement removing a queen-sized duvet from storage. Extra bedding had been shifted here to make room in the linen closet prior to Sorel's birth five months ago. This one was a Black Friday sale special, covered in a pink hibiscus floral print. Dexter said pink was his mother's favorite color. Sharlene thought the flowers would remind her of Trinidad in case she felt homesick. While hauling the bulky duvet in its protective casing up the stairs, tightness welled in her chest. She paused and waited for the sensation to pass. Maybe it was gas, or it could be something more. She made a mental note to arrange a doctor's appointment sometime over the next few weeks and mounted the stairs to the upper floor landing. Dexter was on his knees, affixing a new doorknob to the guest room where his mother would be staying. Screws lay scattered on the carpet beside his feet, next to the old knob.

"Something wrong with the door?"

"Mom likes her privacy. She asked me to put a lock on the door."

"Since when do we have locked doors in this house?"

"I know how you feel, sweetie, but I want her to be comfortable. Just accommodate her request. It's only for a short while, then I'll change it back, alright?" He twisted the screws into place.

"As long as you make a copy of the key, I don't have a problem with that."

"I'll make one. Just promise me that you won't go in there when she's not around."

"Of course, I won't! It just makes sense to have a spare in case of an emergency."

"One more thing; she will change the bedding and clean the room herself. Leave a hamper in the hallway so she can put the sheets there when they need to be washed."

"It's no trouble for me to clean up after her, but if that's the way she wants it, I respect that."

"Thanks for understanding."

"You're welcome. I hope she'll like the room."

"I'm sure she will."

Sharlene sighed. So much for their family's "open door" policy. She carried the duvet into the den. When he was finished, she would prep the spare room.

"Oooh, when is Granny coming?" asked Yunia.

"Tomorrow," Dexter responded. The family was having an orientation session in the living room. Yunia jumped up and down with excitement while Yuquon played with his tablet. Sharlene was rather annoyed with Dexter for letting him access the device while they were having a conversation. The six-year-old was totally immersed in a world of militant fruit madness that was, thankfully, on mute.

"Is she gonna sleep in my room?"

"Granny's going to have her own room," Dexter replied. "I don't want you guys going in there to play. Yuquon, do you hear me?" The boy's fingers tapped the tablet's screen, slicing digital fruit with zigzagging flashes of light. Sharlene gently prised it out of his grip.

"Give it back!" He reached for the device.

"Did you hear what I said? No going into Granny's room to play, even if the door's open."

"Why, Daddy?"

"Because Granny needs her privacy."

"Will she look the same like she does on the phone?" inquired Yunia.

"Yes, baby," he replied.

"I can't wait to show her Nicole!" She held up her tween Black doll with spun-yarn hair and a rock star outfit. Sharlene thought it looked too mature for a girl Yunia's age. It was a birthday gift from Aunty Gloria who insisted on giving the kids whatever they wanted. She secretly wondered whether she was old-fashioned and envied her younger sister's ease with the children. At the twins' fifth birthday party, Yuquon had expressed to a roomful of guests that he wished Gloria was his mother. Kids these days!

"She'll love Nicole." Sharlene smiled at her daughter whose long dual braids bounced on her narrow shoulders as she jigged in place. Her teeth were changing, and she was growing so beautifully. She reminded herself that she was like that once.

Birds trilled in the pear tree that occupied the center of the Bartons' backyard. It was a gorgeous afternoon on 5 July 2024, and Sharlene relished the sounds of soca music while stirring lemonade in the pitcher. She had staged a welcome party for Elsie with pink-themed wardrobe and décor. Flamingos adorned the outdoor cushions on the patio chairs, accompanied by matching paper cups and plates set on the fuchsia tablecloth. Sorel fidgeted in her rocker, her little feet twitching in their pastel-colored booties while her siblings gamed in the air-conditioned living room. Dexter was due to arrive with Elsie in five minutes and lunch was being kept warm on the stove. Everything had turned out well, and Sharlene was chuffed at her ability to hold it down. Some of the credit went to her greens, which she drank daily to give herself a healthy boost of energy.

On the other side of the picket fence, Kyle watered his plants, one hand resting on his lower back, gut protruding slightly over his belted waistband. He wore a peaked blue Yankees baseball cap that shielded his pink skin from the sun. A mild hint of lobster red tinted his freckled forearms. She guessed he hadn't bothered to apply sunblock. Sulfur butterflies flirted with her meticulous flowerbed, sipping nectar at leisure. Sharlene's heart overflowed with contentment for her happy suburban family life that was a far cry from her wild college days. Back then, she never thought that she would ever settle down. She had entertained fantasies of becoming a globe-trotting entrepreneur and then met Dexter in her final year. From that moment on, they were like two pigeon peas in a pod. Though she hardly had time for herself anymore, she had plenty of love.

Kyle waved at her; she returned the gesture. He was a good neighbor and his wife, Isabel, had a two-month-old baby named Alfred. She had seen the little one in his pram when his mother took him out for walks. He resembled Kyle and had fire red lashes. The two women always exchanged bowls of fruit during harvest season. Isabel had an apple tree, and Sharlene's luscious pears were so plentiful, she had to give some away to avoid wastage.

Sharlene heard a car door close at the front. Dexter had arrived. Moments later, luggage wheels scraped across the pavement. The front door opened, and the children screamed with delight.

"Granny! Granny!" they chanted as their father deposited the luggage in the foyer.

Sharlene freed Sorel from the rocker and brought her inside. She was serene and contentedly blowing spit bubbles, having been fed an hour ago. Sharlene had not seen Elsie in person since she and Dexter made an engagement trip to Trinidad in 2008. The old lady was delighted to meet her daughter-in-law but was too sick to attend the Miami wedding. Over the years, video calls addressed the long-distance relationship void, especially when it came to the children. Now, her mother-in-law was here in the flesh.

"Hello darling!" the elderly voice quavered.

"Hi Granny!" the twins chorused as they rushed to hug their grandmother. Elsie laughed and placed her arthritic fingers on their heads. She was hunched and frail, appearing to weigh less than a sack of grain. Her thinning hair was pulled back in a chignon from a bony brown face ravaged by aging. Shiny dougla waves accentuated the fine texture of her hair. She wore a candy pink cardigan over a white sleeveless top with matching pants and shoes. Coral pigment coated her thin lips that parted, revealing uneven teeth stained yellow with age. Gold caps glinted from her upper canines—a hint of old school West Indian Style. She looked at Sharlene and smiled.

"Hello, dear. Long time I ain't see yuh! Aye aye, look the baby!"

Sharlene embraced her mother-in-law. It felt like hugging a baby-powder scented bag of bones. She hoped she wasn't hurting the old lady. Elsie released her and bent down to examine the infant.

"What's her name again?"

"Sorel."

"Ah, Sorel! Like sorrel with one 'r.'"

"Yes. That's exactly right!" Sharlene laughed. "I'm amazed you picked up on that."

"How you expect me not to know? I is Trini!" Elsie caressed Sorel's chin. The baby squinted her round brown eyes and began to cry.

"Sorry about that," Sharlene said. "She was sleeping for a while. Must be the heat."

"Mom, you want something to eat?" Dexter inquired. "You must be hungry by now."

"Not really," she said. "I had some food on the plane."

"That's not real food. Take a little plate of something and eat with us."

"Okay, Dex, I will do it just for you."

"Dexter, can you dish out the food?" said Sharlene. "I need to calm Sorel down."

"Sure, honey." He went to the sink and washed his hands.

"Don't forget the coleslaw in the red bowl on the bottom shelf of the fridge." She went upstairs with the baby screaming in her arms.

Fifteen minutes later, the Bartons were dining on the patio while Sorel dozed upstairs. There was pelau, stew chicken, coleslaw, chow mein, and garden salad. Yuquon and Yunia were devouring pink frosted donuts and chatting with their mouths full. The scent of freshly cut grass wafted on the summer breeze. Lawn sprinklers whirred, hard at work to keep their living carpet lush and green.

"What a lovely home you have here" Elsie ruminated between a mouthful of food. "You've had this place for how long now?"

"Eleven years," Dexter responded. "We've got five bedrooms, three bathrooms, an outdoor whirlpool, swimming pool, and an indoor sauna. I'll take you on a tour of the house afterwards."

"Oh, that sounds like a dream! You all living in a castle."

"Yeah, well it's a small castle in comparison to a real one."

"But look at all the space you have," Elsie marveled, gesturing with her thin hands. "For me, this is a mansion. And I love your backyard. It's so beautiful!"

Dexter's face shone with pride. "Thanks, Mom. I worked hard so you could come and enjoy it."

You mean we worked hard so you could enjoy it, Sharlene chafed silently.

"That's my boy!" She patted him on the shoulder. "I always knew you would make me proud."

"Daddy's a lawyer," Yuquon blurted. "He helps put bad people in jail."

"Yuquon!" Sharlene said, aghast. "Nobody's talking to you!"

"It's okay, let the boy talk." Granny shooed dismissively with her hand. Knobby veins bulged from the volcanic surface of her skin. Yuquon took one look at his mother's face and focused on his meal. "I find he resemble Lennox, your grandfather," Elsie remarked to Dexter. Crick! The old lady cracked a chicken bone with her teeth and sucked out a dark brown substance from the splintered bone. The twins watched in amazement.

"Granny, what are you doing?" asked Yunia.

"I eating the marrow. That's the most nutritious part of the chicken. It will make you strong."

Yuquon picked up a bone from his plate and looked at his father. "Daddy, can I try?"

"Sure, go ahead," he said. "But be careful not to bite down too hard." The boy clenched the bone between his teeth and bore down. Soon, he was sucking on marrow. Yunia followed suit.

"Mmm, tastes good!" Yuquon smacked his greasy lips with approval.

"I'm surprised they haven't tried this before." Granny eyed Dexter and Sharlene, seeking an explanation.

"The chickens out here not like in Trinidad," Sharlene said. "They raise them on hormones and antibiotics, so that's why I don't encourage the children to eat the marrow."

"Nothing perfect in this world," Granny responded. "Better to let them have some marrow than no marrow at all. You should teach the children about our culture. Nothing to be 'shamed of." Granny pulverized the bone, her ancient jowls quivering with every crunch.

"True," Dexter replied. "It's easy to forget, especially living out here."

"Don't worry," his mother said. "I happy to teach them." Grey bone fragments lay in a mangled heap to the side of her plate, bits of residual marrow visible between the cracks. Yunia licked her fingers and made appreciative smacking sounds while Yuquon giggled. Feeling slightly queasy, Sharlene helped herself to an extra serving of coleslaw.

The silver Lexus glided along McKinnon Avenue; a tree-lined residential street of picturesque multi-story homes and dual garages fronted by glistening lawns. The newspaper delivery boy wheeled by on his bike to deliver subscriptions on front porches. Sharlene observed this idyllic scenario and considered herself lucky. Sometimes she had to pinch herself at her remarkable good fortune. So many of her girlfriends were either separated or divorced from their spouses. Some complained about the financial struggles they faced having to support a single-parent household on a reduced income. Others were embroiled in bitter parental custody and child support battles. It was as though society had pitted women and men against each other so that they would forever be at each other's throats. Thankfully, her marriage to Dexter was rock solid. They'd had their ups and downs yet managed to stay focused and committed. The "friendship first" approach was proving to be most effective at helping them navigate the occasional rocky terrain of their sixteen-year marriage.

She reversed into the driveway and parked. Mechanical processes ticked into retirement, and she sat in silence; a rare luxury that would end the moment she set foot in the house. Maternity leave was ending in one month, and it was back to work in September. Having Elsie was a boon; she could babysit Sorel while Sharlene worked and saved them some money.

Sharlene removed her keys from the ignition. A laser-cut palm tree with "Sweet TnT" embossed on a nameplate dangled from the keyring. She exited the car and entered her home. The cloying scent of boiling sugar hung in the air, thick and heavy. The sound of a stirring pot came from the kitchen.

"Next, I going to add the coconut," Elsie announced. "Yunia darling, pass me the bowl please."

Sharlene kicked off her shoes and strolled into the kitchen. Her mother-in-law was at the stove while the twins stood beside her, watching as she stirred the shredded coconut into the bubbling mixture.

"Hi Mom! I see you're making sugar cake."

Elsie looked up from her stirring. "Yes, love—for the children."

"How's Sorel?"

"She upstairs sleeping. I change her diaper half an hour ago."

"Thanks."

"How was your outing?"

"Pretty good. Got my hair and nails done."

"Is good to take some time to yourself every now and then." On the stovetop, the grated coconut had absorbed most of the syrup. Elsie unscrewed a slim glass bottle of colorless liquid and added a few drops to the mixture.

"Mmm, Granny, that smells good!" exclaimed Yunia.

"It's almond essence from Trinidad."

"What's that for?"

"To give the sugar cake a nice flavor." Elsie reached for a small dark bottle on the counter. Moments later, scarlet drops splashed the shredded coconut.

"Granny, what's that?" said Yuquon.

"Food coloring. That will make the sugar cake look pretty."

"Looks like blood in the snow."

"Yuquon," said Sharlene. "Don't be morbid."

"But, Mommy, it's true!"

"Don't worry, I'm not offended," said Elsie while she stirred the mixture. "He's got quite the imagination!" Yuquon stared, fascinated to watch the striated white mass transform into fragrant pink candy.

"Yes, he does," his mother replied. "He's a budding artist too. You should see some of his drawings."

"Can I show her now?" asked Yuquon.

"Later, once she's done with this." Sharlene watched Elsie pour the mixture into a greased dish while Yuquon scraped it out with a spoon. His sister stood by with a spatula and promptly leveled the mixture into a uniform rectangle. Sharlene was amazed that the frail old woman had enough strength to pick up a cast iron pot with both hands. She noted the open package of caster sugar on the counter which Dexter had bought for his mother. Sugar caused hyperactivity in kids and a host of other health issues. Next time, she would ask her to use substitute sweetener.

"Now, we leave this to cool down, and then we can eat it." Elsie rested the pot in the kitchen sink. Yuquon licked the spoon, and Yunia swiped her fingers inside the pot, picking up stray bits of candied coconut and popping them into her mouth. Sharlene felt grateful they were having this experience, as she had never made sugar cake for them. Her mother had passed away shortly after she wed Dexter, so her children didn't have a chance to know their maternal grandmother. Elsie picked up a sponge and squeezed detergent onto the lemon-yellow surface.

"It's okay, Mom. I'll put these into the dishwasher," Sharlene said.

"Thanks, dear." Elsie dropped the sponge in the sink. "I'm going to take a rest now." She slowly made her way to the living room, eased herself onto the love seat and popped the footrest out. Dexter had shown her how to work it, and now it was her go-to favorite.

One hour later, they were all munching on sugar cake and watching Jeopardy. Sharlene restricted herself to one piece while Elsie had a half serving. The twins probably had at least seven squares between them. They sat on the floor and chattered like chickadees, paying hardly any attention to the program. Sharlene made a mental note to vacuum the place tomorrow. Everyone had plates to catch the crumbs, yet she knew some would settle between the carpet fibers. She prided herself on maintaining a clean environment, and the last thing she wanted was critters in her space. Mind you, the roaches in America were like plankton compared to the mammoth variety endemic to the tropics. She thought of the notorious hardback cockroach—the winged terror that reminded her of a humongous, smelly black-eyed pea with antennae—and cringed.

"Thanks for making the sugar cake. I haven't had this in so long! Reminds me of home."

"You're welcome, dear," Elsie replied. Pink crumbs clung like tiny sequins to the edges of her thin lips.

"I hope you like your room. If there's anything you need, let me know."

"The room is perfect. I love the view of the street and those trees with the silvery bark—what are they called?"

"Birch trees."

"They are very lovely. We don't have trees like that in Trinidad."

"Mom, I just want you to know I'm happy to clean your room for you. It's no problem at all."

"It's okay, dear. You mustn't trouble yourself. You have your hands full minding these children. I can look after myself." She looked at the clock on the wall. "It's 8 o'clock now. That's my bedtime. Good night, everybody!"

"Good night, Granny!" the children chorused.

"Good night, Mom," said Sharlene. "You need help getting up the stairs?"

"No thanks, I'm alright." Elsie hobbled out of the room; her body stiffened from sitting down for so long. She ascended the staircase, her hand grasping the railing for support. Thin gold bangles gleamed from the cuff of her cardigan. Sharlene listened for the sound of her mother-in-law's bedroom door being closed and locked for the night. They would not see her again until the following morning.

Sharlene curled her legs beneath her on the sofa and changed the channel to a nature program. She looked forward to watching her scandalous dating reality show, which was set to record and enjoy after the kids went to bed.

At the neighborhood playground, Yuquon climbed the monkey bars while Yunia played pretend with her friends in the jungle gym. It was the first week of back-to-school and back-to-work for Sharlene. She was utterly exhausted and dying for a glass of red wine, which would have to wait until she helped the kids do their homework, shower, and go to bed. Thankfully, Elsie cooked dinner; stew chicken with pelau and salad. Just thinking about wolfing down a plate of Trinidadian soul food after a stressful day lifted her spirits. Going back to her legal secretary role after maternity leave was a discombobulating experience. During lunch break, she had a silent cry in the washroom, feeling the pain of separation from Sorel and the crush of having to practically relearn processes she had previously known by heart. She began to question whether to continue working at the firm or to quit and start her own business. To her relief, she spotted Ann-Marie, a Black mother from the community, wrapped in a knitted poncho at the opposite end of the playground.

"Hey, Annie!"

"Hey, girl!" Ann-Marie beamed her brilliant smile, a flash of lasered pearlies in her glistening mahogany face. "How's it going? Haven't seen you in a minute!"

"Mat leave's over so it's back to reality. You know how that is."

"Don't I know it! A glass of wine at night always helps."

Sharlene chuckled. "Girl, you read my mind! I've been thinking about it all afternoon. Talk about delayed gratification! The kids always come first."

"Yep."

Sharlene stooped down in the sandbox to look at Jericho. He was holding a red plastic shovel and pouring sand into a dug-out pool.

"Hi, Jericho, how are you?"

The boy didn't respond. He remained fixated on his building project, scooping the granulated quartz into a funnel shape that he was creating.

"You'll have to excuse him," Ann-Marie said. "He hasn't been himself lately."

"What's wrong? Is he sick?"

Ann-Marie's eyes flicked around the playground, checking to ensure that no one was listening. "Normally, he would be on the monkey bars, but his energy levels are so low, he's sticking to the sandbox." She leaned closer towards Sharlene and whispered. "The doctor says he has anemia."

"I'm so sorry to hear that," Sharlene said. "Do you know what's causing it?"

"We don't know; no one in my family has it. The doctor says we need to give him iron supplements and organ meats. I've been doing that for the past three weeks, but it doesn't seem to be helping."

"Organ meats are good. I used to eat beef and chicken liver when I was a child. Just make sure they're organic though."

"Of course." Ann-Marie cast a worried glance at her son who was busy shaping the sand with his hands. Sharlene thought Jericho didn't look well at all. He was much thinner than she remembered when she last saw him playing with Yuquon a few weeks ago.

"What are you making, Jericho?" she inquired.

The boy continued to pat the dampened sand into place. She observed the shape that his sculpture was beginning to assume. It resembled a familiar object whose name danced on the tip of her tongue.

"Girrrl, it's so good to see you!" Ann-Marie hugged Sharlene. "Life gets crazy, but we should go out for a drink sometime when our schedules permit."

"Yeah, for sure. I'll text you next week. Have a good eve."

Sharlene whipped scrambled eggs in the skillet while the news blared from the flatscreen television in the living room. Dexter sipped espresso at the kitchen counter and checked his email while Sorel slept upstairs in her crib. A dull ache throbbed in Sharlene's lower back, and she pressed her fingertips against the lumbar region. She needed to book an appointment with the masseuse; it was such a challenge to find the time between the onerous demands of work and motherhood.

"Yunia! Yuquon! Come and have your breakfast now!" Elsie called. The kids sat at the table and wolfed down buttermilk pancakes drenched in maple syrup and organic butter from grass-fed cows, interspersed with sips of orange juice. Sharlene scraped the eggs into a dish layered with sliced tomatoes, cucumbers, bacon, and lettuce. The earthy seductive aroma made her stomach grumble. It was Dexter's favorite breakfast dish and hers as well. The bottom of the eggs was brown, borderline burned yet okay.

"There you go, sweetie."

"Thanks." He dug into the steaming pile of eggs with his fork. Sharlene scrolled through her newsfeed, spatula in one hand, phone in the other. She knew she should focus on eating, but was so addicted to the app that browsing before breakfast had become part of her daily routine. Her thumb paused in mid-scroll on a news item that hit close to home: 'Anemia Epidemic Sickens Falls Heights Kids, Leaving One Child Dead.' She clicked on the article.

"An epidemic of anemia is sweeping the Falls Heights community in New Jersey. Pediatricians say forty-five children have abnormally low blood iron counts from unknown causes. One fatality has been reported for the month of September. Six-year-old Jericho Delaware has died from aplastic anemia after a prolonged bout of illness. State health authorities promise a full investigation into this mysterious epidemic that has left many parents mystified."

Sharlene gasped and dropped the spatula on the floor.

"What's wrong, baby?" asked Dexter.

She glanced over at the twins who were deeply engrossed in their breakfast and picked up the spatula. Specks of egg had landed on the chair legs, giving them a mottled appearance.

She lowered her voice to a whisper. "It's Jericho, Ann-Marie's son. You know the little Black boy with the purple frohawk who bikes with Yuquon?"

"Yeah, what about him?"

"He... he passed away."

"Snap! I'm so sorry to hear that."

"He died of aplastic anemia."

Dexter bit into his sandwich. A strip of bacon dangled from the edge of his toast, tiny pools of grease gleaming from the marcelled crevices. "People rarely die from anemia. It must have been quite severe."

"Yes, I'm sure it was." Sharlene texted her condolences to Ann-Marie. A lump of grief swelled in her throat, depriving her of appetite. Crying in front of the family at breakfast time was out of the question. She drank her coffee and focused on the bird-of-paradise floral centerpiece that breathed fresh tropical vibes into their living space.

"She must be taking it hard," said Dexter.

"How are we going to tell the kids? That's their friend; I don't want to upset them."

"They're gonna find out sooner or later. We'll have a family meeting after breakfast and break the news to them."

Sharlene's phone pinged. Ann-Marie had texted back to thank her for the well wishes.

"The funeral's on Sunday. I'll go and show my support. Can you keep the kids? I think it's best they stay out of this."

"Sure, darling, no problem."

Packed to the rafters, St. Mary's Episcopal Baptist Church swam in a sea of yellow. Sharlene sat among mourners, radiant in a double-breasted dress suit. Yellow was Jericho's favorite color, and Ann-Marie chose to honor her son's love of life and the sun, evinced by the sunflowers and yellow lilies that elevated the church's somber ambience. Mourners queued to view the body, and Sharlene stepped forward, moving closer to say farewell. Ann-Marie sat in the front pew with her immediate family and offered a nod of appreciation. Her face looked drawn but otherwise, she seemed to be holding up fine. Jericho's grandmother sobbed uncontrollably, her large body heaving while a relative comforted her.

As Sharlene drew closer, she caught a glimpse of Jericho's purple frohawk which contrasted sharply with the casket's white satin lining. Beneath his hairline, there was a surprising hint of beige. Jericho's complexion was the color of dark chocolate; it must be the reflection from the lining that made his skin seem off. She tried to convince herself that he was now in a land of sunshine and rainbows where suffering had been replaced by eternal joy. There was no way to know for sure; that was the thing about death. No one ever came back to tell you how nice it was on the other side.

The corpulent mourner ahead of her stepped aside to reveal Jericho's body swathed in canary yellow. Sharlene's feet wobbled in her golden high heels, and she put a hand on the casket's edge to steady herself. Jericho's rich dark complexion was now the color of rice paper; a depleted husk of his formerly round face, now sunken and hollowed beyond recognition. The mortician's brush could neither disguise the dark under-eye hollows closed in perpetual sleep, nor conceal the gaunt cheekbones of his wasted frame. The boy's yellow silk tie lay flush against his white dress shirt, encased in a tailored sunshine print jacket. Across the stomach, his blanched hands clutched an action figurine. Blue veins threaded the translucent skin that reminded her of onion paper. He was pale—so pale!

Sharlene sobbed and pressed a tissue to her eyes. He had suffered and slipped away despite intensive efforts from his parents and doctors. Never again would he swing from the monkey bars, play with the twins, or grow up and go to college. Ann-Marie sat with a resolute expression on her mocha face. The woman seemed calm, almost peaceful about the loss of her only child. Sharlene doubted whether she would have had the strength to bear it like she did.

She touched the little boy's hand. It was shockingly cold. "Bye, Jericho," Sharlene said. "Rest in peace, little darling. Yuquon and Yunia will miss you. We will always love you."

Sharlene opened the door to her home, smelling sugar cake intermingled with the savory smell of pizza and wings. Dexter had taken the family to church, and they were all in high spirits. 'Cook Curry Ochroe' by Shadow played in the background. The calypsonian's reference to a vegetarian dish proved an ironic counterpoint to the greasy food her family was consuming. A plate of buttermilk biscuits sat beside the bowl of sugar cake squares. Although she was stuffed to the gills from the funeral's reception dinner, Sharlene could not pass on the biscuits.

"Hey, guys! How was church?"

"Boring!" Yuquon replied, a chicken wing grasped between his fingers.

"I liked the singing," Yunia said through a mouthful of pizza. "That was the best part."

"Well, at least somebody got something out of it." Sharlene washed her hands at the sink and helped herself to a biscuit.

"I prayed for Jericho. Hope the angels will take care of him," Yuquon said.

"It was a very nice service," said Elsie. "Reverend Jones gave such a good sermon! The Holy Spirit was strong in him! You could tell he was preaching from the heart."

"I'm glad you enjoyed it," said Sharlene.

"Did you see Jericho?" Yuquon inquired.

Sharlene swallowed a piece of biscuit that felt like a boulder going down. "Yes, I did, honey."

"What did he look like?"

"Like he was sleeping."

"I'm going to miss him."

"We all will, baby."

"Is Jericho going to heaven?" asked Yunia, her eyes bright with guileless curiosity.

"Yes, I'm sure he's in heaven," Sharlene replied, washing the biscuit down with iced tea. "He was a good boy and he's in a better place now."

Later, after the children and their grandmother were asleep, Sharlene and Dexter relaxed in bed. She was engrossed in Housewives of Atlanta with a glass of wine, while he perused a sports magazine. After several minutes, he looked at his wife's fixed gaze and set the magazine aside.

"Talk to me, baby—what's on your mind? Something troubling you?"

"Dex, you should have seen the body. He was so pale that he was almost beige."

"Seriously? How come?"

"I don't know. He died from aplastic anemia; that's when your bone marrow gets so damaged it can't make enough blood cells. Ann-Marie said no one in her family has a history of anemia. I wanted to speak with her privately after the funeral but didn't get the chance."

"Man, oh man! That's so sad. I don't know what to say."

"I'm glad the kids didn't go; it wouldn't have been good for them to see him that way. Because honestly, he looked as if he had the life sucked right out of him." Tears brimmed in her eyes.

Dexter put his arm around her shoulders. "I know this is hard, honey. Grief takes time to process. Just remember I'm here for you."

"It's not just grief." She wiped a tear with the heel of her hand and rested her glass on the side table. "All these kids in our community have anemia, all of a sudden. Forty-five cases between August and September. Something's wrong. I don't want anything to happen to our kids."

"The kids will be fine." Dexter smiled and kissed her on the forehead. "You shouldn't worry too much."

"That's easy for you to say. You didn't see the body!" She tensed up within his embrace. "Maybe you should call and express your condolences. Let them know you care."

"I'll do that tomorrow. I just wanted to give them some space." He kissed her neck. "Anything else you want to tell me?"

"No, that's it for now."

"I'm going to get some shut eye. The firm's got a big case coming up bright and early tomorrow morning. Ah, Mondays suck!" He kissed her on the lips. "Good night, baby."

"Night, Dex."

He rolled over on his side. Sharlene resumed watching her show. Images moved. Folks argued; she did not hear them. Her mind harkened back to the first time they had lunch with Elsie in July. How the old lady had crunched that chicken bone with her teeth, sucked out the marrow and said, "That's the most nutritious part of the chicken. It will make you strong." She thought of how repulsive it was to watch her eat that day, and how she got the kids involved.

Two months into her stay, Elsie gained weight. Dexter was elated that his mother had adjusted so well. Even Marlon commented that she was looking rosy during their last group chat, and indeed she was. Her face had plumped out as though she had gotten fillers. A newly expanded waistline meant she had to go shopping for new clothes. Sharlene dozed off and saw Jericho's emaciated corpse lying in his casket. Startled awake, she reached for her wine glass. Nightmares were the last thing she needed. Dexter snored beside her, and she envied his easy rest.

"Dex?" He didn't respond. She got out of bed and went down the hallway to Elsie's room. Sharlene pressed her ear against the door and listened. All she heard were the familiar sounds of the house settling down for the night and the low drone of the television from her room. It was after ten-thirty and her mother-in-law always went to bed at eight. She rapped on the door and was greeted with silence. Perhaps the old lady slept soundly just like her son. She turned the knob.

"Mommy?"

Sharlene whirled around and saw Yuquon standing behind her.

"What are you doing out here?"

"I can't sleep."

Sharlene stooped down and gently took her son by the shoulders. "What's wrong baby?"

"I dreamed about Jericho."

"What did you dream?"

"We were at the playground on the swing. He tried to tell me something."

Sharlene could tell her son was scared. "What did he say?"

"He couldn't say anything. Blood came out of his mouth. There was blood everywhere." Yuquon began to cry. Sharlene took him into her arms.

"Sssh, it's okay." She led him into the den and sat him on her lap. Yuquon thought himself a sophisticated gentleman and announced that he was too big for 'baby stuff.' Sharlene cradled him, feeling the fuzzy texture of his pajamas and sang. "Hush little baby, don't you cry, cause Mama's gonna buy you a mockingbird. And if that mockingbird don't sing, Mama's gonna buy you a diamond ring. And if that diamond ring turns to brass, Mama's gonna buy you a looking glass."

His sobs subsided and he curled up in his mother's arms. As Sharlene continued the lullaby, he dozed off. She carried him to the kids' room, where Yunia was sound asleep in her bed, and deposited Yuquon into his. She pulled the covers over him and crept out, closing the door behind her. She checked on Sorel who slept peacefully in her crib and went back to her bedroom. She turned off the TV, climbed in beside Dexter and prayed silently, asking the Lord to bless her family and protect them while they rested.

On Tuesday night, the couple dined at LobStars, their favorite seafood restaurant, at a table with a lakeside view. This was their date night, which had been postponed after Sorel's birth, and Sharlene was elated to stoke their romantic connection while her body continued to recover. After weaning Sorel over a month ago, her breasts finally felt like they belonged to her again. She wasn't quite ready for sex yet, but she understood the importance of keeping Dexter engaged so he didn't think she was neglecting him.

"So, how's work coming along?" he asked while tackling the snow crab.

"I can't lie; it's stressful at times. I'm getting back into the flow but it's not exactly like riding a bicycle." She sampled her lobster bisque and decided to let it cool further. "I'm thinking of quitting so I can start an online business and spend more time watching my kids grow."

"If that's what you really want to do, go for it."

"My body's different now—it's not like when I had the twins. Back then I bounced back quick. This time it's taking longer. Plus, I feel like upper management are way more critical of my performance than my White colleagues. The executive assistant asks me to do work she should be doing, as if I don't already have enough on my plate!"

"Honey, if you're really not happy, then you shouldn't continue with the job." Dexter sipped his wine. "We'll be fine for money. At the end of the day, the important thing is you're happy."

Sharlene sampled the crab. "Mmm... oh gosh! I forgot how good this is."

"Mom makes a wicked crab and callaloo. You should do it with her some time."

"Speaking of which," she put her fork down. "I meant to ask you about her. Dex, she's so quiet! A really nice lady, but she doesn't talk much."

"She's never been the talkative type."

"Can you tell me more about her? What was she like when you were growing up?"

"Mom was a hardworking woman. We weren't rich, but she always made sure we had enough to eat and clothes on our backs. She used to work in a factory in Sangre Grande to support us while Dad worked in construction. It's not easy when you have five mouths to feed, but she did it. She was real strict at times, but that helped to keep us out of trouble. My parents made sure we got a good education so we could have an easier time than they did."

"That's good to know." Sharlene tried the bisque which had cooled to a reasonable temperature. "I don't want you to get defensive, but when you were growing up, did she always keep her bedroom door locked?"

"That only start happening when she was in her fifties, after Dad died from cancer. I think she was depressed. Life can be hard especially when you lose someone you love, like your husband. I was a hardhead teenage boy, but me, my brothers, and sister loved my mother, so we didn't bother her at night."

"Okay." Sharlene mulled over this tidbit of information. "Did you ever ask her why?"

"No. Mom always kept to herself and stayed out of people's business. Sometimes, I wish she remarried, but I guess she wasn't interested."

The waiter brought the peach cobbler to their table. "Thanks!" Dexter said. "Oooh, that looks good." He helped himself to the dessert. "You sure you don't want some?"

"That's not going to help me slim down anytime soon."

"I always like meh women thick you know!" he joked. "Life too short." He dropped a slice of cobbler into Sharlene's empty dessert plate. "Go on—I know you want some!"

"You know me too well," she laughed. "I'll have it later."

They dined in silence for several minutes. Sharlene pondered how to raise the topic that was foremost on her mind as she didn't want to spoil the romantic mood. Dexter was relaxed and not preoccupied with clients; his phone was silenced.

"I saw Yuquon standing outside Elsie's room on Sunday night."

Dexter raised his eyebrows. "Oh yeah? What was he doing there?"

"He couldn't sleep. He dreamed that he saw Jericho at the playground and blood came out of his mouth when he tried to talk."

"Do you have to bring this up while we're eating?"

"Look, I know this probably isn't the best time, but I'm really concerned for our kids. They haven't been sleeping well this past week. Even Sorel's waking up in the middle of the night when normally she sleeps right through."

"They'll get over it." Dexter chewed his cobbler and avoided eye contact with his wife. Sharlene knew he was upset. "I know a good child psychologist. If you want, I can give you her number."

"Sure, honey, I appreciate that." She reached across the table and grasped his hand. "I'm sorry if I upset you but I just want what's best for our children."

He looked at her with a grave expression usually reserved for the courtroom. "I know it's hard for you to understand my mother but believe me, she loves her grandchildren. I just want her to enjoy the time she has left here before she goes back home." He squeezed Sharlene's hand affectionately. "Please help her enjoy her stay. It means the world to me."

"I'll do my best," she replied. A tiny patch of gray was beginning to sprout from his goatee. Though the passage of time was beginning to wear on him, at thirty-eight he was still holding it down in the looks department. Elsie would be leaving for Trinidad at the end of September, three weeks from now. Everything would return to normal; Sharlene just had to be patient.

Greta lay in her crib, marble blue eyes observing the galaxy night light on the ceiling. She gurgled happily, her plump arms reaching out to touch green laser stars that swirled beyond her reach. No one was available to play with her, so she grabbed her feet, the tiny toes curling beneath her fingers. Soon she would fall asleep and wake up three hours later screaming for sustenance. Her protest would prompt the exhausted yet adoring creature to pick her up and push a swollen protuberance into her mouth. She would suck the warm nourishing liquid out while squeezing the fleshy pump with one hand. These sensations bestowed such comfort that she often fell asleep while she drank to her heart's content.

From the corner of her eye, she detected movement. Through the wooden slats of her crib, she saw a tiny flame slip through the keyhole of the bedroom door and swell to the size of a tennis ball. She felt the urge to scream and get the milk dispenser's attention, yet she was compelled to remain silent. The flame drew closer until it hovered beside her. She tried to touch it. A shriveled thing that resembled her mother appeared, except this creature had wrinkled dispensers that drooped down to its waist. It grinned hideously, its eyes glowing like coals in a firepit. Something sharp sank into her wrist. She tried to cry, but the sound died in her throat before it even began. The creature was enjoying from her arm the same comfort she got while feeding from her mother's breast. She made a feeble attempt to pull away; it held fast, the withered mouth battened greedily onto its tender target. Drunk on this fresh new taste, it sank its teeth into her upper arm between a fatty fold of flesh. Gradually, Greta became very sleepy as the needle-like pain ebbed to a dull throb. She fixed her eyes on the galaxy lights, her consciousness mingling with them until she could no longer stay awake.

At work, Sharlene sipped her latte near the staff lounge window and scrolled through Anne-Marie's feed. Her page was clogged with condolence messages, yet she hadn't posted anything since the funeral. Sharlene couldn't imagine anything more devastating than having to bury one of her children. Anne-Marie looked fine at the funeral; who knew how she was holding up now? Sharlene pictured her at home, vegging out before the TV in a soiled bathrobe and hair that hadn't been washed in weeks.

Suddenly, a riveting post made her stop in mid-scroll. 'Has your child suddenly developed anemia? Concerned about the Judas tick explosion in New Jersey State and what this means for our children's safety? Falls Heights Mother Hens are holding a meeting at Ari Golde Hall on Tuesday September 19 at 7 PM. Come to a safe space for mothers to freely discuss what's on our minds. Time is tick-ing (pun intended) and we must take action! Light refreshments will be served. Click on link to register.'

Sharlene went to the sign-up page and input her details. She avoided joining the Mother Hens committee because it mainly comprised upper middle class White women with zero common ground with her Black, West Indian self. She also couldn't stop thinking about Sorel who remained in Elsie's care while she worked. Dexter would give her hell if she suggested they employ a babysitter. 'Why you doing that for? You don't trust my mother or what?' Heated questions would erupt, and the resultant stress wasn't worth it.

Later that evening at Ari Golde Hall, she took a seat in the auditorium. A gang of loquacious mothers mobbed the snack table stacked with cupcakes, donuts, and tea. Sharlene sipped on orange juice while waiting for the meeting to begin. There were close to sixty women there, with more checking in at the front door. On the stage was a podium with a laptop and projection screen. She searched for a familiar face; there was none she recognized. She texted Dexter who confirmed he was at home helping the kids with their homework. Coming back to clean and showered lambkins ready for bedtime would be a bonus, but because Dex was spent after a long day, she knew it was impossible to escape bathtime duty altogether.

A manicured White woman sporting a sleek dark ponytail and dressed in a yoga suit took to the podium. She stood before the laptop and smiled, her gleaming teeth and green eyes sparkling beneath the spotlight.

"Hello, everyone, and thank you for coming! I'm Chelsea Greenridge, coordinator for Falls Heights Mother Hens. I'm acutely aware that mothers are extremely busy, so I aim to wrap this meeting in one hour so we can all get back to doing what we do best; looking after everyone else before we look after ourselves."

Laughter erupted across the room, with Sharlene adding her chuckles to the chorus.

"So, without much further ado, let's dive right into the reason why we're here tonight. I'm sure most of you have heard about the pediatrician-in-chief at Falls Heights Hospital, Dr. Jonathan Gainesburg's statement on the Judas tick invasion." She presented a news article slide featuring the doctor speaking to news media. "Earlier this week, he held a press conference and revealed that due to extended periods of warm weather fueled by climate change, the tick's population has exploded, and doctors are reporting an increase in bites, especially among small children. Apparently, these ticks are voracious feeders that leave telltale blue marks." Chelsea selected a photo of a White child's arm, bearing bite marks on the wrist, and another of an Asian toddler who had been bitten on the lower back.

"On darker skinned complexions, the bites look dark brown or purplish." She projected an image of bite marks on an Indian child's foot near the ankle. "There's itching and swelling at the site, but that's not the worst of it. The Judas tick can transmit a disease known as babesiosis, which causes hemolytic anemia. That's a condition where red blood cells are destroyed so quickly that the body can't make enough cells to replace them. Symptoms include dizziness, fatigue, yellowing skin and whites of the eyes. As you know, over the past two months, there has been a sharp increase in hemolytic anemia among children ages 2 to 10 in our community. Personally, my kids have not been affected, but as a community of concerned parents, we all want to know what the heck is really going on, especially since four-month-old Greta Harwicke died of hemolytic anemia just three days ago."

Sympathetic murmurs rolled through the audience. Sharlene jolted upright in shock. My God, a four-month-old baby killed by a tick?

"That's the second fatality in two months. Our community recently lost 6-year-old Jericho Delaware to aplastic anemia one month ago. The good news is we finally have answers. Dr. Gainesburg advised to exercise caution when going into wooded areas with kids and pets. Use tick repellent and thoroughly check clothing and belongings before you enter your home. As of this week, New Jersey Department of Health will spray the area, but this is not a magic bullet as Judas ticks are tough sonsabitches and have been known to resist spraying. Awareness and taking proactive measures to keep our kids safe is crucial in these times of unprecedented change. I open the floor for questions. Please raise your hand so the facilitator can pass the mic to you and introduce yourself."

A White woman's hand shot up in the audience. The facilitator, a portly White man in a checkered shirt and jeans waddled over to the woman and gave her the mic. She stood up, a forty-something, large blonde woman with a blotchy complexion, dressed in a mint green velour tracksuit and thick wedding bands on her finger.

"Hi, I'm Sally. My child got bitten two weeks ago, and now he has the anemia Chelsea just talked about. The doctor prescribed medication, but he doesn't really seem to be getting better. I don't know if there's anyone else here whose child got bitten, but I'm really scared for him." Tears glimmered in her eyes. "The doctor said he'll recover but he's so weak and pale. I had to take him out of school because he doesn't have enough strength to even hold a pen to write. I just want to know, does anyone else here have a kid who has hemolytic anemia, and how are you coping with it?"

Another hand went up. The mic was passed to an immaculately groomed White lady who looked like she'd had one Botox too many, a permanent expression of surprise etched across her babydoll smooth brow.

"Hey, Sally! I'm Rebecca. Both of my kids were bitten and developed fever and extreme loss of appetite, in addition to the lack of energy you just talked about. So, I've been giving them liquid iron supplements, fresh vegetable juices and soups plus the meds our doctor recommended. They had it rough at first, but now they're settling down and the bite marks are healing."

"My son's bites aren't healing," Sally replied. "It's like they're infected or something. They scabbed over at first, but the scabs broke a few days ago, and now they've swelled up again."

"That's the first time I've heard about that," Chelsea interjected. "Other parents I've spoken to say the bites heal after a few days, but some say their child gets bitten again in a different spot. Those ticks are a real terror, I'll tell ya!"

"What's wrong with you people?" a woman shouted in an African accent. Sharlene cranked her head to see where she was seated. At the far-right corner of the room stood a rotund ebony lady with close cropped hair. "Does anyone here know what's really going on?"

"There's no need to yell," said Chelsea. "Harris, please pass her the mic."

"I don't need a mic! I know everybody can hear me," said the woman. "My name is Hanna, and I have four kids. My 3-year-old boy was bitten. What I can tell all of you tonight is that no tick is responsible for any of this, okay? The truth is the authorities have no idea what they're dealing with, so they blame it on something else and none of you have any sense to recognize that."

The Mother Hens clucked with disapproval at the interloper's remarks. A White woman stood up and countered. "If New Jersey Health said it was the Judas tick, then they know what they're talking about. You're not a doctor! Who do you think you are?"

"Everyone, please calm down," Chelsea admonished. "And please don't speak out of turn. This is a safe space, and everyone's opinions have value." She gestured towards the Black woman whose chest heaved with anger. "Please continue with what you're saying." Harris handed her the mic.

"My son has puncture wounds on his leg that couldn't have possibly been made by a tick, because they are three times larger than an insect bite." She paused for effect, allowing this revelation to sink into the gathering. "And I'm sure if you all were to measure the marks on your children you would find this is the case, plus ticks leave one mark where they bite, not two. The photos show the bites come in pairs."

"Okay," replied Chelsea. "So, if the Judas tick isn't responsible, then what do you think it is?"

Hanna's dark eyes swept across the audience like searchlights, beads of sweat forming on her ebony brow. "I know what I'm going to say sounds crazy, and none of you will believe me but I'll say it anyway. I'm from West Africa, and in my culture, we say these bites are the work of the obayifo—people who turn into blood sucking creatures at night."

Gasps of astonishment swept through the audience. Hanna continued, "Did you know that baby girl who died was completely drained of blood when they found her? I know a nurse who saw the body and said it was white like paper. Stop believing the bullshit propaganda on the news and use your heads, people! A monster walks among us!"

Indignation erupted in the auditorium with various exclamations of "Nonsense!" and "She's out of her mind!" while Chelsea called for order to be restored. Sharlene felt like she'd been struck by a lightning bolt.

In Trinidadian folklore, there was such a creature: the soucouyant.

"Everyone, please settle down!" Chelsea pleaded, her face flushed with agitation.

"That's right, I don't expect you all to believe me," Hanna laughed bitterly. "To you, I'm just a crazy Black woman. I'll tell you what though; doctor's medicine won't help. As long as the obayifo lives among you, your children aren't safe! They're not like the vampires in your silly Hollywood movies. They walk around in daytime just like us. At night, they shed their skin and turn into a ball of fire and suck human blood. I never thought I would come to America and meet one of those things."

"Why you don't take your superstitious nonsense and go back to Africa?" an Asian woman shouted, her face twisted with rage. "You scaring everybody for no reason!"

Hanna looked at the woman as though she had broken the heel of her patent leather pump. "I hope the obayifo doesn't come for your children," she replied with chilling finality. "Because if it does, you'll wish you stayed in China."

"Korea!" the woman screamed. "I'm Korean, you dumb bitch!"

Chelsea chastised the Korean woman. "That was completely uncalled for!"

Hanna grabbed her purse and headed for the exit. Sharlene got up and ran after her as she barged out the side door, her three-quarter length cardigan billowing in the breeze.

"Hey wait!" said Sharlene. "Wait please! I want to talk to you!"

Hanna whipped around, ready to combat an army of skeptics. Fight mode blazed in her eyes as she assessed the threat level of this potential adversary.

"I just want to say that I believe you," Sharlene continued. "I believe everything you said out there tonight, and I'm sorry they treated you that way."

Hanna uttered a sigh of resignation. Her war mask dissolved to reveal the sad expression of a spent warrior. "What a bunch of idiots! Waste of time trying to tell them anything."

"I'm Sharlene." She stuck her hand out and Hanna shook it. "I'm from Trinidad and Tobago. Where are you from?"

"Ghana," Hanna replied. "I work with a Trini girl. You like rum and roti, no?"

"Roti for sure, but I'm not a big fan of rum."

"Me, I prefer beer." Hanna chuckled. "It gets very hot in Ghana. Hotter than Trinidad!"

The ladies shared a good belly laugh. Hanna's eyes twinkled with good-natured mischief. She was at ease with a melanated sister who knew she was not off the rocker.

"So, tell me more about the obayifo. Can you protect yourself from it?"

"Salt is best. I sprinkle it by my front door and in the corners of the children's rooms. It hasn't come back since. I can't tell that to those fools in there. They'll probably tell the cops I'm a mad lady and send social services to take the kids from me!" She exploded with laughter and Sharlene joined, relieved to know that she could retain a sense of humor in a terrifying situation.

"How do you destroy it?"

"One must find where it put its skin and rub it with salt," said Hanna. "If you can find it at all. Obayifo are very crafty. The bloodsucking ones are good at hiding their skins, so care must be taken not to even let them know that you are looking for it, else they can kill you right away." Hanna mopped her sweaty face with a wad of tissue. "I thought I left those things behind in Africa, but it seems like they're everywhere." She shrugged noncommittally. "What is one to do? We live in a strange world filled with many strange things. No one really knows how the obayifo came to be or why they exist. They just do, and we have to deal with them." She glanced at Sharlene sideways. "Has it attacked any of your kids?"

"No, it hasn't, thank God. But I believe it killed my friend's little boy."

"Ahh yes, I heard about him." Hanna shook her head with despair.

"What a shame! It's probably a female obayifo."

"What makes you say that?"

"You know that saying, 'opposites attract?' Well, it's something like that when it starts a new feeding cycle. Lately though, it seems to have developed a taste for White babies." Hanna dropped a conspiratorial wink. "I think it came into America from another country. All these different nationalities here—it's like ice cream flavors to this thing! Anyways, I'm going to get going. God bless you and your kids. Bye!"

Hanna unlocked her car and got in. Sharlene watched her drive out of the parking lot, her black SUV shining like a jaguar in the night.

Sharlene tweaked the final sentences that the AI chatbot helped her write: 'Thank you for your understanding during this difficult time. I appreciate having the opportunity to serve your organization and look forward to continuing my service upon my return.'

She hit 'Send' and leaned back in her chair. She had just taken one week's personal leave from work, starting from the twenty-third of September to the first of October, which covered the final week of Elsie's stay. Management was not thrilled with her decision, coming on the heels of her return from maternity leave.

Family comes first before everything. My children's safety is my number one priority. To hell with work!

She told Dexter that she was taking a trial leave of absence to consider alternative career options, which conveniently solved any friction that might arise if she brought up the subject of hiring a babysitter. From now on, she would be keeping a close eye on Sorel and her mother-in-law until she boarded her plane and departed from their lives. Elsie had gained more weight in the past two weeks; a double chin had formed beneath her previously lean jawline. Day by day, the old lady looked jollier and rosier, and expressed to Dexter how much she would miss America when she returned to Trinidad.

I'm sure bone marrow and French fries aren't the only things fattening you up. Who the hell are you, Elsie Barton? Did you kill Jericho? What in God's name have we invited into our home?

After Sharlene arrived home from the Mother Hens meeting, she checked her children's extremities for bite marks and found none. She thought about sprinkling salt in their bedroom and the nursery, but nixed the idea. What if her suspicions—outlandish as they seemed—proved correct? Must avoid mashing anyone's corns in this precarious situation.

Spirited banter floated upstairs from the TV in the living room where Elsie was watching a popular courtroom reality show. A visit to the mall for ice cream was scheduled before Sharlene picked the kids up from school and took them to the psychologist. She would leave Sorel until the session was over. The baby crawled on the floor and gurgled happily. She had entered her chatting phase and was already attempting to form sentences. Sharlene was relieved that she had recovered from the latest round of teething, which involved a fever and fitful crying that had made life difficult for her and Dexter these past two weeks. Gloria would have cussed her out if she dared to dump a cranky baby deep in the throes of teething hell on her doorstep.

Sharlene closed her laptop, picked Sorel up and went downstairs, passing a family portrait that hung on the wall in a gilded frame. Yunia and Yuquon stood on either side of her in matching sailor outfits while she sat in a black ruffled chiffon dress, holding Sorel in her lap. A suited-up Dexter rested his hands on the rear of the high-backed chair. Elsie stood beside him dressed in a mauve pink blazer-skirt combo, grinning wide with those gold teeth of hers catching the light flare from the studio flash. A sapling of anger wormed its way through Sharlene's ribcage, watered by growing resentment. She only went along with the portrait session to please her husband, secretly wishing that he would consign the photos to an album as opposed to a wall portrait. Elsie was a stranger in their midst except to the man she loved dearly—her son.

At the food court, both women enjoyed bowls of ice cream, their large shopping bags resting on the floor beside them while Sorel relaxed in her stroller. Elsie scored bargains on socks, pants and shirts for her grandchildren back home. Dexter was organizing a barrel for shipment stocked with eagerly anticipated commodities to fulfill the wish lists of various relatives. The return flight would be here before they knew it, and Sharlene thought it wise to get a jumpstart on the shopping.

"So how many people we have to shop for now?" she inquired.

"We don't have much again, you know." Elsie consulted her list, a creased slip of ledger paper with names scribbled in blue ink. "Lystra and her five children, Marlon's daughter, Wendy and she nieces and nephews and... I have some more things to get."

Sharlene already saved the checklist on her phone for convenience. She savored her guilt-laden strawberry-vanilla swirl ice cream topped with berries and whipped cream. Yes, there was that pouch of stretch-mark-riddled mommy flap sitting beneath her waistline that she must address before it got out of hand, but dammn—not today! She watched Elsie eat her raspberry-white-chocolate ice cream with delicate dips of her faux-silver spoon, laughing shyly, truly delighted with her decadent dessert. After all, ice cream was a centuries-old favorite, loved by everyone from Roman emperors to grandmothers; Elsie was no exception.

'They're not like the vampires in your silly Hollywood movies; they walk around in daytime just like us,' Hanna had said. Was her mother-in-law the sweet old lady she appeared to be, or did she change into a bloodsucking baby killer at night?

"Eeeeeiiiii-aaaah!" Sorel shrieked and shifted in her stroller. A subtle yet discernible cloud of stink drifted over to Sharlene's nostrils and sent a jarring left hook to the upper floor of sweetness, destroying flavors that, up until now, had been heavenly. The baby scrunched up her face to cry mode, her black eyes shining with tears of indignation. Sharlene steeled herself for oncoming siren wails that gradually increased in volume, interspersed with angry bursts of baby babble buildup.

Dammit Sorel! Why you have   to do that now when I'm enjoying my ice cream? Sharlene's hand drifted to the bootied foot that twitched in annoyance as the baby screamed. She rubbed the dimpled skin of Sorel's leg, knowing the touch would soothe her while she finished her race with sublime indulgence, willing herself not to rush her treat because of the baby. She recognized in that moment of self-awareness that she needed to put herself first because ice cream was her guilty pleasure.

"Poor baby! I think her diaper needs changing," Elsie said.

"I'll change it when I'm done eating."

"I'll do it. You enjoy your ice cream."

"No, Mom, it's okay. I'll handle it."

Sharlene finished her treat and pushed the stroller to the washroom, past the noise and bustle of the food court. Sorel calmed yet visibly perturbed. Ahead stood a familiar figure in a pinstriped shirt dress, waiting for her order.

"Oh my god—Ann-Marie! How are you?" Her friend turned around, and in delighted shock, they embraced each other. Ann-Marie laughed heartily, as though they hadn't seen each other in years.

"Good some days, not so good the next. I'm hanging in there with the gracious help of my husband."

"I need to ask you something if you don't mind."

"Okay."

"Did you ever find marks on Jericho's body?"

Anne-Marie stared at her as if she'd been shot. "What kind of marks are you talking about?"

"Blue marks, like insect bites"

"Yes, I did, as a matter of fact. Why do you ask?"

"Mother Hens had a meeting to discuss the spike in anemia cases the other night. Some people believe the Judas tick is making kids sick; others don't buy it."

"That damn tick bit my boy and gave him a disease. He's gone, and there's nothing I or anyone can do about it, except pack our shit up and leave." A tear glimmered from the corner of Ann-Marie's eye. "We're selling the house and gonna move out west and try for another baby while there's still time. Life gotta go on living, and that's what Jerry would want me to do if he were here right now."

"Order 689!" a server yelled from the counter.

"That's mine." Anne-Marie opened her strong brown arms and enfolded Sharlene like a sausage roll. "Bye, girlfriend! We'll stay in touch."

"Bye, hun!" Sharlene knew this might well be the last time they would speak to each other unless their paths serendipitously crossed. "You take care, and best of luck with the move."

"How's school coming along, Yunia?" asked Dr. Browne.

"Fine." The girl held her doll and sat in a neon green beanbag chair beside her brother who was busy coloring a sketch with crayons. Sharlene monitored her children's reactions as they received counseling from the psychologist Dexter had recommended. Dr. Browne's office was spacious and cheerfully decorated with paintings, plush toys and a child-friendly palette, including the tangerine-colored walls. She was a forty-something Black woman with neatly groomed locs and an adorable gap-toothed smile. Sharlene thought Dexter made the right choice. This was the children's third session. They were finally warming up to Dr. Browne. Building trust was essential to making headway, so she could work more effectively.

"Your mother told me your teacher says that you haven't really been paying attention to your lessons lately. Can you tell me why?"

Yunia trained her soft brown eyes on the doctor, who reclined in an ergonomic chair beside them with a notepad on her lap. Framed photos of her smiling children were artfully arranged on her desk. "I don't like school."

"That's not true," Sharlene interjected. "She's an excellent student with good grades, and she's popular with the students. The teacher said for the past month, she's been disengaged from her studies. Honey, you like school, don't you?"

"Not anymore."

"Why is that?" inquired Dr. Browne. "Is someone bothering you?"

A hint of fear clouded Yunia's eyes as her fingers yanked the curly strands of Nicole's hair. Sharlene tensed in her seat, hands clasped together so tightly that they felt stapled together. Yunia opened her mouth, then closed it. Her eyes flicked over to her mother as if seeking permission to speak.

"It's okay, Yunia," Dr. Browne assured in a gentle tone of voice. "You don't have to be afraid. You can tell me anything you want."

"I saw Jericho."

Dr. Browne's eyebrows arched in surprise, her pen poised above the notepad. Sharlene's blood turned to ice water in her veins.

"Where did you see him?" asked the doctor.

"Outside the window, in the playground at school."

My child seeing jumbie now? Lord, what trouble is this?

"What was he doing?"

"Standing there, looking at me. Now he's so skinny! I don't think he has anybody to play with." Yunia regarded her mother sharply. "You said that he went to heaven. I don't think he's in heaven, Mommy." The girl twisted Nicole's hair with such force that Sharlene thought she might pull it out. "I think he's still here."

Her mother was at a loss for words. She looked at Dr. Browne with a pleading expression: I'm up to my eyeballs with this one. Help me out!

"Did he say anything to you?" said the doctor.

"No. I think he wants something."

"Do you know what he wants?"

"I don't know." Yunia looked agitated. "Maybe he misses when we took computer lessons together at school." She eased her grip on Nicole. "I wish I could help him."

"It's okay Yunia," Dr. Browne said. "When you lose a friend, it's normal to feel sad for a while. But one day, you'll feel much better, and you won't feel so sad anymore. You can help Jericho by remembering all the good times you had together."

"Do you know why he didn't go to heaven?"

"I'm afraid I don't have an answer for you." The doctor's forehead creased with genuine sympathy. "When people we love die, we hope they go to heaven, because we're told it's a good place. The truth is no one knows exactly where they go. When you get older, you'll understand this a little better. Are you feeling okay?"

Yunia hesitated before answering. "Yes, I mean... not really. But I'll feel better soon." She smiled bravely, her changing teeth on full display.

"That's good to know." Dr. Browne scribbled in her notepad.

"Dr. Browne?"

"Yes, Yunia?"

"What should I do if I see Jericho again?"

The doctor gazed at Yunia with compassion. "Just close your eyes and count to ten. When you open them, he'll be gone. Remember Jericho is no longer here with us. Whenever you see him, he's not really there at all—it's like seeing a picture that you're going to put back into an album when you count to ten. There is absolutely nothing to be afraid of, Yunia. You'll be fine."

I hope you're right about that. My daughter doesn't need to know that poor boy's stuck in limbo because his soul's not at rest!

"Finished!" Yuquon rested the crayons on the table before him.

"Great! Do you want to show me what you drew?" asked Dr. Browne.

The boy held up his sketch with artistic pride. What the doctor saw caused her to recoil in her chair.

"Yuquon, who is that?"

"The sugar cake lady."

Sharlene's heart somersaulted in her chest as she observed the doctor's horrified expression. "Yuquon, honey, show me what you drew."

Reluctance riddled the boy's face like a noontime shadow. "Okay, but you have to promise me you won't get mad."

"I promise you I won't get mad."

He paused to consider the veracity of her oath, then passed the sketchpad to her. Despite her vow to remain equipoised, her mouth fell open in shock. Though she had become somewhat inured to Yuquon's interest in graphical material—sword wielding samurais, battle crazed Vikings—this drawing threw her for a loop. It was an artfully rendered composition of Elsie making sugar cake in the kitchen, except this was a bald ogre-sized monstrosity that loomed over the stove, its naked body horribly wrinkled like a paper bag that had been reused too many times. Blood-stained canines bulged beneath the ruby red lips that looked like lipstick had been carelessly applied, a frantic coloring outside the lines. Ever the detail-oriented artist, Yuquon was mindful to portray the gold teeth with lurid splotches of yellow. A cooking pot bubbled on the stove, filled with white grainy material drenched in a gooey red substance that was not food coloring, judging from its sordid viscosity. Blood was also splashed on the floor and the walls, as if an unhinged style advisor decided to update the color scheme of the Bartons' kitchen for Halloween.

Father in heaven, look what this boy gone and draw!

"Can I see, Mommy?" Yunia craned her head in their direction.

"No!" Sharlene tore the sheet from the sketch pad, folded it and shoved it in her purse. An uncomfortable silence settled over the room. The twins exchanged telepathic glances that acknowledged Mommy had just broken her promise.

"That will be all for today." Sharlene stood up. "Thanks, Dr. Browne."

"I think we made significant progress. Would you like to schedule the next session now?"

"No, thanks, I'll let you know when I'm ready. Yuquon and Yunia, time to go."

"I knew you'd get mad," her son exclaimed with righteous indignation. "You lied to me!"

"I'm not mad at you, Yuquon."

"Yes, you are. You took my drawing! Give it back!"

"Your drawing stays with me for now. And I don't want you drawing any more pictures like that again—you hear me?"

"It's not fair!" He stood up, fists clenched at his sides. "I want my drawing back!"

"Yuquon, listen to your mother," said Dr. Browne. "She's not angry with you; she just needs to hold onto the drawing for a while." The psychologist looked at Sharlene with unfiltered concern. Yuquon frowned angrily, looking from the doctor to his mother, as if he didn't know who to believe. It was tough to pull a fast one on kids who were astonishingly smart for their age. Even Yunia gave her an accusatory stare. Yuquon's shoulders slumped with defeat as though he was certain he wouldn't see his sketch again.

"Let's go." Sharlene opened the door, and the children filed out.

"Bye, Dr. Browne!" Yunia waved at the psychologist with Nicole clutched securely in the other hand. "See you next time!"

The doctor smiled. "Bye, Yunia!"

That night, Sharlene lay awake in bed beside Dexter, her mind racing. After three glasses of wine, she was not even close to drowsy. The disastrous session kept replaying in her head. That hideous sketch... there was no way she could show that to Dexter! It confirmed everything she had begun to suspect over the last few days.

I must be out of my mind! How this thing possible? A soucouyant living in meh house? Lord, why me? Though familiar with the legends, she researched the creature on the internet and discovered some nonsensical tales, yet much of what she found corroborated with what Hanna had revealed about the obayifo.

Elsie's flight home was only four days away and the sweet scent of the toolum candy she had made earlier lingered in Sharlene's nostrils. In four days, the old lady would be gone and that would be the end. Would that really be the case? Would she return home emboldened by her experience in America to embark on another feeding frenzy? Or could it be that her mother-in-law was no monster, but a lonely old woman longing for love?

She thought about Jericho's wasted corpse, photographs of bluish puncture wounds on the children's bodies, Yuquon's grotesque drawing, Elsie's locked guest bedroom door. The arrows seemed to point in one direction. She would be a fool to ignore the signs.

Maybe I shouldn't bother. It hasn't harmed my children. But what if it does?

Sharlene heard a muffled scream come from next door. She went to the window and peeked through a gap in the curtain. The light was on in the upper floor nursery of Kyle and Isabel's home. It sounded like they were having an argument while the baby wailed at the top of his lungs. Had he been bitten by the soucouyant? She hoped not, yet the fact that he was alive gave her some reassurance. At least there was no dead baby drained of blood next door, just a couple whose quarrelling apparently woke the infant. Sharlene returned to bed and lay down, feeling immense relief as her mind settled and the wine worked its magic on her senses.

Lowered voices deep in conversation stirred Sharlene from sleep. Reluctantly, she opened eyes that felt grainy, and glanced at the alarm clock. It was 6:03 AM. Normally, she would be downstairs having coffee with Dexter, but last night's wine had her in its clutches. She moaned and rolled over in bed, her head spinning like a top. Sorel was probably lying awake in her crib, soon to start crowing for attention, and the twins would be up shortly. She felt like going back to sleep and knew that was impossible. Dexter and his mother were downstairs talking. She crept to the bedroom door which was ajar and listened.

"Anything else we need to get before you go back?"

"Just the sneakers in a size twelve for Andy, and a bookbag—that's it."

"I'll ask Sharlene to pick it up for you since she's home now."

"Son, I feel like I don't have long again on this Earth."

"Don't say that, Mom."

"Is true. I old. My body feels tired."

"You've been saying that for years now, and you still here."

"When the time comes, no matter how it happens, know that I will be at peace with God."

"You really shouldn't talk like that."

A long pause. "I'm eighty-two. Anytime the Maker calls me home... I glad I had the chance to spend time with meh grandchildren. They're so nice."

"I glad you enjoyed your time with them. I'm gonna miss you."

"I'll miss you too."

"I love you, Mom."

"Love you too, Dexi."

Another long pause. Sharlene knew mother and son were sharing a hug. She went into the nursery and checked Sorel's body for bite marks. Negative. Next, she entered the twins' room where they were fast asleep, rolled up their pajama sleeves and cuffs, examined their arms and legs. Everything looked fine so far. She would scrutinize them in more detail when it was time for their shower. This practice had become part of her daily routine since the Mother Hens Meeting. She hadn't thought about what she would do if she found puncture wounds on her children.

If anyone ever hurts my kids, I'll go apeshit on their ass!

Her head throbbed with the onset of a mild hangover headache. She went to the master bathroom, grabbed a bottle of painkillers and went downstairs. Dexter and Elsie were seated at the kitchen counter with steaming mugs of coffee and black tea.

"Morning!" said Sharlene.

"Morning!" they responded cheerily.

Sharlene took a bottle of baby formula out of the fridge and warmed it on the stove while she made herself an espresso.

"Taking the strong stuff I see," Dexter observed. "Didn't sleep well last night?"

"I got carried away with the wine. Now, I pay the price."

"Thou hast shewed thy people hard things: thou hast made us to drink the wine of astonishment," Elsie uttered. "Sixtieth Psalm, verse three."

"Mom giving Bible lessons now!" Dexter joked. "She going and give Reverend Pringle plenty competition."

You bloodsucking bitch! I go show you wine of astonishment. Watch me.

"A little indulgence is good every now and then—right, Elsie?" said Sharlene with a smile.

"Yes, of course, dear! I don't drink anymore, but I enjoy a good glass of wine on special occasions." Elsie sipped her tea and munched on a slice of toast with butter and jam. Sharlene took the veggie dip with hummus out of the fridge. Eggs were definitely off the menu this morning.

"Sharlo, can you pick up the shoes and the backpack for Andy?" asked Dexter.

"Sure. I'll swing by the mall later, and I'll text you about the shoes. That style sells out fast, so if they don't have his size, you might have to try the store near your office."

"Okay." Dexter looked put off, as if he shouldn't have to be the one to run that particular errand. "I just thought since you're home now—"

"—That I should be the one to do everything? I have to look after my kids and your mother too while you go to work. Last time I checked on this marriage, we were a team."

Elsie looked uncomfortable, as though she had walked in on them having sex.

"I'm not asking you to do everything. Just to pick up a pair of shoes and a backpack. Is that so difficult?"

"You're supposed to be helping your mother get stuff for her relatives. Why is it that I'm the one taking her shopping most of the time? I don't have a problem helping, but you can do your part every now and then, Dexter." Sharlene took her espresso from the machine and turned her attention to the veggie dip. Tension hung thick in the air like smoke from burned toast. Head pounding, she sat at the island counter and munched on carrots and celery.

Elsie stared into her cup, as if searching for a remedy to the unpleasant turn of the couple's conversation, while Dexter looked at his wife as though she had morphed into a Venusian.

"I'm sorry, that was harsh. I've got a bit of a hangover this morning." Sharlene sipped her espresso. It was important to maintain an air of civility—especially now.

"You want me to help get the kids ready for school?" Elsie offered.

"It's okay, Mom. I'll take some aspirin, and I'll be fine." She popped the pills and chased them down with coffee. Silence reigned supreme while the trio ate, interrupted only by the drone of the television. Sorel screamed upstairs, demanding her breakfast. Sharlene rescued the baby bottle from the boiling water on the stove and left.

After dropping the kids off to school, Sharlene came home, showered and spent a few hours researching how to start an online business while Elsie rested. She cleaned Sorel and prepared to take her out for a walk, knocking on the guest room door on her way out.

"Mom, I'm stepping out with Sorel for a while. I'll be back in an hour."

No response. Usually, her mother-in-law would reply. Sharlene guessed she was either tired or upset over what had transpired this morning. She went downstairs, took the stroller, and went for a leisurely walk with Sorel. It was a beautiful morning, and the trees were aflame with rustic red, burgundy, and earthy orange fall colors. She noticed a large white van parked outside Kyle and Isabel's house, but no sign of activity in the residence.

I hope everything's alright with them.

She circled the block, past rows of orderly homes and lawns that retained their lushness, thanks to a wetter than usual summer. Climate change really was a thing, and the Judas ticks were apparently having a field day in New Jersey state, though she had yet to spot a single one. She made a mental note to check Sorel's stroller and her clothing before they re-entered the house, though they never ventured near wooded areas.

Her daughter chatted happily in the stroller, enjoying the fresh air and sunshine. The headache had subsided to a dull throb that would soon cease altogether. Sharlene zipped her windbreaker open to cool down as she was beginning to perspire. She hadn't seen a gym now in almost a year and felt allergic to weightlifting of any kind except for laundry hampers. She rested at the playground and gazed at the empty sandbox where she had last seen Jericho. It made her wonder if the twins reminisced about their friend when she brought them here to play. If so, they never mentioned it.

One hour later, she returned to her block and saw men loading household items into the van outside Kyle's home. She drew closer and saw Isabel standing on the front lawn, holding the baby in her arms with a pinched expression on her face. Sharlene waved. Their eyes met, and Isabel said nothing; just held little Alfie close to her sizeable bosom.

"Hey, Isabel, everything okay?"

The woman offered a wan smile that vanished almost as quickly as it materialized. Sharlene pushed the stroller onto the lawn, away from the busy driveway, and approached her. Bags of sleep deprivation pooled beneath her reddened blue eyes. She looked paler than usual.

"Isabel, what's wrong? Where's Kyle?"

"He'll be back soon. Just left to drop off some stuff."

"Are you moving?"

"We're leaving, alright. For the time being until we decide exactly what we're gonna do." She seemed squirrelly, as though she had seen something that had kept her up all night.

"Do you mind telling me what happened?"

Isabel wavered, as if that question was too much to ask, and said, "Kyle and I, we picked this area because we thought it was a safe place to start a family. New homes with lots of space, good roads and nature trails. You and I have been neighbors for eight years and you were always good to me, so I think I can tell you the truth." Isabel licked her lips nervously before continuing. "Last night, I woke up around quarter past twelve, feeling that I should go check on Alfie. That's never happened before so I got up and went into the nursery. And that's when I saw it." She clammed up as though regretting what she had just said.

"Saw what? It's okay Isabel, I won't tell anyone."

"I... I saw a fireball floating next to his crib," she stammered. "I swear to God I've never seen anything like that my entire life! I screamed, and the thing just vanished—poof! It was gone. Just like that. The noise woke Kyle right up, and he asked what went on, and I told him. He didn't want to believe me, but he knows I've always been a straight shooter; never smoked or did drugs or nothing like that. Alfie was scared too but he was okay. I told Kyle I wanna leave right away because whatever that thing was, it wasn't natural! I don't feel safe here anymore, and I don't want anything to happen to Alfie. He's my firstborn son." She kissed the baby on the top of his red curly head and looked at Sharlene. "Have you seen anything like that around here?"

"No, I haven't."

"Lock all your doors and windows at night. You've got young kids to think about. First, we get a tick invasion and now this? Whatever this is, I don't like it. Not one bit."

"Thanks for sharing that with me, Isabel. I'll take your advice and be extra vigilant with my kids." Sharlene offered her hand. "Take care."

"Oh, don't be so formal! Gimme a hug." Isabel wrapped a free arm around her neighbor's shoulders. "You're a good woman, Sharlene. Kyle and I will come back, but we're not sure when. We're gonna pray with our pastor and ask for guidance."

"Bye, Isabel, take care of yourself. Give my regards to Kyle."

"Will do. Enjoy the rest of your day!"

Sharlene walked back to her house on stiff cardboard legs, pushing the stroller with hands made of sawdust, background noise reduced to a muted volume; wind, birdsong, traffic, dump trucks collecting garbage two streets away.

No way this is happening here in my backyard. But it is.

Her ears popped from the sudden release of pressure and her hearing returned to normal. What Isabel just revealed changed everything. There was no more time to waste.

"Did you remember to take your science project?"

"Yes, Mommy," Yunia replied dutifully. She and Yuquon were going to spend the night with Aunty Gloria. Cool! She is so much fun. The last time they slept over, Yunia came back with nail polish, which her mother forced her to take off. Sometimes, she wished she didn't have to leave Aunty Gloria at all.

"Yuquon, please check and make sure you have your tablet. I don't want you calling me later to say you forgot it."

"Yes, Mom." Her brother had been pretty quiet around Mommy since the visit to Dr. Browne. He was still mad that his drawing had been taken away. They both knew that he wasn't going to get it back. Her mother's phone pinged with a message from Aunty Gloria: 'I'm here!' She opened the front door, and Yunia saw Aunty Gloria emerge from her shiny red jeep. A boxing glove accessory in Trinidad and Tobago colors dangled from the rearview mirror. Encased in a neon pink pantsuit and platform kicks, Aunty Gloria came up the walkway covered in bling, her blue-streaked perm swept to one side, heliconia versus avians tattoo sleeve on display.

"Aunty Gloria!" Yuquon shouted and ran out to embrace her.

"Hey, Yu-key, how's it going?" She rubbed his hair affectionately. "Hey, sis!" She beamed at Sharlene. "Everything cool?"

"Yes, everything's fine. Thanks for taking them last minute."

"No problem. It's practice for me until I have mine."

"If I were you, I would enjoy my freedom while I have it!"

"Single life does get lonely sometimes, you know," Aunty Gloria replied wistfully. "Kids are fun, especially when they go back to their parents at the end of the night."

"Alright, don't rub it in!" her mother chuckled. "I'll bring out their bags."

"I'll come and help you." Aunty Gloria stepped inside and gathered some belongings while their mother led the way to the car.

"Hi, Aunty Gloria, I missed you!" Yunia hugged her aunt's chunky waist. "Can we play Twister tonight?"

"Sure, sweetie. As long as I don't get twisted out of shape!"

Yunia giggled with delight. "I'm gonna beat you again!"

"Wait 'til you're my age! You'll find Twister ain't so easy."

"Are you sure you've got everything, Yunia?" Sharlene inquired. Yunia frowned in concentration as she reviewed a mental checklist. Her mouth dropped open.

"Nicole! I left her upstairs!" She dashed up the staircase, ran to the kids' bedroom and grabbed the doll from her bed. On her way out, she noticed her grandmother's door stood partially open. She paused on tiptoe, knowing she wasn't supposed to peek into Granny's room. Curiosity got the better of her and she peered through the gap. Granny was lying on her side, back towards the door. Yunia wrinkled her nose at the funny odor emanating from the room. If someone asked her to describe it, she would say it smelled like Yuquon's dirty socks.

"Yunia, darling, is that you?" Granny croaked in a raspy voice.

The little girl was astonished. How did Granny know it was her? The old woman had not moved from her position. Yunia froze on the spot, her heart now finding a new home inside the roof of her mouth. Maybe if she said nothing, Granny would go back to sleep.

"Come inside, darling. Don't be scared."

Yunia looked over her shoulder to ensure no one was coming

upstairs and slowly pushed the door open. Overwhelmed by the room's funky odor, she sneezed. Granny lay there in a pink and black houndstooth dress, her thin feet clad in white frilly cotton socks. Yunia tottered forward, her legs seeming to move of their own volition. She wished she hadn't peeked in Granny's room. She tried to scream. All that came out was a tiny squeak, similar to that of a plastic toy being mashed by a giant.

She stopped in front of the bed. Slowly, her grandmother pushed herself up and turned around to face her. She smiled, and Yunia gasped in terror. Granny's upper and lower front teeth were missing. Her gold capped canines glinted in the shadows of her ruined mouth. Yunia thought the gold teeth looked cool. She wished she could have some too when she grew up.

"You scared, baby? Granny wears dentures. I take them out before I go to bed."

"Huh... how did you lose your teeth, Granny?" Yunia stammered.

"Through my pregnancies. Sometimes women does lose their teeth when they have plenty children. You must take good care of yours, so you don't end up like Granny, you hear?"

"Okay."

"Yunia!" Sharlene yelled from downstairs. "Aunty Gloria's ready to go!"

"I have to go, Granny. Bye bye!"

"Bye, sweetheart! Come give Granny a hug."

Yunia wanted to bolt out of the room. Again, she tried to make her legs obey her silent command, but they remained glued to the ground. Her grandmother leaned forward and embraced her. Saggy breasts pressed against her head like soft balloons. The old woman's heart beat steadily beneath her gown, lightly perfumed with fabric softener, as her thin arms gently wrapped around her granddaughter's shoulders. To Yunia, her aged body felt warm and comforting. The little girl returned the gesture, feeling her grandmother's love envelop her like a cozy blanket.

"I love you, Granny."

"I love you too, baby."

"Will you make sugar cake again before you go back to Trinidad?"

"Yes, I will. I'll make you some vanilla fudge too."

Yunia kissed her on the cheek. "Sounds yummy! Ok, Granny, see you when I get back!" She dashed out the room.

"Close the door behind you please!"

Yunia did as told and dashed down the stairs. Outside, Aunty Gloria waited behind the wheel of her jeep that was pumping loud soca music. Yuquon sat in the passenger seat, which she had hoped to score. She climbed in the back beside Sorel who was strapped in the car seat.

"Take care and drive safely!" said their mother.

"I will. Everything okay, sis?"

"Yes. Dex and I just need some time alone together."

Aunty Gloria gave her sister a skeptical eye. "No, it's not. Anyways, lemme mind my own business, you hear? I go text you when we get in."

She put the jeep in reverse and backed out of the driveway. The twins waved goodbye as their aunt drove off. Their mother waved until they were out of sight, then went back inside and closed the door.

Inside Elsie's room, Sharlene snapped a photo for visual reference so she could rearrange everything exactly as she found it. Then, the search began. She pulled back the covers, looked under the mattress and the bed. Searched between layers of clothing on the woven hamper. Every nook and cranny must be thoroughly explored for the precious cargo that she sought. Perversely, she thought of treasure hunting, like searching for chocolate eggs at Easter time.

She listened for any sound of activity from her bedroom. Dexter had been effectively dispatched to Dreamland after she slipped a sleeping pill into his drink before bedtime. According to her research, soucouyants usually returned from their nightly excursions before sunrise, which gave her plenty of time as it was now 12:23 AM. These notorious creatures of habit were sometimes unpredictable, so the sooner she completed this operation, the better. She yanked open the wardrobe, removed Elsie's belongings and examined every fold of fabric. Shook out sweater sleeves, searched shoes and sneakers, peeked inside the dress hats her mother-in-law wore to church. Stood on a step ladder and felt along the back of the top shelf. History might very well prove her wrong if nothing of consequence turned up tonight.

Ten minutes later, the wardrobe had been emptied of its contents, articles piled high on the bed. She searched every corner of the guest room without success. Was there a spot she might have overlooked? Two suitcases stood like silent sentinels beside the bed. It didn't make sense to search them because the soucouyant would most likely keep her skin not only carefully hidden, but within easy reach. Besides, Elsie would know that someone had disturbed their contents as she was still in the process of packing. Sharlene racked her brains, trying to determine if there was anywhere she might have missed. She'd already been through the dresser drawers and looked behind the unit. There were no loose boards to pry open.

Frustrated with her fruitless search, she returned Elsie's items to the wardrobe and compared the tidied room to her reference photo to ensure she had put everything back into its proper place. It was obvious that the search failed to produce results, because her mother-in-law was not a soucouyant, which meant it was either someone else within the community, or she had been completely fooled by a cock and bull story. Her teeth chattered from the chilly draft blowing through the open window near the dresser. She caught a strong whiff of the offensive odor she had initially encountered upon entering the bedroom. Elsie's gold jewelry rested on top of the unit next to a large porcelain vase that held artificial flowers. A jolt of realization hit her with unexpected force. Jericho had been sculpting an object from sand that closely resembled a mortar, the traditional vessel where soucouyants hid their skin. What if the creature had chosen a suitable facsimile? Her own skin crawled with the sensation of thousands of ants moving beneath its nerve-wracked surface.

Do you really want to look inside that vase, Sharlo? Afraid of what you might find?

"Yes, I'm scared. Oh Lord Jesus, have mercy upon me." Her cold hands trembled as they removed the flowers and set them on the dresser. She could turn around and go back to her bed right now. In two days, Elsie would fly back to Trinidad and probably die before she could ever make another trip overseas. But her treacherous fingers couldn't abandon their mission. No, not now.

She gagged, feeling her stomach revolt at the sickening stench emanating from within the vase. At last, all the flowers were gone. She put her hand inside and felt something moist, papery, somewhat sticky, and began to pull at this mystery material. Clamped between her right thumb and index finger was a dark brown wrinkled substance creased upon itself like folds of ancient parchment. As she eased it out, she realized, though extremely fragile, it weighed a few ounces. Her mind desperately tried to make sense of what she was seeing... something with one, two, three tiny club shaped formations with little nails that resembled—

A foot!

Sharlene screamed and dropped the vase. It hit the dresser with a loud thunk and rolled on the wooden surface. The crinkled foot skin dangled from the rim as though looking to play football with Elsie's gold earrings.

Oh God, oh God, oh God, ohhhh!

She clapped a hand to her mouth and slid to the floor. Her heart beat with such force she thought it would explode from her chest as the tight elastic band of tension returned, constricting the area with excruciating pressure. She struggled to breathe, silently cursing herself for neglecting to book the checkup with her physician she had promised herself months ago.

Dear God, please don't let me have a heart attack now! Don't let me die in this room please! Nausea overtook her and she began to retch, exerting all the self-control she could muster. She put her head between her legs and breathed deeply. No, it wouldn't do to pass out. There was no telling what might happen if the soucouyant returned and found her lying unconscious on the floor.

Several minutes passed before the nausea dissipated and her chest pain eased. A burning sensation lingered there, and her left arm throbbed with a prickling sensation. Not a good sign, yet she couldn't stop now. She got up and gently grasped the skin, suppressing the gag reflex that even now, threatened to usurp her mission. Here was a crinkled thigh, just below the vulva peppered with grey pubic hairs. The arms were folded beside the chest whose empty breasts resembled shriveled raisins. And finally, the head emerged—a grotesque eyeless mask that seemed to mock her. Yes, it was a fine joke; a monster had been living right under her nose all along! A monster that loved to watch courtroom dramas, admire silvery birch trees outside its window, and eat raspberry white chocolate ice cream. A monster that had changed Sorel's diaper and made sugar cake for her children.

She cleared a space on the dresser and carefully unrolled the skin, then reached into the pocket of her robe and produced a container of salt. She sprinkled it onto the skin, feeling completely disconnected from her body as though someone else was salting the soucouyant's shell. The Elsie skinsuit didn't seem to mind at all. In fact, it appeared to be in on the scheme, its empty eye sockets winking with good humor. Sharlene thought the salt crystals resembled granulated sugar. A wild giggle escaped her lips. Would the soucouyant know its skin had been tampered with? Apparently not, according to the old folk tales. Tonight, she would surely find out. She had concealed a baseball bat in her bedroom closet just in case things went sideways. It was always best to prepare for the unexpected.

After returning the skin to the vase, she swept the remaining salt crystals off the dresser and rearranged Elsie's items. Washed her hands with soap and steaming hot water. A slight trace of the cockroach stench remained. She sank to her knees, spat saliva into the toilet, and waited for the nausea to pass. When she stopped trembling, she returned to her bedroom. Dexter dozed like a little boy worn out from too much playtime. Another giggle erupted. What she just pulled off was almost too easy, like a child stealing candy from the kitchen late at night while their parents were asleep.

Tonight, I salted a soucouyant's skin! Aye-ya-yie! Who would ever believe?

She got in beside her husband. The time was now 1:18 AM. She should try to get some sleep if that was even possible in this bent scenario. At least her kids would be shielded from the worst of it. Life was complicated and oftentimes messy. Protecting them from the unsavory bits so they could enjoy their short-lived innocence was her mission as a parent. After tonight though, that might change. How could she explain the truth about their grandmother to them? They didn't need to know about such a hideous family secret that, as it turned out, was an abomination. Yuquon's sketch had been secreted in a lockbox where she stashed her valuables. Though she had considered burning it in the fireplace, she couldn't bring herself to destroy it. Maybe one day, when enough time had passed, she would take it out of hiding, light a match, and reduce it to ashes. Let the flakes quietly settle in the fireplace like a bad dream consigned to forgotten memory...

"Aiiiiiiiieeeee! Ohhhhh, Gawd, help meh! Aiiiiiiieeeeeeeee!"

Sharlene immediately shot out of sleep. There was no mistaking where those bloodcurdling screams were coming from. Thwump! A loud noise that sounded like an object hitting the floor emanated from down the hall. She could smell something burning, like roast beef left too long in the oven. The moment had arrived, yet she was pinioned to her sheets, unable to move. Terrible and tremulous, the screams continued to ring like the cries of a tortured animal unable to comprehend its ghastly fate.

"Skiiiinn! Yuh nah know mehhhh! Nah know mehhhhh!"

Sharlene clutched the bedsheets to her bosom like a frightened child and feared the worst. What if the monster escaped the confines of its death trap to exact revenge on its destroyer?

"Sharlo?" Dexter rasped. "Where that noise coming from? What's that smell?" Confused, he looked at her, still groggy from his drug induced slumber. She returned his gaze, eyes wide and scared, mouth glued shut from the shock of knowing the horror that was unfolding just down the hall. He sat up, threw back the duvet and stumbled out of bed, falling onto the floor.

"Maaa!" he screamed. "MAMMMYYYYY!" He staggered out the bedroom door towards the guest room.

"You nah know mehhh! Skiiiinnn! Aaaaa oooooohhhh, GAWD!"

BOOM! Sharlene heard him kicking the locked door open. BOOM! The screams sounded syrupy, as though the monster was gargling through a mouthful of molasses. BOOM! Stubborn and sturdy, the teak wood refused to budge. Sharlene crawled out from beneath the covers and went down the hall just in time to see the door give way to Dexter's relentless onslaught.

"Mammyyy! Oh God, MAMMYY, NOOOO!" Dexter wailed.

"MAMMY, NOOOO!"

Sharlene approached the guest room. Her husband's heart wrenching sobs shredded her ears, a grown baby boy crying for his mama, the love of his life, light of his soul, being devoured by hellfire. A sooty black figure that had once been a woman was being consumed by blue flames that licked its shriveled form, causing it to curl into itself like a dry leaf in a pile of garden refuse. The soucouyant's hair was on fire, melting to a tarry substance on its scalp, teeth gleaming white in the blackened face. Pools of grease congealed on the wooden floor, and the air was thick with the aroma of cooked flesh—a sickly sweetish smell that Sharlene would remember for the rest of her days.

The soucouyant's eyes were darts of burning fury submerged in sorrow that pierced the heart of the traitor who, even now, bore witness to the fruit of her betrayal. They clouded over and turned milky before they popped from the heat, ending the soucouyant's sight forever. Nothing else in the room caught fire. Dexter snatched the duvet off the bed, cocooned his mother and rolled her on the ground in an attempt to extinguish the flames while smoke curled from the quilted fabric.

"Mammy, you alright? Mammy, can you hear me? Talk to me, Maammy!" The monster was incapable of speech, its tongue dissolved to mush as it smoldered within the duvet. Dexter sobbed and cradled his mother to his bosom, rocking her slowly.

"Ssshhh, Mammy, it's alright! I here with you now. Ssshh... ssshhh..." He kissed the charred forehead. Burned flesh flaked off the skull, peeling back to reveal raw red tissue beneath. Outside, the smoke alarm shrieked, and sprinklers deployed. Sharlene stood there, speechless, arms wrapped around her body in a desperate bid to hold herself together. Blue flames sprouted from the duvet, rapidly growing in size until Dexter was forced to leave the body on the floor where it continued to burn. He stood up and faced his wife, fists clenched at his side, eyes dark with murderous hate.

"I told you to stay out of her room! Why you didn't listen?"

He's probably going to kill me. She braced herself for whatever was coming next.

"I didn't ask for much—just one simple request! All I wanted was for Mom to enjoy herself. And you…" He choked on his words. "You with your fas' self had to go and spoil it! She just needed to feed for a little while."

"Fuh-feed? What you talking 'bout? You mean to say you knew—"

"—You stupid bitch! She would have never hurt her grandchildren! I told you they would be fine, but you didn't listen! How I will explain this to Marlon?" he shouted. "You killed my mother! You killed my heart!"

"But she was a soucou yant!"

"She was my MOTHER! Damn you, selfish cow! How I go tell my children? What we go tell the police?" Tears streamed down his face. "Get out!"

"Dex, please!"

"OUT!" he bellowed. Sharlene fled down the hall and into the bedroom. She grabbed a duffel bag from the closet and began to pack. The neighbors must have called the cops after hearing the commotion. She would wait until they arrived to give her statement and then go to Gloria. Using his courtroom savvy, Dex would come up with an explanation. Today, the firmament had shattered, raining brimstone on her marriage, searing it beyond recognition.

All this time he knew! He knew we had a monster living right under our roof with our children!

Something inside her chest jackknifed like a sixteen-wheeler careening off the interstate. She screamed and collapsed on the bed, clawing at her breast, unable to rise or call for help. Black specks swirled before her eyes.

He knew! Even when children in the neighborhood were sick and dying… he knew.

The room faded to black, and Sharlene knew no more.

Dexter closed the door to his office and walked to the elevator. He was relieved to go home after yet another harrowing day of back-to-back meetings and a never-ending sea of paperwork. The official investigation had concluded; Elsie's cause of death was ruled as spontaneous human combustion. No evidence of foul play had been discovered at the scene, though detectives had initially suspected that either himself or Sharlene may have had a motive. Despite being grilled relentlessly, they stuck to the story that he had cooked up to keep them both out of jail. As much as he hated his wife for what she had done, she was still the mother of his children, and they had already suffered tremendously from the loss of their grandmother. Unable to return home immediately following "Granny's accident," they had been shuttled between Gloria's house and their aunt in upstate New York while Sharlene recovered from a panic attack at the hospital.

Forensics confirmed that the cause of Elsie's 'combustion' was not an external source as no trace of flammable liquid had been found in her room. It was simply an unfortunate tragedy caused by a rare yet mysterious phenomenon that had yet to be fully understood by science. As far as his immediate family was concerned, he was an excommunicated villain responsible for the death of their beloved matriarch. A pompous pariah who had failed them miserably, unworthy of even their disdain. Banished from group chats, his number blocked, they were dead to him now except for his compassionate Uncle Kelvin, and would remain that way for the foreseeable future.

When Sharlene returned home from the hospital, he filed for a separation and moved out. After the guest room had been renovated, they agreed to sell the home and split the proceeds. He felt like a dead man walking, merely going through the motions of being a good father and a productive employee. Life had lost its flavorful zest, and he was unsure whether he would recover his mojo. Since his mother's death, he avoided after-work mixers with colleagues and his weekly meetup with 'the boys,' friends he had known since university. Such activities seemed perfunctory considering what had recently unfolded.

The kids. I have to think about them, but I need to put myself first.

The elevator bell chimed, and he got into the empty lift and pressed 'G.' Dexter rarely dreamed, and when he did, he always found himself transported to that fateful night, hearing his mother scream and scrambling out of bed only to find the bedsheets wrapped around his feet that refused to let him go. A thick barbecue scent hung in the air when he finally lumbered down the hall towards the guest room on feet weighted with lead. Sharlene was always absent, and when he arrived, his mother had been reduced to a smoking pile of ash. There was nothing left of her to hold. He had missed her final moments. He was an incompetent fool, incapable of protecting the woman he loved. He would fall to his knees, and Marlon would be there, cussing him out for his shortcomings before putting a gun to his head and pulling the trigger.

His psychiatrist said recurring dreams were normal after traumatic events and would resolve in time. It was easy for him to say because he never had to wake up thrashing under the covers, unable to escape a nightmare so convincing that his brain could not differentiate between illusion and reality. The barbecue smell actually made his mouth water while dreaming which he found highly disturbing. He didn't share that one with Dr. Henry who believed that every Black man in America needed therapy, just by the sheer dint of living in a society inimical to their very existence. A course of antidepressants and weekly sessions had been prescribed. So far, he was able to function, although he often felt like he was trudging underwater. Daily conversations assumed the consistency of thought bubbles; light, fluffy, of little consequence really, compared to the night terrors that made him weep like a little boy.

Dr. Henry noted Sharlene's absence in the dream. He believed that indicated Dexter held repressed anger towards her. If there was something he could tell his wife right now, what would it be?

It would have been perfect if you had just played along and stayed out of her room! Mom would have eaten enough to keep her healthy for a while until it was time to meet her Maker and be freed from this terrible curse. So a few kids fell sick, and two had died... a rather insignificant death toll, all things considered. He wished she hadn't picked on poor Jericho, but he had no say in the matter. Sacrifices had to be made for the greater good. Everyone died eventually because that was the way of the world. Life was not fair and little children certainly weren't exempt from that cardinal rule.

How could he tell the doctor—or anyone—the truth? No one outside the family or even the Caribbean would understand that these so-called 'folklore characters' had their basis in a reality that defied explanation. In Dr. Henry's mind, reality was a delineated construct to be tidily assigned to neatly labelled drawers called logic and rationality. Instead, he told the psychiatrist that he would tell his wife she could have done more to make his mother happy by listening to his advice more often. She was stubborn as a goat, and in the end, it cost them their marriage.

Dexter emerged from the elevator into the carpeted lobby and out the building's double glass doors. Bleak mid-December weather greeted him as he descended the ice-encrusted steps. Dirty piles of snow dotted a lonely parking lot below a uniform slate grey sky that made him pine for the tropical blue heaven of Trinidad. He considered booking an all-inclusive carnival vacay with his boys to dance off the aggravation from these past two months, when a figure wrapped in a knee-length navy winter coat swiftly approached him from the left. He spun around and confronted the intruder.

"What are you doing here?!" he snapped.

"You haven't been returning my texts."

"I told you not to contact me about anything else besides the kids."

"I need to talk to you!"

"There's nothing to discuss, Sharlene. Please leave and don't come back to my workplace again, or I will file a restraining order against you."

She pulled a folded piece of paper out of her pocket. "Before I go, I want to give you this."

"I'm not interested."

"It's from your son. And if you think I'm lying, ask him yourself. I did my best, Dexter. I really wish things could have been different, but it's too late to turn back now."

"You're damn right about that!"

"I did what I had to do to protect our kids. You never took them to a therapy session—not even once! Just remember—I was the one who was always there with them, early in the morning and at night, cleaning and putting them to bed. Your kids need to see more of their father. Don't punish them because of something I did." She pushed the paper into his coat pocket, walked back to her car, and drove away.

Dexter stared at the vacant spot where his wife's vehicle had been. He had not seen her in over a month, and quite frankly, never wished to see her again. Christmas was around the corner, so he would have to find a way to tolerate her presence for the children's sake. He entered his Mercedes, which had been remote warmed to a toasty temperature, and put his briefcase in the back. He rested his hands on the steering wheel and sat in silence.

I hope she's not having some sort of breakdown, or I might have to file for sole parental custody.

He reached into his pocket and retrieved the paper. Maybe this wasn't a ruse to win him back, but a letter from his son, telling his father how much he missed him. Yuquon loved composing short stories and poems that he often presented to his parents. Dexter even had some of his creations on display in his office. He unfolded the paper and noticed it had been dated prior to Elsie's passing. Saw a large splotch of red on the upper left corner of the page that reminded him of crudely rendered ketchup; opened the sheet to its full dimensions and sat there speechless at what his talented son had drawn.

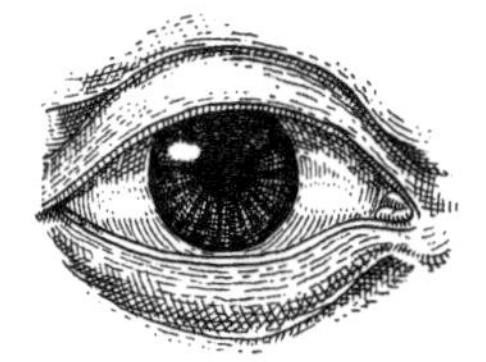

Tired Eyes
Anthony Martinez

Nick took a shot of tequila. It burned as it went down his throat but filled him with warmth and sense of familiarity. Freshly twenty-one, he'd never been one to appreciate alcohol. Now, it was his nightly routine to take a shot before his shift in the back room.

He glanced around the old-timey bar, which hadn't changed since Nick first walked into this place. Each round table sat under a low hanging light fixture with a puke-green shade covering the light bulb. Off to the right, up a couple of rickety, wooden stairs, were three pool tables bereft of any cue sticks or billiard balls. Red polyester carpet covered the concrete floor, which has begun showing in a few places where the carpet was beginning to tear. The wooden walls gave the image of a cozy log cabin, but these days the slats of wood felt more like a prison.

Nick stood behind the bar, which was located against the back wall. The only entrance and exit were straight ahead. He thought, for the millionth time, about trying it. If he could leave, if he could just successfully exit, then everything would be alright.

How long had it been? Nick couldn't remember. Between the sleep deprivation and the looming threat of overall destruction, Nick had no idea how long it had been since he'd stepped outside of the bar. There were times since this all began when he struggled to remember the significant details of his own life, like his mom's maiden name and the shape of her face under her blond hair. These days, he spent a lot of effort attempting to remember if his birthday was March 21st, March 22nd, or March 23rd.

Nick heard the sound of a toilet flush to his left. He only had a few more seconds before Maria came out of the bathroom. He glanced at the bottle of tequila like a person looks at a photo of their long-lost lover. Another shot called out to Nick, but he found the strength to put the bottle away for now.

The door to the single-stall bathroom creaked open and nearly hit the outdated jukebox against the wall. Maria stepped out of the bathroom, still drying her damp hands on her shirt. Her black hair fell to her shoulders, greasy, stringy and reeking of sweat. The dark circles under Maria's eyes were less visible, indicating she'd slept well, but her resting face was a permanent frown every time she was awake.

Nick didn't even bother to look in the mirror anymore. He feared he wouldn't recognize his light blond hair and his lopsided smile.

"You ready?" Maria asked. Her voice, low and determined, filled Nick with warm and cold thoughts. Her voice was both the angel and devil sitting upon his shoulders, intriguing and frightening him at every turn.

Wordlessly, Nick nodded.

He stepped out from around the bar. Maria met him at the opening, and they walked through the swinging door to the hallway, which led to the kitchen, the liquor backroom, and the employee breakroom. The two of them turned left down the hallway to the breakroom.

The room was lit more harshly than any other room in the bar. The ceiling was lined with white fluorescent lights, causing a momentary need to squint upon transitioning into the room from the rest of the bar.

Jack and Christian sat inside the breakroom under the bright lights. They sat at the singular table—Jack with his elbows on the table, his head resting in his palms, and Christian slumped over like the Hunchback of Notre Dame. Their backs were to the door, and they both stared straight ahead at the refrigerator, which was pushed up against the wall and otherwise devoid of appliances. On the right side of the emotionless room was a counter with storage below and a plain white microwave directly in the center. On the left side of the room, an old black couch was lined up against the wall. Nobody lay on that couch anymore—the four lone stragglers avoided this room at all costs when they could. Instead, when they needed to rest, they slept on the pool tables back in the main bar.

Without a doubt, Jack and Christian heard Nick and Maria enter the room, but they didn't move. Maria walked up to them and tapped them both on the shoulder. They stood up, synchronously, their eyes remaining on the refrigerator. Nick took Jack's chair, and Maria took Chrstian's. Nick and Maria focused their eyes on the refrigerator, and the two men knew their shift was over.

"Good luck," Christian said. He always said that at the end of his shift.

"I'm gonna go have a drink," Jack informed the group. "We survived another round, friends."

Despite his upbeat words, Jack's voice was monotone and lifeless. Nick had a faint memory of Jack trying to keep the mood funny and uplifting, but his demeanor gave the opposite effect due to the despair that filled each of them with each passing day.

Except, there were no days anymore. Not really. The windows in the bar always showed darkness and mysterious fog outside. Seeing more than five feet outside of the bar was a challenge in and of itself.

"Go get some sleep," Maria told the two men. And with that, it was just the two of them, sitting in the uncomfortable steel chairs and staring ahead at their object of fatality.

The refrigerator was rectangular, with a standard lower level to keep food cool and an upper level for frozen goods. It was white and plain; without any magnets or pictures. The only interesting aspect of the fridge was the dent directly in the center of the bottom half. Nick liked to imagine that someone had kicked the fridge hard enough to deface it. He often felt like kicking it himself to worsen the dent and fill his heart with some mediocre sense of satisfaction. The two handles, long and white, had faded in color due to the frequent use by bar employees grabbing their food, but that was no longer an issue. Nick had no idea how long it had been since someone had opened the fridge. He had no idea if there was even food inside of it or what would happen if someone decided to rummage through its insides.

"What is your name? I am Maria Lucas." Maria asked, beginning their ritual of call and response. Maria always went through the questions; when Nick watched with Jack or Christian, they often forwent the exercise that Maria began. Typically, when Nick was paired with Jack, they would chat about alcohol for a few minutes before falling into silence. When paired with Christian, neither of them spoke at all.

"Nick Golding."

"How old are you? I am twenty-nine."

"Twenty-one."

"What do you do for work? I am a waitress."

"College student."

"How...?" Maria trailed off.

"Where do you live?" Nick corrected her.

"Where do you live?" Maria repeated, affirming the question. "I live in Arizona."

"Colorado."

The questions stopped. Usually, there were more, but Maria clearly wasn't in her right mind this evening. The weight of the situation was getting to her. "It's important to remember who we are," she used to say adamantly about the questions, but Nick hadn't heard her say those words in a long while.

Nick stared at the refrigerator. His eyes grew heavy and weary, unable to wander as he stared at the fridge that defined his existence. The beginning of the shift wasn't too bad, but as time went on, his mind fell into darker, more dangerous thoughts. It was a strange feeling, that of driving yourself insane with your own mind. His thoughts would become violent and angry as he would curse himself and think about giving up, giving it all up, and rejoicing in the thoughts of his own death. All the while, his eyes would grow restless and he would begin seeing visions of shapes and colors in his peripheral vision that he would not, could not, look at because his eyes needed to remain on the fridge at all times. This ugly fridge without any distinguishable features, other than the dent, haunted him. His eyes would be so focused and exhausted that he would often forget Maria was even next to him, and he would feel alone, frightened, and panicked. His mind would scream at him to look away, to go to sleep, to just let whatever would happen, happen, but he couldn't. For now, he would remain strong. But as his eyes begged desperately to give up, he wondered how much longer he could last like this. How much longer could he stare at this appliance and let his mind disintegrate? How much longer could any of them continue this and not become husks of their former selves, as if they weren't already?

Nick could not tell how much time passed. It could have been seconds, minutes, or hours. The only thing Nick was sure of was nothing. His eyes and his mind needed rest, but he could not stop. He blinked and forced his eyelids open so wide he felt like his eyeballs would pop out. He thought about using his own fingers to dig them out of his head, placing them on the table to watch the fridge while he went to sleep.

Out in the bar, there was a thump.

Nick wasn't used to hearing strange noises. He fought the urge to turn around, wondering if Jack or Christian were playing a game of pool or moving stuff around. It had been so long since any of them did anything other than stare and sleep, but he supposed it was possible one of them decided to liven things up a bit.

More time passed. Time was both consequential and irrelevant. It had no meaning as a social construct, yet each second felt like the most important moment of Nick's life. His eyes burned, the fluorescent light in the room and the whiteness of the fridge stinging his retinas with unforgivable madness.

And then, for the first time in a thousand years, something happened—someone screamed.

Turn around, Nick thought, but he did not. He kept his eyes peeled on the refrigerator, suddenly determined to use all of the strength he had left inside of his body. Someone needed to watch the fridge, and he would not let the world down.

"Jack! Christian!" Maria yelled.

The noise to Nick's right startled him, causing him to jump up from his seat. Still, his eyes did not wander.

From the bar came a sob. The cry shook Nick to his core.

"I have to go see what's going on," Maria said hurriedly. "Nick, do not take your eyes off of the fridge."

"But there's always—"

Always supposed to be two in here, I know," Maria scolded. "But there's an emergency. I need to be able to trust you, Nick."

Before he could respond, Maria's chair scraped against the floor, and he heard her run out of the room.

Nick had never been alone in this room before. He was alone with the one object he detested more than anything else in this world. His heartbeat accelerated, but his body grew numb as he could do nothing with the surprising input of adrenaline. He did his job with haggard breathing, hoping that somebody would come relieve him of duties soon.

He heard the pounding of footsteps and the sound of Jack's ragged breathing as he entered the room and took Maria's seat.

"Maria needs you out there. I'll keep watch."

"But we're always supposed to be in pairs," Nick argued.

"Not anymore. Go, Nick. Now."

The exhaustion made Jack's words sound like a riddle. Nick tried to decipher the meaning, but he couldn't. He stood and removed his eyes from the refrigerator. He was overcome with a sense of relief that quickly faded once he looked at Jack. His gray shirt was covered in blood and tears were streaming down his chubby cheeks as he sat and stared in complete silence. Nick knew, against his better judgment, that he should not leave Jack in here all alone. His state of mind was too fragile, and yet...

Nick left the room. He rushed to the bar, where he instantly found Maria kneeling next to the fallen body of Christian. Blood covered his body and seeped onto the carpeted floor. Christian's throat had been slit by the glass shards of a broken bottle. The remains of the bottle remained in his left hand; he hadn't even dropped it upon his death.

"No," Nick whispered.

Maria's hands covered the bloody wound on Christian's neck, but it was no use. Even if he wasn't already dead, they had no way to fix a wound this serious.

Something switched in Nick's brain. He couldn't do this anymore. He wouldn't. His mind was rotting, his eyes felt like someone had rubbed salt in them until they bled. And now, one of the only three people he had in this world had taken the only way out that he could imagine.

Nick turned and began walking straight toward the exit.

"Nick, stop!" Maria yelled as Nick placed his hand on the cold, metal doorknob.

"Why can't I just leave, Maria?"

"You know why. You know there is no way out of here. Going through that door is certain death. There is only darkness and fog and you will die, Nick. Do not leave it up to just me and Jack. Do not do that to us, Nick. The world depends on it. The world depends on you."

Nick knew Maria was right. He would die if he stepped outside of the bar. He'd seen it before. There was another, someone besides Nick or Maria or Jack or Christian, who attempted to leave. He couldn't remember their face, but he remembered watching through the window as they were killed by the mysterious darkness.

He took his hand off of the doorknob.

Just then, the bar began to shake. It was slight, beginning with the floors, but it quickly felt like a small earthquake as the walls shook and the light fixtures swung back and forth.

Without hesitation, Nick and Maria ran to the break room, where they'd left Jack all by himself. They knew what they were going to find as they pushed into the room.

The refrigerator was shaking as if it had a fever, causing ripples across the rest of the bar. Jack had taken his eyes off of it, and because of that he'd paid the ultimate price.

Jack was gone. His body turned into a mushy puddle, like he'd melted. A pile of blood, organs, and bones took his place on the table and chairs. His remains left nothing of relevance as to his identity. Nick thought that, in time, he would only remember the gore and forget the name of who the remains belonged to.

Both Nick and Maria aimed their eyes at the refrigerator. The shaking began to slow and, after thirty seconds, calmed completely. They were safe, again, for now.

"This can't be happening," Nick said.

"I expected something like this from Christian. He was always a mystery. He would not answer my questions. And Jack was strong, until now." Maria paused. "More will come to replace them. We just have to survive until then."

"How do you know that?"

"I just do."

"What do we do until then?"

"We wait. And we take turns watching."

Nick shook his head, but not enough to remove his eyes from the refrigerator. "We can't do this alone. If one of us falls asleep or takes our eyes off of the fridge, it could all be over."

"I know that. But until there are more of us, it is just you and me. If we do not take turns, we will both be too tired to watch."

She was right. There was too much at stake, and Nick knew it. This was their only option for now, aside from death.

"Nick, can I trust you?"

He paused. It was a simple question, but as he stared at the fridge he couldn't help but wonder if the two men who'd died were finally at peace. At the very least, he knew that their eyes were no longer burning with fatigue.

"Yes. Yes. You can trust me."

With that, Nick's double shift began. Maria went to clean the mess in the bar. Nick felt more pressure than he ever had before. It was all up to him and Maria now. He could no longer depend on someone else to continually keep watch alongside him.

Time passed. He couldn't feel it passing and yet each second in excruciating pain. He could no longer remember how long his shifts were. He couldn't remember sleeping, or if Maria had come to replace him. His eyes itched as he felt his brain become mush. He stared at the refrigerator as he would have to do for the rest of his life. He stared and started until his eyes grew heavy and the time finally came to stop.

The Hinge Fort

Jeff Thompson

"It's time I told you the story of what happened at this cabin. You know that we are very near the old Hinge Fort? I know you have heard things from your brother and sisters and I am sure you remember the day your father died, but this will be different. This will be the true story behind it. Less ghosts and ghouls, more to the heart of it all. The Shadow People own this land—dark and more dangerous than anything that ever could be. And you know it for true, what else could have made your father do those things?"

Nanna paused then, her age-clouded eyes looking back to before she lost her son, back to a time when her features were not cracked and weathered by age and hardship. Her lips fidgeted around the teeth she no longer had, she wet them slowly and continued on.

"When my parents first brought me here it was so very different. Not just the cabin itself, but the land was different. Not so wild as it is now. No less tame mind you, but there wasn't the ravenous hunger that lingers between shadows. You know of it, I've seen it in your eyes and felt it in your gentle heart. That heart of yours is what will be the death of you, just as it was the death of your father. No, say what you will about him, he had a gentle heart down behind all the anger. He never meant to hurt you. You of course know that much, but it's the rest that remains muddied and wrong."

Benjamin didn't interrupt. He knew better than to interrupt Nanna when she started in like this. His hands clutched the heavy blanket close to his chin, his eyes unable to leave the wizened old woman. Her voice continued, an unstoppable drone underlining and demanding that he hang on each and every word.

"The hanged fort, that's what they called it back then. I don't know when they started calling it that, but there you have it. I know your father found those old papers claiming it was the Hinge Fort, but I think it held closer to the other name and that was what I always knew it as. During the day it was normal enough, but if you caught it by moonlight, there were shadows of the men they hung there, all staring out with hateful eyes. I think that's what called the Shadow People there in the first place."

A shadow loomed down the hall, Benjamin watched it with wide eyes. He knew Nanna shouldn't mention them. If you talked about them, you drew their attention. She said their name too many times and they heard it. Nanna didn't notice the darkness that inched closer down the hall at an almost imperceptible pace, she continued with her story.

"Benny, you know about them don't you? You must have seen them around here at some time or another? They always liked to roam down from what became known as the "hanged fort" and creep into the house at night. I remember when I was very young, they would crawl along the porch out front. Probably why I never liked the creaks and groans this old place makes as the wind whispered through the trees. They like standing in the room at night, watching as we pretended to sleep. Your father saw them. That I know for true. When he was but five years old we had him up here one summer. I told him to stay away from the cellar door but, well you know your father, always so curious and not about to be stopped by anyone saying he couldn't do a thing. We found him curled up in the corner of the kitchen, bawling his little eyes out. I, of course, saw the shadow then. It stood there like a great angry thing wanting to pull my child down into the cellar with the rest of them. But I wouldn't let them take him. I don't suppose he ever told you about that, did he?"

Benjamin shook his head behind the blankets, his eyes jumped between Nanna and the shadow that was now growing large in the doorway. He had never been down in the cellar, it had terrified him and he never had reason to be down there. Nanna continued her story, oblivious to the shadow that drew closer behind her. Benjamin wanted to cry out; he wanted to tell her that he knew about them and they were coming. He sat silent in the bed, the sheets pulled up around his chin, watching Nanna.

"Your father was never the same after that. I think that thing did something to him, made him a bit strange at times, you know? I stopped coming up here shortly after that. Your grandfather still liked it up here, they never seemed to bother him. He was never much for believing in such things. I just wish he hadn't taken your father with him. I can't help but think whatever evil that roams the Fort has reason to occasionally come down here, and when it comes, it leaves death in its wake.

"You know, your father didn't hang himself, oh I don't care what the police said and what the family whispered. You know he didn't. The shadows can make people do the most horrible things. And don't think you're safe just because you leave this cabin. They can follow you anywhere. Distance and walls mean nothing to them; they are the shadows and if you speak of them, they will come. I suppose we should be careful, talking about them tonight as we are, here in the cabin so close to the hanged fort, I wouldn't be surprised if one came calling down. Best we save the rest of this story for tomorrow night. I can see that you're tired."

Nanna paused just then, her head turning slightly to the side as if she just now noticed the pillar of midnight behind her. Anger pooled out from it in ripples that splashed hot against Benjamin's face. He felt a cold tear trace its way down his cheek.

Nanna looked back at him with eyes more clouded with death than age. She stared sightlessly at nothing as the shadow moved impossibly slow, coming up behind her. Benjamin didn't see it move, instead it seemed to grow larger. It loomed over her, darkness seeping all around its human-like shape. Hateful eyes looked back at Benjamin, eyes that froze his breath and sent shivers running down the back of his head and neck. His hands were shaking. He couldn't breathe. They didn't like that she was talking about them. Benjamin felt the hatred deepen and a small cry escaped his throat.

Nanna's skin hung off her in cold, dead, sagging mounds. Her mouth slowly opened as if she were about to speak. Her mouth continued to open wider until her jaw cracked, splitting her face in half and revealing missing and rotten teeth. Her face contorted into an angry, hideous mask of what it once was, as her jaw sagged to the side.

Out from that horrid mask came a hissing noise, like that of a feral cat that's been cornered by hunting dogs. She shook her head, spitting and hissing angrily, then a wail shuttered its way up her throat. It grew in pitch, turning into an otherworldly piercing shriek that ripped through Benjamin's mind, driving everything else from it to the point of blinding terror. He realized he was screaming with her, his lungs erupting in absolute certainty of his death.

The dark shape came forward and took hold of Benjamin's head and leaned down low, the shadowed mass was an inch from his face.

He could feel coarse rope coiling around his neck. The darkness was a congealed patch of oil, writhing and churning like a whirlpool. Out from impenetrable blackness stared dead eyes that lanced through his soul. They knew his every thought and there was nothing he could do to escape. He was going to die. The thing that killed his father was going to kill him. His father hadn't hung himself, Nanna had been right. It was a fleeting, whispered thought.

The rope bit into his neck and slowly started dragging him up towards the wooden beam rafters. He gagged and pulled with bloodied nails at the rope that cut into his throat. He struggled against the weight of his own body, his legs kicking uselessly in the air as he was pulled higher up. Faceless dark forms crowded the room, filling every corner. They watched, excited that he was going to die, excited they would soon have him. The ceiling rafters came closer as the rope continued to drag him upward. He felt his nose brush the wood-paneled ceiling, like a thunderclap he fell. The rope came up tight, snapping his neck.

"Ben, wake up! Wake up, Ben, it's only a dream," Tess said as she pulled his face towards her own, her green eyes wide with fear.

Benjamin drew a ragged breath through a mouth that was too dry to form words. A numbness spread all through his body and he shook with fear. His neck burned from the rope that had suspended him. He felt his neck and was relieved to find neither rope nor blood.

"Was it your Nanna again?" Tess asked softly. Benjamin made no response, knowing how Nanna didn't like people talking about her. "It only happens when we visit here, why don't we just sell this place?"

Ben coughed and cleared his throat, wiping his tear stained cheeks.

"It's been in the family for years. I can't just—" Benjamin cut off as he saw the spectre of his dead grandmother slowly creep down the hall, away from the open bedroom door. Another shiver shook through him.

"Go back to sleep, sweetie," Tess said as she rolled over.

Benjamin lay awake, fearing what would come next. He felt better with Tess next to him, but her breathing started to slow, and eventually fell into the deep rhythmic breaths of sleep. He was alone again. He heard the creaking of the front porch as a cold wind kissed the eaves. The groans of the old cabin sounded almost like footsteps. The shadows remained in each corner, watching Ben, waiting for him to close his eyes, daring him to look away so they could crawl their way closer to him.

He finally did close his eyes, only to open them immediately. The darkness hadn't moved, stillness sat heavy in the room as the creaking continued downstairs. He heard a cat yowling high and angry in the night. There were no cats in the area. He felt his heartbeat heavy in his ears, his mouth was too dry. He wanted to reach for a glass of water kept next to the bed, but he felt the old familiar fear holding him fast. It was a fear he had felt since he was a child, a paralyzing, cold, sight-blinding fear. Irrational, raw, feral, and unconquerable.

Benjamin forced his eyes closed and pretended to sleep. He felt their eyes on him just the same. He could almost taste the putrid decay of death against his cheek as they hovered inches from his face, daring him to open his eyes again, daring him to cry out or give any indication that he felt them there. Benjamin would not give in, he remained in the same position for the rest of the night, his legs cramping and cold sweat drenching the sheets. All the while thinking of the old Hinge Fort ghosts that gathered within the cabin.

In Orbit

V.M. Sawh

Up here, in orbit around the Moon, I learn that I am now alone in the world. Wasn't supposed to find out this way, but the Sri Rama Temple newsletter found its way into my inbox. Not Mission Control. Just a stray email from a random busybody auntie. A hastily written obituary was how I found out that my cancer-ridden mother is dead.

That my handlers kept it from me isn't all that surprising. Probably assumed that a lone astronaut in a single spacecraft wouldn't handle the news very well. Despite the many psych evals specifying my emotional autism, they don't want to take the risk of jeopardizing the moon survey mission. Cutbacks have already reduced the crew count to one in this rickety Soviet-era SOL4CE bucket. Since all the funding for space exploration's gone private, we've had to scrounge for cheap, proven designs. Yes, we're taking considerable shortcuts by using outdated tech, but believe-it-or-not, that's not why my mother didn't want me to go on this mission.

"Why do you want to isolate yourself like this, Devika? Everything you need to have a future is here on *this* planet. I must be a failure if you still haven't learned this, despite all that I have tried to teach you. Being a mother is the highest of achievements you can have in this life. Beta, you would not be here if I had not done my duty."

"I have a duty to my ambition, Amma." This made my mother's eyes crease with anger. In her, I saw the distillation of tradition passed down from every mother who came before. She was the torchbearer for Indian culture for our whole family; by denying her, I was responsible for the downfall of my entire generation. I was her only child, and unfortunately for me, I happened to be a girl. That meant all her hopes for a grandchild rested upon my shoulders. While she had always expressed her deep love for me as her daughter, she openly admitted to marrying my father because an engineer made for a 'proper provider'.

I was seventeen when he died, which meant that Amma and I were stuck with each other. The daughter who was so much like the man she married for his money. Oh, I think they loved each other enough over time, but I know my Papa loved me more. I was his only child, and he was delighted to discover that I had my eyes set on the stars, just like his had been. On the day of his funeral, Amma had turned to me and said, "All we have is each other now, Beta. Your father didn't live to see you flourish. He will never hold his grandchild in his arms."

The hot sting of parental guilt burned my throat. She could have slapped me across the face and it would have hurt less. I needed my mother to loosen the noose of expectation from around my neck; instead, she threw it over the banister and let me dangle. Resentful tears trickled down my cheeks. Did she want me to squeeze out a child right then and there? And even if I did, would that child grow to resent me the way I resented Amma? If my spite and pride kept a child out of her clutches, then so be it.

But then Amma would touch the back of her hand against my cheek and say, "You are so smart, Devika. With brains like yours, you could figure out how to find a husband. But you don't try. Why don't you try? Do you really want to spend the rest of your life alone? What will you do when I am gone?" This was her version of loving concern. I only wished it didn't smell like fear.

What do you have to lose, Amma? I wanted to ask. Do you really think your legacy is one I want to carry? I'm not like you and I don't think I can be.

Even through the recycled air and endless void of space, orbiting on the dark side of the moon, I can feel her disappointment reaching for me.

I stare at the cobbled-together mash of words in the newsletter, not really reading the results of the temple's latest fundraising dinner. My mother, after all of her decades of service, gets a three inch square in the corner with her picture. The obituary lists all of the functions she's been a part of and I find it ironic. That she so opposed my joining this mission because she felt I would just be a cog in a machine. A tool for cheap exploration.

But the temple exploited your soul, Amma. You just didn't know it.

In my mind's eye, her face creases with concern. She gazes at the lights, switches, toggles, and dials of my command console in absolute bewilderment.

I'm not surprised. Science was never her forte.

A signal wakes me from a fitful slumber and I sit up in the sweat-stained bedchamber. Unbuckling straps that look like they're from a last century land-boat takes longer than I'd prefer, but it allows me time to wonder.

NASA doesn't encourage wonderment so much. They're more interested in hard data instead of things like... ghosts.

Is that what Amma is now? Of course, spectral phenomena are common in space; it's all just light and particulate matter and energy anyway. But visitors from beyond the grave? Mission Control would consider that troubling. It would require a video eval from a certified psychiatric professional. But there are no mind-altering controlled substances on board that they could prescribe.

I don't believe in ghosts. That I've seen my dead mother in my spacecraft when I know objectively that I'm alone just means that my mind is conjuring images of her from my memories. Ask an AI to generate art, it has to draw from some source material, if you'll excuse the pun. Most will scour the internet and reference different artists, trying to most closely match what you want them to create. Maybe that's what my brain is doing now.

I refuse to consider that I'm simply losing my mind. That my subconscious grief is somehow punishing me for not living up to her expectations, now that it's too late to meet them. I wish Papa was still here. He would know what to say to Amma to get her to back off. He'd get up from the recliner where he'd be watching some deep sea documentary on angler-fish or something, and touch us both on the shoulder. He'd tell us not to fight, because family is all we have in this world. At that, Amma would relent. Papa protected me.

In that state between wake and sleep, where I can't be sure whether it's a dream or a memory, he's saying something to me. But all I can hear is the damn tv, *"... the anglerfish is relatively unique in its approach to luring its prey..."*

Mission Control lies right to my face when I ask them if they have any news for me. Of course, that's probably what their psych advisor told them to do. Don't want to upset their lone astronaut. Can't afford to send another to replace me, and they're counting on me to carry out the survey of previously unmapped moon craters. The last thing they want to hear is that I'm seeing my dead mother's reflection in the porthole glass behind me. A great gray sadness accumulates under her sun-kissed skin, like a portrait of moving sand. Haggard loss and wretched ineptitude dangles from the ends of the stress-curled strands of hair framing her face. She looks as lost as ever. Is this how she was, at the end? Am I witnessing her as she was at the end? Cold and alone. With no family by her side while she battles against the hungry sickness consuming her body?

Would my presence have made any difference? She might have reached for me, and let me hold her hand to give her some of my strength. She'd always maligned my will as stubbornness; the irony of its source within her was entirely missed. Still, I could have been by her side at the hospital while she went through cancer treatments. Not that we had the money for her to afford the best. A sick sliver in my stomach tells me that wouldn't have been good for either of us. I would have been performing a daughter's duty, while she would be trying to hide her vulnerability from me. Afraid to need me. Far too late for her to admit that she regretted having me, or rather, that I didn't turn out the way she hoped. But what good would that kind of daughter be for her? I'd have been carrying a child on my hip, and holding onto the hand of another. My lawyer husband would be there, talking away on his cellphone.

Would that have brought her comfort? To know that I lived on, carrying on her legacy in the way she'd wanted me to?

Instead, I am here, but not here, staring at sonic-rendered topographic maps of the Erlanger crater, and its shadowed sisters. It's nearly ten kilometers across and shrouded in perpetual darkness.

I see Amma's lips part in the lines of data pouring in from the survey. Her down-turned cheekbones fit the curves of the crater's arched edges.

I'm monitoring the bounce back frequency of the sonic scan, which amounts to a series of harmonic pulses registered on an old-style seismograph, when I detect a voice between the tones.

Come to me.

Despite being weightless, I feel my legs slip out from under me. My soul has been wrenched loose. This can't be her. I am imagining things. Spectral phenomenon belongs to the realm of pseudoscience. Like most fictional 'discoveries', it matters only to those who believe in it. But I am my father's daughter—I don't believe in such things. I'm not searching for forgiveness from a ghost.

For what?

You're just a voice in my head now, Amma. The real Isha Mistry died back on Earth.

Alone.

I know dammit! What are you, my conscience? NASA would not approve of this conversation.

My chest aches and my eyes burn throughout the rest of the sonic scan. I diligently make my notes and collate the data. I refuse to respond to anything else, no matter how many times she screams my name.

I try and remember to smile during NASA's next video check-up. The crow's feet lines around their eyes crinkle and flex; they've never seen me smile before. Had to be careful about that. *It's the man's world, Devika. No matter how often they tell you it isn't. You can't give them any excuse to think you fancy them. That is how you get assaulted, then all of this science-study and stargazing will be for what?*

When Papa saw my indignant, humiliated face, he took her to task. I heard him lecturing her from outside the door of their bedroom. Amma would never back down, and my sweet, gentle elephant of a father tried his best. But as she said, she did not marry him for his passion. Up against the iron will of a proud Indian immigrant that came to the West and never sacrificed an ounce of her culture, Papa's efforts were futile. He came out afterwards, head hung, with the slumped shoulders of a ceramic Buddha. He knew I had been listening, and from the hissed exhalations coming out of my mother, I knew he had lost. He put his thick, heavy hand on my shoulder, "Want to come for a drink of lassi?" I was fifteen.

The lassi shop was our private little escape, adorned with palm-leaf potted plants and digital menus overrun with ads for skin-brightening cream and Neem toothpaste. Friendly, rotund shopkeepers adorned their coloured turbans with straws to match the lassi cups they sold. Things you had to do to be accepted as American. Be a useful fool in society. At least NASA wasn't like that, Papa assured me. "You can do anything you want to do, as long as you study hard and get good grades. Your Amma only wants the best for you, but she might not know what that is in today's world. She comes from... a different time."

I'd sipped my lassi, thinking that maybe I was outgrowing this kind of treat. I wasn't a kid anymore. Most other places had candy-infused soda-flavoured fro-yo by then. Papa still clung to some of the more traditional ways, which I don't think he acknowledged. So, I'd tested the depths of his self-conception.

"Is that why she still believes in stuff like reincarnation? Or *karma*? Or *dharma*? I forget which one that is."

Papa had laughed, which was always comforting to me. He had a grin like a chimp, and his coconut beard made him look like a rather wise one. "You believe what you want to believe, Beta. The important thing is your conviction. You must be willing to see yourself through all of the obstacles that will come. Your Amma is right in some aspects, but wrong in how to approach them. You will not be favoured when it comes to any kind of selection, so you must make up for this with your brains. Devika, you must shine so bright that any organization would feel like they are missing out not to take you. It starts with schools now, but eventually, it will be the selection committee at your dream job."

"In space?" I gave him a toothy grin, daring him to deny me my dreams. And of course, he did not.

"On any planet in the solar system. In the whole galaxy. In the whole universe even!"

I stuck my tongue out at him. "You're saying I'm Miss Universe then?"

"You are to me," Papa said.

It's morning or afternoon when I wake aboard the SOL4CE, and the sonic scanner has detected a new anomaly. The Erlanger crater is registering something it did not previously detect. Something new. At least, I think that's what it is. My vision's hazy and I haven't slept well. Drowsiness hangs from my eyelids and clings to my back like a well-meaning demon. Why haven't I rested?

Devika.

Oh, right. Amma. At least... no it isn't! You know it isn't her!

Then how does she know my name?

You're tired and you're grieving. Things that can be worked out with the therapist appointed to you when you return.

Back to Earth, right?

What was I doing out here? Why did I come here? Toggling through the controls and computer analysis of last night's scan doesn't give me the answer. I should reach for my headset, reach out to Mission Control. But they won't give me what I'm looking for.

What are you looking for, Devika?

Amma is sitting on the edge of my cot. But she shouldn't be, she should float in zero gravity. That would be real, that would mean she... exists in this space—this place—with me. I rub the spiky ball of nerves behind my eyelids and blink. Pigment halos circle her form like errant hula-hoops and now she hovers above the bed, the flat ends of her silken *dupatta* ripple out to touch me. I fall back, and let them drift past. Swallow past the grindstone in my throat and reach for the water. I suck from the straw and swish it around my mouth, letting the cold sting my brain out of this state between dream and reality. When I open my eyes again, she is gone, and a palpable sense of sadness settles over me.

Why do I deny her? Is it me asking that question, or the voice inside? Is that even my voice? If so, why does it sound like her? Why do I see the corner of her temple in the side of the console?

Why is she looking at me behind my reflection?

Just... let me go!

I should... take my own advice.

When Mission Control checks in on me again, they are now accompanied by a mental health specialist as well as a medical doctor, who are both concerned about the spikes in my cerebro-chemicals.

I tell them I'm fine, but they don't believe me. They insist I begin low-dose supplementation and start my return trip. When I yell at them to look at the data, their faces go pale.

Instead, I tell them I'm going to do my job. It's why I'm up here. I have a spacewalk scheduled in a few hours. Despite their protests, I go prepare.

Amma watches me from the porthole, with what seems like distant approval. Behind her, the Erlanger crater beckons, its velvet darkness more inviting than my bed.

It was only when I went out into space for the first time that I understood how to properly explain Amma's embrace. She hadn't embraced me often, but, like the empty expanse all around me, each one had both meant everything and nothing. Not performative, I'd never accuse her of that, but hollow and endless all the same. You see, people think that in space you see all these stars and twinkling lights from our distant neighbours. It must be beautiful, I've heard more than one well-wisher say. But those photos you get from trillion-dollar space telescopes that show all of the endless tapestries of form and colour are all a lie. They're computer generated and enhanced with vivid splashes to make space seem more enticing than it is.

But now you know. Space is nothing. It is cold. Dark. There is you, your ship, and the void. There are no stars. On the dark side of the moon, you can see the great gravitic rock that keeps you in orbit, but Earth is too far to perceive.

You, I, we are alone. Only our thoughts remain to comfort us.

I see Amma's bangle-covered arm slide down the outside of my extravehicular activity suit. Her fingers encircle mine. I can feel the pressure from her grip. Tendrils of her hair dance into my vision. I brush them aside and focus on inspecting the SOL4CE's exterior panels for micro-meteor strikes. Moon dust and debris have clogged the antenna. So that's why I haven't received any calls today. But what would kick dust all the way up here?

I look down into the crater. It's as big as the world now, from this viewpoint. Its infinite center is as black as the surrounding space. The rest of the moon might as well be the ring of the iris.

Amma touches my faceplate. Caresses the outside of my helmet. She mouths words to me.

I'm sorry, Devika.

What are you sorry for, Amma? For not loving me the way I am?

You could not perceive the depths of my love, Beta. All I ever did was want the best for you. It's not too late for us to be together, to be the mother and daughter we should have been.

I haven't thought of myself as your daughter in so long. I'm an astronaut. This is my purpose in life; I am here because of my choices.

Then it hits me. I'm not as different from her as I thought. Our conviction binds us, even in death. Did I come all the way out into space to get away from what... from who I should have embraced?

My lower lip trembles. The drill I'm holding floats free from my grasp. I forgot to secure the strap. It tumbles round the bend, and disappears behind the curve of the moon. I am no different from it. Just a tool in orbit around a thing that does not need me. I am the long-handled extension of the cheapest kind. Devika Mistry means nothing; I am the least of NASA's investments out here. Only the SOL4CE matters, and it's a relic.

What am I doing?

You are searching. I can give you the answers now, that I could not in life.

How are you doing this?

There are things in this life beyond our understanding. Did you not trust me? Look where that got us. This is our last chance.

My cheeks swell with grief. Amma, don't do this to me.

Despite all of her flaws, she would never intentionally hurt you. Why are you so afraid to trust her? Can't you see that there are some things that don't require an explanation?

None of these questions have a good answer, for they can't strike at the central conceit at my core. I can't deny that part of my father inside of me, the part that led me up here all along: I have to know.

I can't return to Earth with numbers as my answer. What I need lies beyond them.

When I sleep that night, I dream of Papa.

I have my eye pressed to the peephole of the telescope he bought me. I'm excitedly pointing out a star I see. He is glued to the TV though, and won't respond to me the way I know he should. I am disappointed at the wall of his indifference. He would never act this way. But I step into the living room where he sits, transfixed by the glowing screen. Amma is draped over the TV like melting candle wax. Her teeth frame the edges of the screen, her lips hang from the corners. Her eyes flick up to me, backlit by LEDs.

I rush to Papa, and curl my anxious hands around the sleeves of his shirt, pulling with all of my strength. His shirt stays intact, but he tears at the shoulder. He turns to me, wide-eyed and sweating, and opens his mouth to say something, but his jaw falls into the gap I've opened in him. He blinks in terror as his head slides down the curve of his collarbone, and into the wetness inside of him. He glances at the screen, and back at me.

I already know, Papa! Amma is never going to be okay again, not with you gone. Don't abandon me! I need you!

The whites of his eyes are suspended by veins of bright red panic. His pupils shiver. He wants me to see.

I look at the screen. The anglerfish opens its mouth, and pulses its blinking lure. A little fish flits around it, stark in its loneliness; its tiny fins look like cherub wings against the inky ocean.

Amma's tongue flops out of the bottom frame. She tries to close her lips, to use that mouth to say my name. I don't want her to.

I awake to static. The SOL4CE is spinning in one direction, but I tumble in another. Controls seem to drift further away every time I reach for them.

Lights dim around my home in space. More like a dwelling, the SOL4CE was never where I was supposed to be, was it? I know Amma would agree.

Somewhere out there, among the millions of Indian women who look like me, many are embracing the future their Ammas lay out for them. If there is other life in the universe, if they have love between them, they have expectations. One cannot travel without the other. If guilt exists in other worlds, and is felt by other forms of life, then I am not alone out here. Perhaps somewhere, on some distant planet, someone else is feeling the way I do.

Amma smiles at me and I can feel her warmth radiating in my chest. She waits for me by the airlock. I float past the distant, tinny echoes of voices from my headset, and don my EVA suit. This tin capsule finally feels too small for my ambitions.

I'm doing what you wanted, Amma. Not what you told me my whole life, what you've realized now. If you can forgive me, then I can do the same. There's something you want to show me, up here in my world.

You've never shown an interest in space before.

Yet now you guide me through the airlock with the tenderest of touches. You pull me into your arms and I feel your heartbeat in my ear. A tiny part of my brain itches with a familiar sonic frequency, but that is just part of my scientific mind that refuses to let go. It was standing in my way.

Like Papa? No, that doesn't seem right.

I just couldn't feel you before, but I do now. Maybe that's what I needed to do all along. Just trust that you knew something I didn't. About dharma, karma, reincarnation... it doesn't matter that I don't fully believe. You do, and out here, flying free from the last tether, that's what matters. You're going to show me something new.

I let go of the SOL4CE and drift toward the moon.

Darkness surrounds me, but it is warm. Welcoming. The very opposite of the endless, frigid expanse of space. The edges of the crater reach for me, close around me, and envelop.

I am in its warm embrace. And all is well.

Amma?
Amma?
Amma!
When the response comes, it's from some... thing... I don't know.
No.

Oil

Ihsan Sim

Orang Minyak (translated to "Oily Man") is a notorious entity in Malay urban legend. Characterised by his slick, oil-covered skin and glowing red eyes, the Orang Minyak is believed to terrorise and abduct young women in their sleep. Although the legend of the Orang Minyak has largely faded from the rear-view mirror of glittering, metropolitan Singapore, the odd sighting of the figure persists to this very day...

"Sit down my friend, you look terrible!" George gestured to the chair.

Maz collapsed into his seat, face buried in his hands. His hair was dishevelled, work uniform crumpled, and a scruffy 5 o'clock shadow had begun to sneak its way onto his cheeks. And by the looks of things, a shower hadn't been in the cards for a while either. No, this was more than just your average 'end of the workday' type fatigue.

"Rough day at work, huh?" George probed as he raised a glass of *teh* to his lips.

"No," Maz said in a distant tone. "Not work."

George contemplated his words for a second while discreetly signalling a waitress with one raised index finger and pointing it towards Maz. The waitress nodded in understanding. "So uh, tell me about it, man. What's eating you?"

Maz unstuck his hands from his face for the first time that evening, and as the golden sun cast a feverish glow across the coffeeshop, George was struck by a pair of bloodshot eyes and the suitcase worth of eyebags that completed the dreadful picture.

At first, George wasn't entirely sure that Maz heard him, and when a dry, croaky voice emerged from the man across from him, George nearly choked on his drink.

"Where do I start?"

"Mmm, the beginning usually works."

Maz hesitated.

"You remember the night we had to work late?"

George scrambled through his memory bank for a moment.

"The one where the oil pipes broke and we had to repair them on the fly? Hell yea, I remember."

"This was after we knocked off around 11.30 pm. I was in my car, driving along the old cemetery road... I can't recall the name. You know the one, right?"

"The dark one with potholes and the jungle?"

"Yea, that one. Anyway, I was driving..."

...And there were no other cars on the road except for mine. I know this isn't unusual, especially at such a late hour, but something felt different about that night. Something felt... off. I don't know how many times you've driven down that road, but it gets super dark even with the streetlights. I can't explain it; it was almost like there was a dark cloud hanging over me that—Hey, stop laughing! No, I can see you smiling.

Look man, I know it sounds *gila* but please hear me out before you conclude it as crazy.

This road was a long, narrow stretch of road. Like a good 20-, maybe 30-minute drive. If your car broke down halfway, you're basically screwed. And good luck getting any type of signal. So, I was driving, and it was just one long stretch of darkness, only interrupted by my headlights and the odd streetlight. All of a sudden, I saw a figure leap out in front of my car. I screamed and slammed on the brakes, but it was too late, and the impact shattered my windshield. At first, I thought I'd hit a wild boar or maybe even an armadillo; they were not unheard of in this area. But after realising neither animal is tall enough to strike my windshield, I started to fear the worst.

I got out of the car, and if I wasn't certain about the strangeness in the air before, I was now. The humidity shocked me. The air felt so thick, I swore I could punch through it with one fist and tear a hole right through this world... and if I did, all the unseen horrors of this world and the next one over would come spilling through like seawater through the hull of a ship.

There was no sign of any animal when I inspected the damage—not even a shred of fur. There was no way an animal hit by a car going 70 km per hour could survive that kind of impact, let alone get very far. But what really scared me was that there wasn't a drop of blood on the front of my car... only some splotches of oil that probably spilled out of the hood on impact. And then I saw it.

My eyes followed the dripping patches of oil where the headlights shone—thick, wet pools of black stuff that reflected the rainbow if you shone the light just right. Too thick, in fact. And I knew something was wrong when it seemed to get thicker and fresher the further, I moved away from my car. I stopped right by the edge of the roadside, but I could barely make out the oil tracks ending somewhere in the treeline, where they blended completely into the shadows. At that moment, my heart raced, and a voice in my head screamed at me to leave. I ran straight back to my car. Animal or no animal, this was no place to be in the dead of night.

Sitting in the driver's seat, I was about to turn the key and drive away, ready to forget any of this ever happened when I heard the most awful sound. I still curse myself every day for not being a little quicker, for not putting the car in drive a little sooner so that the roar of the engine would muffle the horrific scream I heard from the treeline, for not listening to that voice in my head. Actually, I'm not even sure if it was a scream. It was angry for sure, but definitely not like any animal I'd heard before. But it also sounded like it was laughing, mocking me.

Do animals laugh? Don't answer that, George. The noise was barely human either, almost like a deep, gurgling choking sound that sputtered from the depths of hell... like the sound of someone laughing while choking to death, if you can imagine that. The sound echoed from somewhere behind the trees, crystal clear even from the inside of my car, and I wondered how loud it must have really been.

I knew it was time to go. I drove as fast and as far as I could. And as I did, that little voice kept screaming from the back of my mind.

Don't look back. Don't look back. Don't even think about looking back. Go home to your wife. Go home to your children. Never speak about this to anyone. Take this to your grave! Over and over the voice repeated until...

"...I pulled into the parking lot half an hour later."

The waitress returned with another cup of *teh*. Maz muttered a thanks and chugged the drink down gratefully. He placed the empty cup back on the table with an audible *clang*, snapping George out of his stupor.

"That's... that's quite a tale, my friend." George had heard many crazy things in his life. This was probably at the top of the list.

"No tale. It's real."

"How much sleep have you gotten lately?" George bit his lip. Stupid question.

"Almost none. I've been having... nightmares."

"Oh?"

"Of a man, or at least I think it's a man. In my nightmare, I'll always be looking out the window. And when I look out the window, I see a tree. On the tree, there's a man squatting on one of its branches. But he's all... wrong. You see, he's covered in oil, every inch of him. And even though it's dark, I see him there, oily black skin shining against the moonlight. He has this pair of horrible, red eyes like burning lumps of coal. But worst of all is his smile. When he eventually smiles, it's like the crescent moon itself on a sea of darkness... and when I look at it, I feel like I'll never know peace again. That's how the dream always goes, and I wake up screaming and drenched in sweat. Siti always has to calm me down after that, and when she asks me what's wrong... I'm too ashamed to tell her. What would she think of me?"

"God, Maz. I didn't know it was that bad."

"George... this will sound crazy, but I think I hit an Orang Minyak."

"What's that?" George's understanding of Malay was rudimentary at best. His knowledge of Malay folklore, virtually non-existent.

As Maz explained, George's eyes grew wide with disbelief. Now this was at the top of the crazy list.

"Look, Maz, you know I'm your friend and I care about you but... I think you're having a breakdown."

"You think I'm crazy."

"Come on man, you know that's not what I mean! I'm not doubting you had a weird experience on the road that night, or that you've been having nightmares. But maybe you're a little stressed out right now. You know? Overworked. We gotta look at things rationally."

Maz drummed his fingers on the table frantically, hunched over as a bead of sweat rolled down his brow. Suddenly, he shot up. There was a strange, intense look on his face that George didn't like very much.

"George, you remember Afifah right? My eldest daughter?"

"Afifah? Yeah, I met her when I came over to your place for dinner a few years ago. Smart girl. She must be what now? 17? 18?"

"19. She just turned in August."

"Ah right... but Maz, what does that have to do with anything?"

"George, she's gone."

George blinked, dumbfounded.

"What do you mean gone?"

"Gone, George. She's vanished!"

"Maz, people don't just vanish in Singapore. Besides, you always did say Afifah was a bit... rebellious," George said, choosing his words carefully. "Maybe she just ran away for a few days. You know how teenagers are."

Maz shook his head.

"You remember how I said the Orang Minyak terrorises young girls in their sleep?"

"Yes—?" George replied cautiously, following but not quite enjoying the direction this conversation was headed.

"George, the Orang Minyak. It took her."

With one hand cupped over his mouth in both shock and contemplation, George considered the incredulity of what his old friend was telling him.

"Assuming what you're saying is true, why don't you report it to the police?" he quizzed. "They wouldn't believe me." Maz looked up. "I mean, you don't."

"Well, you're not exactly making it easy for me, man."

Maz retracted his hand from where he drummed the table, and

George noticed that a small pool of sweat had formed on its shiny, plastic surface.

"When Siti and I went into Afifah's room that night, the curtains were pulled back and the windows were wide open. She always slept with the curtains drawn. And in her bed..." Maz paused, struggling to articulate himself. "...In her bed was nothing but a thick puddle of oil." Now, the tears rolled freely.

The two men sat in silence, the cacophonous bustle of the dinnertime crowd a world and a half away.

It was late by the time George hit the road, and as he traversed down that same, hauntingly lonely route he had a thousand times before, Maz's story clung to him like an itch that would not quit.

He couldn't believe it. He wouldn't! It was simply ridiculous. Clearly something very wrong had happened, but the Orang Minyak was a rationalisation... an excuse for cold hard facts. Add a series of unfortunate events to an urban legend and what do you get? A convenient cover-up for a bitter, ugly truth. Afifah had run away, plain and simple.

As his old Toyota Corolla sped over a pothole, the old Al Pacino bobblehead on George's dashboard nodded its head vigorously in agreement. Maz was his best friend. Hell, he was George's *only* friend in his twenty years in Singapore... but he couldn't stand by and watch him be consumed by his own delusions. His friend clearly needed help, but where to sta—

George's train of thought evaporated by the sudden screech of tires and a rogue steering wheel that spiralled helplessly into oblivion. The surrounding view meshed into an incoherent blend of shadows and asphalt as his car careened wildly into the darkness. And when it seemed the carousel from hell would never end, the sound of crushed glass and metal ordered the car to a sudden and violent stop.

Accompanied by nothing but the bobblehead that seemed to shake its noggin to the rhythm of the car's turn signals, George sat silently in the pulsating yellow glow for what felt like a very long time. Eventually, as though his little friend would inexplicably come to life and bite his fingers off, George gingerly placed a palm on the crown of Pacino's head, bringing the hypnotic cranial jig to an end.

The warmness of the night greeted George as he stepped out of the car to survey the damage. Almost instantly, the cool air conditioning was a distant memory, and a dark patch of sweat had begun to pool across his back. But that wasn't the only reason why George was sweating. Despite the humid air, he was acutely aware of a cold shiver that began to worm its way from deep within the trees and onto his spine. There, it latched onto the nape of his neck with vicious intent... and fear was all he knew.

George edged towards the side of the road, subconsciously staying within the beams of light from the Corolla as a sickly, dark trail of liquid caught his eye. Starting from the front right tire of his car, the goo snaked its way back home to the darkness, only made slightly visible by the lights that reflected off its shiny, black surface—*rainbows.*

George found himself unable to tear his eyes away from this accursed trail of crumbs, every twist and turn crying out at him to walk away and never return. And yet, a pair of frightened yet curious eyes continued to follow the trail... till they met its chilling conclusion.

It was like looking in a mirror, if the mirror was crafted by Satan himself. A pair of glowing red eyes sitting among the trees, bestial yet intelligent, locked with George's own. An upturned row of infinite teeth, human but too numerous to be, made a mockery of George's mouth, which was agape with horror. And like the trail of oil that led to its owner, the Orang Minyak glistened ferociously, his wet, shiny skin the only thing that separated him from the shadows he called home.

Sometimes, seeing was believing, and George would miss those blissful days of ignorance.

Coincidences

Arvee Fantilagan

I still don't know how it happens, Doc, or why. Frankly, I've given up wondering.

I remember when it first did, though. It was another Friday night, my Ate, Amelia, begged me to deal with our parents while she met yet another guy from the internet. She was twenty then, but you know how Filipino boomers are: "Get home from school by six, from work by eight, and date your first at twenty-five."

Hehe, that wasn't a problem for me, as you can see. My face had always repelled girls just fine.

My sister, on the other hand, hogged all the attractiveness God meant for siblings to share. I've even stopped telling people we're related because nobody believed me anyway. But I adored her too; when she finally got a sales job at that mall an hour away, it became my own job to defend her frequent nights-out from mom and dad.

And boy, did they stomp around fuming when it was already 10 p.m. and she still wasn't home. I often piped up that she was probably just stuck at work doing so-and-so, and that since she was pitching in with the bills, they should cut her some slack and so-and-so.

In exchange, Amelia would give me a hundred pesos as soon as she got home.

Except, for some reason that night, I texted her that this sneaking around was going to get her murdered someday. She just lol'd.

We didn't hear from her again until a few days later, when police directed us to a morgue two hours away. They found her violated and strangled in an alley somewhere in Pasig.

Mom fainted right there beside her body.

Even Dad, who had always prided himself on his macho stoicism, spent each day of my sister's wake weeping and drinking. And when all the visitors left, he'd burst into my room and beat me until one of us passed out.

Still, that hurt a lot less than being told they didn't want me at her funeral.

I realize now I should have started seeing someone like you back then, Doc. But I was sure they would just say it was a waste of money, that I should pray harder if I wanted solace, or just tough it out like they were doing—to just be a man.

And anyway, they probably would've sent me straight to a mental hospital had I told them I could still see my sister. Might as well get rid of the demented black sheep who got their favorite child killed rather than reward him with college. Like they weren't basically smothering Amelia on the way to that dumpster.

... uhh, yeah, that's right, Doc. Her corpse still hangs out with me. Like, right now, she's down there, slumped by your feet.

Well, obviously, she's not doing much. Her mouth's frozen in that helpless gasp as usual. Her neck is too mangled, so she's just leaning her bloated head against your knee and, like always, staring at me, even with her eyes gouged out.

Don't worry, Doc. She won't hurt you. She's just bullying me as usual. Even in the afterlife.

Sure—her case didn't go anywhere. This is the Philippines, after all; unless you have the right surname, why would you expect justice?

We did go and see the guy Amelia was supposed to have met a few days after he was cleared by the police. Some call center agent in a slum in Quezon. My parents had been pushing Amelia to be one if she didn't mind being a saleslady. You know how they got paid those days. And no surprise, his house was the only one on his street with a cable satellite dish on the roof and a car on the side. A dirty goat in a princess outfit.

So, as he told us, they first met on Yahoo chat. He was funny, she was flirty. They hit it off, sent each other pics, added each other on Friendster, yada yada yada. Then, after a while, they decided to meet up.

I barely listened. I was too distracted by my sister's pale, contorted remains on his couch, demanding our guilt.

He showed us the last text message she sent him: "Just got on the bus!" Winking emoji.

Then, in his outbox, a string of unanswered texts: "Already here!"

"I'm the guy in Hawaiian and flip-flops."

"Where are you?"

"Are we still on?"

And the last: "Thanks for wasting my time, bitch."

Right around the time Amelia was getting the life strangled out of her.

Nothing we didn't already hear from the police.

In hindsight, my parents probably weren't expecting much. They just wanted closure. Sucks that all they got was a half-hearted apology and a shrug.

None of us said anything on the way home. I suppose they were grieving; they probably knew that that was it. On the other hand, I dreaded how it was a Saturday, and that they'd still drag me out of bed the next morning and into church. This time without Amelia's cranky Sunday morning mouth snapping at us.

Because that's what Catholics do, you know. Rain or shine, famine or feast, you're supposed to attend Mass, listen to the word of the Lord, praise His will. And when a loved one dies, drop in a few more coins so they don't end up in hell.

But man, I said to myself, if anyone deserved to die in pain and agony, shouldn't it have been that smug playboy back there and not my church-going sister?

I woke up the next day with his burnt carcass standing next to my bed. I'm telling you, Doc, I almost shat myself—hahaha.

Well, I didn't know at the time that it was him. I just opened my eyes and saw this blackened mass of flesh staring down at me. I'm sure I screamed. My mother rushed in, but when she yelled at me for not being dressed for church, I figured he wasn't really there—kind of like my sister slouched and decomposing by the door.

We saw on the news later: that same alley in Quezon we visited, now razed to the ground. Just the typical fire here in the Metro, you know. 'Jumpers' stealing electricity from neighbors. Then a transformer exploded, lit up a few houses; soon, the entire neighborhood was on fire.

The footage caught it all: people screaming in terror, clogging that narrow street; children wailing; men cursing; washing machines, TVs, couches being carried away. And behind them, giant flames were devouring the world.

Then they zoomed in, just as this one house in the background caved in and burst into a fireball—the only one with a satellite dish on the top.

My mother crossed herself, mumbling to Jesus. Dad's mouth was agape. Me? I was just like, good riddance!

Hehe. I guess that sounds so mean, but I was just a kid, Doc. Okay?

And can you blame me? If only this asshole had chatted with a different girl on a different server that night, then my sister could've ended up with some other guy in a different corner of Manila! Then, who knows? She might have been able to come back alive—still cranky—with my hundred peso bribe.

So, that news actually cheered me up, I can't lie. Sure, he's still here, this huge lump of coal glaring at the side of my head, but I always thought he deserved it. And he's just another mirage to me now. A tinnitus I've gotten used to.

... Amelia? Well, of course, Doc, it still hurts. Seeing her ghost every day—it still hurts.

And I don't really want to admit it, but sometimes I think my parents were right: that if I didn't keep lying for her and enabling her, then maybe she would still be around, instead of down there, crumpled and rotting by your legs.

So yeah, she makes me feel guilty. But this cadaver next to me? Why should I feel bad for him?

Of course, whoever did those things to my sister deserves a whole lot worse, but this guy was no angel himself. He had it coming. It was karma!

Alright, let me tell you about this neighbor we had once, Doc—the one just above the apartment Heidy and I first lived in. I bet she even mentioned him to you before. We liked to call him Bane: the Bane of our Sleep.

Christ, this dude would wake up at five in the morning and shake our entire lives, doing jumping jacks and tossing dumbbells around.

And on weekends—my god—he would have the most obnoxiously loud sex, our ceiling shaking from some fat slob trying to work out. Okay, good for him, but this guy would also curse, moan, and howl like a hyena. It was repulsive.

But days before we moved out, police came to our building to cordon off his apartment. Apparently, right after he and a girlfriend got home from a date, she decided to pick up the kitchen knife and slice his throat open. Who knows why?

Was it my fault that I finally bumped into them on the stairs that day? All I did was fantasize about her gutting him, but it was her dumb ass who actually did it.

Or when I told my parents it's time they finally made it up to Amelia. Should I feel bad because they decided to go to my sister's room later and hang themselves there? You think any judge would convict me for that?

Well, that's nice of Heidy to leave me to tell the details. But yes, Doc. They both did.

Almost as soon as we left the Christmas Eve dinner, too. They didn't even finish their spaghetti, the police said. When we were questioned, we just said it was our first visit in years, so Mom and Dad actually started off in pretty high spirits.

They even brought out their wedding glassware Amelia and I weren't allowed to touch. They asked for so many updates about me and Heidy, our life, our careers, about a baby someday. But as soon as my sister was brought up, they started losing it. They babbled on and on about how much my wife resembled Amelia. That she was a lovely daughter, and that she would've been an even lovelier mother. And as usual, that little spiel on how lucky I was that her insurance basically paid for my college.

Our Christmas dinner kinda devolved into a shouting match after that. Poor Heidy had to drag me out of there. She even apologized.

Just parents being parents, I guess.

Well, they went on to lynch themselves and now they're finally with their favorite child again. I truly hope they're happy, reunited at long last, even if they all look so miserable. They were probably hoping for an afterlife with Mary, Peter, all the angels—not cramped in rooms together with me, Heidy, and all these other randoms. But hey, corpses can't be choosers.

... Yes, Doc. They're all here.

Mom and Dad are actually why I've been fidgeting so much. All I want is to sit here in peace and look you in the eyes, but their gnarly feet just keep swaying in front of your face. Of all the spots in my daily life they could have chosen to dangle from.

... What? Of course I haven't told Heidy, Doctor. Are you crazy? You know how delicate she is! How do you think she'd react if she knew our bedroom was full of dead bodies watching us sleep?

But yeah, that's the other reason I agreed to come see you, Doc. I wanted to personally thank you for everything you've done for Heidy. I've never seen her this happy and at ease before, and I'm so glad! And that's all I want: my wife's joy. Especially when I remember what a wreck she was back then. I'm sure you already know this, but she used to come to work for weeks crying. She would sit at her desk, compute, tabulate—sobbing and sniffing the entire time. She broke all our hearts at the bank, but she didn't want to let any of us in.

Except for you, apparently.

So even if none of these things bother me anymore, I understand why she kept insisting that I see you as soon as possible—pleading, even. I mean, from her perspective, her husband's parents just killed themselves!

She probably thought that I needed the support, you know. Someone else who could listen, like what you did for her.

I guess growing up in an orphanage makes you wary of people, right? Heidy said she didn't really like it there, so she basically had no one else in her life. And Christ, her first few years trying to survive on her own—going door to door asking if she could do laundry, cleaning up old neighbors shitting themselves. She's always been proud of that part of her life, putting herself through college and the board. And yeah, it's incredible, but honestly, Doc, it all just sounds so pathetic.

So maybe that's why it really destroyed her when her boyfriend decided to jump in front of a train one day—just a few weeks before their wedding, too. She'd already suffered so much, but he was still her very first loss—her crutch and anchor for the longest time, she told me. And she was three months pregnant.

But I didn't know that. Not at the time. If I did, I would have recommended him something else.

He told me he liked to go hiking. I've found that outdoorsy dudes are talkative like that. Light their cigarette, and they'll yammer on about their hobbies and shit. I suppose, if I told him to walk into the Sierra wilderness or jump off Mt. Pulag, then maybe it wouldn't have been so bad. Maybe she would have agonized much less.

Like this burnt up ghoul looming next to me over here. As soon as my sister stopped replying, he was already chatting with someone else.

Not saying Heidy would have moved on as quickly as that, but if she thought she was just ghosted, then maybe she could have moved on faster, chalking it up to her fiance being a coward. Then, she could open up her heart to somebody else later.

Maybe she could've even had a healthy birth, because I can stomach the shredded chunks of her ex-boyfriend's face splattered all over my floor. You know, I already got stiff parents dangling in front of me, and here on this side, my neighbor moaning out of his gaping, bloody throat. I don't mind them anymore; there's not much that scares me these days. What's another random body to add to my morgue?

What bothers me though, is Heidy's disgusting three-month fetus just plopped down there on the floor. Right between Amelia's cold dead legs. My wife's tiny monstrosity in front of my sister's violated body.

It's sick, however the hell this happened. She doesn't deserve this. And of course, neither did Heidy. For a few weeks after her ex's death, she looked so ghastly, I was afraid she would one day follow him to those train tracks herself.

But I took my shot—offered myself in case she needed someone to talk to. She said, "No, thanks," she was already seeing a therapist.

But she gave me a call later, anyway—crying. And for a long, long time, that's how all our calls went—just her crying.

But you know what, these days, I think I can safely say she's wiped her last tears. My love, Heidy—happy as she could ever be.

And you were a big part of that, Doc, just holding her hand and helping her through all that pain. I know she's probably already said this a million times, but thank you. Thank you, thank you so much, Doctor—for saving my wife.

Speaking of, I have to get going. We're seeing a movie tonight.

Sorry I took up so much of your time. It does feel good, though. I can see why Heidy still likes coming here every week. I might as well. Of course, everything stays just between us, right, Doc? I think you will agree that she finally deserves this peace of mind.

Thanks again, Doctor! Good night, and you drive safe, okay? Lots of drunk drivers on Friday nights, you know.

Meet the

Authors

Mir Aziz
"Shadows on the Frontier"

Mir Aziz, author of "Shadows on the Frontier," has been captivated by history and folklore since childhood. He often writes horror— or horror-adjacent—stories that intertwine these themes. Drawn to the mythology of his ancestral highlands in Pakistan, he uses history and the supernatural as a lens to explore the region's traumas, both past and present. In his spare time, Mir enjoys wandering through new locations, rural or urban, reflecting on their often grim histories and imagining how to weave them into ghost stories. When not writing, he's likely exploring new cafés around London.

(Stock photos are used for authors like Mir who prefer anonymity.)

Mei Davis
"In the Grip"

Mei Davis, author of "In the Grip," currently lives in the cold wilds of Metro Detroit with her family. When not wrangling either her literary or literal children, she can be found binging procedural dramas, collecting rupees in Hyrule, or skipping to the last pages of a book. She has been previously published by *Prairiefire, Translunar Traveler's Lounge, Sans Press, Parsec Ink,* and others.

(Stock photos are used for authors like Mei who prefer anonymity.)

Jonathan Brònico
"The Spirit Board"

Jonathan Brònico is a neurodivergent writer, poet, and game designer. His fiction has been recognized by *L. Ron Hubbard's Writers of the Future* and the *New England Science Fiction Association.* His work appears in *Secret Stairs: A Tribute to Urban Legend* and *Gothic Tales: Agents & Spies.* Jonathan designs storytelling-focused games, many available for free at lionsheadpress.itch.io.

Justin Alcala
"A Bridge of Bones"

Justin Carlos Alcala is an award-winning American novelist and short story writer featured in *Publisher's Weekly, the SLF Foundation Awards,* and the University of British Columbia archives. A folklore fanatic, history nerd, and tabletop gamer, Alcala has published over 30 short stories, novellas, and novels in various anthologies, magazines, and journals. He lives with his dark queen, Mallory, their fey daughter, Lily, changeling son, Ronan, goblin-baby, Asher, and hounds of Ragnarök, Fenrir and Hilda, in Bigfoot's domain.

Alishia Dauterive
"The Guardian"

Alishia is a Black-multiethnic writer, cat lover, and mental health professional who sparks conversations about oppressive healthcare systems. Originally from a small coastal California town, she willingly traded paradise for a bustling capital city offering seasoned food, diverse faces, and reasonable prices. With an abstract but consistent creative process, she rarely goes a day without writing. Her work explores identity, self-discovery, magic, and relationships. Her essays and fiction works appear on various websites, and she is currently finalizing her first novel.

John Sieber
"The Sweetest Fruit"

John Sieber is a queer poet, fiction writer, and hopeless romantic based in Northern Indiana. His work appears in *Literary Heist*, *Oakland Arts Review*, and *Marathon Literary Review*. Inspired by religious philosophy, personal relationships, and nature, John spends his time traveling, exploring the outdoors, teaching, and reflecting on the curious world around him. In March, he will join the U.S. Peace Corps as an Education Volunteer in Costa Rica, teaching English as a Second Language.

Anthony Martinez
"Tired Eyes"

Anthony Martinez is a horror writer based in Flagstaff, Arizona, where he lives with his partner and two dogs. Holding a Master's Degree in Teaching English as a Second Language, Anthony weaves fantastical elements into his chilling tales, aiming to carve a niche in the horror genre. When he's not crafting stories, he enjoys exploring the outdoors with his dogs, immersing himself in video games, and dreaming up his next dark creation. Anthony aspires to expand his publications and share his unique blend of horror and fantasy with a wider audience.

Franka Zeph
"Sugar Cake Lady"

Franka Zeph, author of the novella *Sugar Cake Lady*, hails from Trinidad and Tobago and is now based in Toronto, Canada. Raised on a steady diet of horror and sci-fi since childhood, she has developed a fertile imagination. An SFWA member and winner of the "Clash of the Query Letters" 2022 competition, her upcoming 2024 publications include the Caribbean horror tale "The Banyan Tree" (in African Ghost Short Stories) and "One Eye Weeps Alone" for the clean water project Yemoja's Tears. Her military sci-fi story "Door Crashers" was published by Tor in the award-winning anthology *Africa Risen*. Other works have been published under the pseudonym Frankie Diamond in *Augur Magazine Issue 3.2* and on a dance music blog. Find her on Twitter and Instagram @frankazeph.

Jeff Thompson
"The Hinge Fort"

Jeff Thompson is a versatile writer whose work has been featured in *The Bangalore Review*, *The Write Launch*, *On the Run Press*, and the forthcoming *Wordfire Press Cryptid Anthology*. He has self-published two books on Amazon, with a third in progress. A passionate reader and writer, Jeff dedicates every spare moment to honing his craft, drawing inspiration from the support of his incredible friends and family. With a love for storytelling and a drive to share his unique voice, Jeff continues to expand his creative horizons.

V.M. Sawh
"In Orbit"

Originally from the West Indies and now residing in Calgary, Alberta, V.M. Sawh is an award-winning author who blazes his own trail in storytelling and identity. Inspired by a chance meeting with Guillermo Del Toro, V.M. published his debut short story "Cinders," which reached #1 on Amazon and launched the acclaimed *Good Tales for Bad Dreams* series. His work has appeared in literary magazines, and his short story "Till Death Do Us Part" was adapted into an audio play by *The Morbid Forest* podcast. A champion of indie creators, V.M. is compiling the "Good Tales for Bad Dreams" collected edition.

Ihsan Sim
"Oil"

Ihsan is a political science major with minors in history and sociology. Writing for over six years, he has earned recognition in competitions like the *Writers of the Future* contest and *The Writers College Short Story Competition*. Influenced by authors like Stephen King and H.P. Lovecraft, Ihsan's first love is horror, though he also enjoys pulp noir and science fiction. In his free time, he listens to country music and unwinds at Sembawang Park, one of Singapore's last natural beaches. Passionate about storytelling, Ihsan continues to explore genres that spark his imagination.

Arvee Fantilagan
"Coincidences"

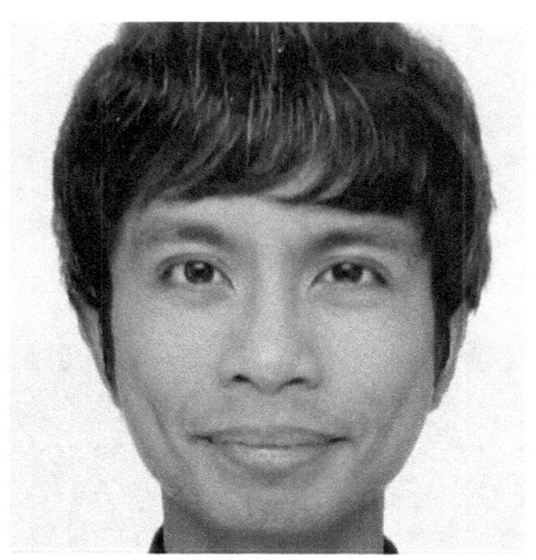

Arvee Fantilagan is a versatile writer whose work spans psychological horror, science fiction, fantasy, and mythology. He is the author of Coincidences, a chilling psychological horror piece, as well as imaginative tales like "The Butterfly, the Flower," and "Pollen and Her Cute Little Hellspawn." Born and raised in the Philippines, Arvee draws inspiration from his cultural roots and his current life in Japan, weaving these influences into his speculative fiction. His stories explore the surreal, the mysterious, and the profound.